About the author

Ian McFadyen was born in Liverpool and has enjoyed a successful career in marketing. He lives in Hertfordshire with his wife and his retired greyhound. He has three grown-up children. *Killing Time* is the fifth in the series featuring DI Steve Carmichael, all published by Book Guild.

By the same author:

Little White Lies, Book Guild Publishing, 2008. (Paperback edition 2012)

Little White Lies (large print edition), Magna Large Print Books, 2010.

Lillia's Diary, Book Guild Publishing, 2009. (Paperback edition 2012)

Lillia's Diary (large print edition), Magna Large Print Books, 2014.

Frozen to Death, Book Guild Publishing, 2010

Frozen to Death (large print edition), Magna Large Print Books, 2014.

Deadly Secrets, Book Guild Publishing, 2012

Deadly Secrets (large print edition), Magna Large Print Books, 2014.

Deadly Secrets (Italian edition), Miraviglia Editore, 2014

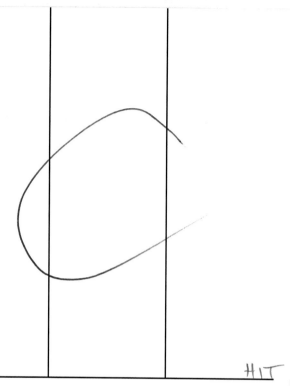

HIT

Please renew/return items by last date shown. Please call the number below:

Renewals and enquiries: 0300 1234049

Textphone for hearing or
speech impaired users: 01992 555506

www.hertfordshire.gov.uk/libraries   Hertfordshire
L32

53 142 132 3

First published in Great Britain in 2015 by
The Book Guild Ltd
The Werks
45 Church Road
Hove
BN3 2BE

Typesetting in Baskerville by
Nat-Type, Cheshire

Printed in Great Britain by
CPI Antony Rowe

A catalogue record for this book is available from
The British Library.

ISBN 978 1 910508 14 5

To Emma Sparks
(my glamorous hedgehog lady xx)

Chapter 1

Tuesday 3rd June

To look at her it was difficult to believe that Patricia Elizabeth Wilbraham was only fifty-two years old. Her dishevelled appearance, tangled grey hair, and weathered, wrinkled face made 'Betty the hedgehog lady', as the locals called her, look at least ten years older.

Even though Betty had lived in a small end-of-terrace house in the tiny hamlet of Hasslebury for over twenty years, few people knew much about her. Her accent was certainly not Lancastrian, causing those who actually gave her any thought to believe she had to be a southerner. But in that part of Lancashire a southerner could refer to anyone whose origin was outside the Red Rose county.

As her nickname suggested, Betty was fanatical about hedgehogs. Her passion being so well known that few days would pass without her receiving a call or visit from either the RSPCA or one of the veterinary practices in the area, asking her to take in yet another prickly waif and stray. Her obsession with and commitment to these creatures was such that at any one time Betty could easily have a couple of dozen animals in her care, and she would nurse her little babies back into good health, before releasing them into the wild at one of a variety of locations in and around the village.

It was just before 7 p.m. on that warm June evening when Betty heard a loud knock on her front door.

'That will be that handsome, Mr Preston,' said Betty to the tiny young hedgehog which she had, for the last twenty minutes, been patiently feeding goat's milk through a tiny plastic pipette.

Dennis Preston, the local RSPCA officer, had called Betty earlier that day to enquire whether she could take on yet another spiny patient. So when Betty answered the door she fully expected to see a tall, young, well-turned-out RSPCA warden, but to her surprise the sight that confronted her was of a decidedly more elderly and distinctly scruffier man.

'How are you, Patsy?' he enquired as if he knew her well. 'I bet you never expected to see me again.'

Chapter 2

Tuesday 15th July

Inspector Steve Carmichael was in a foul mood by the time he arrived at Kirkwood Police Station. It had taken him almost an hour to travel the 23.2 miles from his house in Moulton Bank, a journey time almost twice as long as normal.

'What the hell is happening on the roads this morning,' he moaned to the duty sergeant as he entered the station.

'It's an incident on the railway line down in Alcar,' replied the sergeant. 'It looks like we have a jumper. Sergeant Cooper and DC Dalton are at the scene now. I suspect that's got a lot to do with the roads being so congested.'

'Bloody inconvenient,' snapped Carmichael uncharitably. 'If people want to kill themselves, why can't they just take an overdose or something that's less problematic to the rest of us? Jumping on the rails is such a selfish thing to do.'

The duty sergeant wisely decided not to respond. He could see Carmichael was in no frame of mind to hear a contrary opinion.

* * * *

The scene at Alcar train station was one of utter chaos. They had not had a suicide on that stretch of track for over twenty years and unfortunately the macabre interest of many locals had kicked in. By the time Paul Cooper and Rachel Dalton arrived, dozens of them had already congregated as they tried to catch a glimpse of the grisly scene.

Cooper, normally the most placid of individuals, was thoroughly disgusted at the way these people seemed to view the incident as little more than a source of entertainment, and he was going to have none of it.

'Get those damn people away from here!' he barked angrily at a lone young PC who, other than Cooper and Dalton, was the only officer in attendance.

'I want them at least fifty metres away,' he said in full earshot of the gathered throng. 'And if anyone doesn't cooperate, charge them immediately, Constable.'

'Shall I help him?' enquired Rachel Dalton, who in truth was dreading seeing what remained of the body after a high-speed train strike.

'Yes,' replied Cooper more calmly. 'I hate voyeurs.'

Rachel didn't need to be told a second time. Without another word she strode over to join her uniformed colleague and the two law enforcers unceremoniously started to herd the onlookers back to a more acceptable distance.

*   *   *   *

Being the editor and the lead reporter on a small provincial newspaper, Norfolk George was not used to receiving information from anonymous sources, and when he had, it had rarely been sent by text and had never been associated with local murders.

He read the text over and over again while he decided what to do next.

Within the space of a couple of minutes he had made up his mind. He'd certainly print the story but he'd also call his friend Inspector Carmichael and pass over the information he'd just received. He elected to forward the text message and then make the call to Carmichael as he drove to Alcar to see one of the alleged crime scenes.

* * * *

Dr Stock and the SOCOs arrived at Alcar twenty minutes after Cooper and Dalton.

'Where is he?' he asked Cooper as if he was enquiring about nothing more than a worthless, mislaid possession.

'Most of him is over there,' replied Cooper, pointing at the deep grassy bank about ten metres down the track. 'But there's bits of him all over the place.'

'It's definitely a *him* then?' Stock asked impertinently.

'I'll let you be the judge of that,' Cooper responded. 'I'm just going by his clothing, I've not got that close, if you want to know the truth.'

Stock sniggered. 'Good job I had a hearty breakfast this morning. This one sounds like it may take some time and I may have to miss lunch.'

* * * *

Norfolk George had only just started up his engine when his mobile rang and the name Carmichael came up on the small screen in the consul of his navy-blue Nissan Qashqai.

'Hi, Carmichael. I was just about to call you,' announced Norfolk George before Carmichael had time to utter a word. 'I guess you got the text.'

'When did you receive it?' Carmichael enquired sternly.

'About thirty minutes ago,' replied the reporter. 'Is it true?'

Carmichael paused before responding. 'Someone has been killed on the line today, but at this stage I've no details to either confirm or deny who it was, let alone the circumstances.'

'Why don't we meet down at the railway line?' suggested Norfolk George. 'I am just on my way there now.'

'Oh no you're not!' snapped Carmichael. 'You can head on straight to Kirkwood Station and bring your mobile with you. I need to trace the person who sent you the text message.' Carmichael glanced at his watch. 'I'll expect you here in twenty minutes tops.'

'What!' exclaimed Norfolk George angrily. 'I'm a reporter, I need to ...'

Carmichael hung up. He had no desire to argue with his reporter friend.

'Damn it,' cried the exasperated village hack. 'How does that bloody man expect me to earn a decent living?'

Having curtailed the call and without a shred of remorse for ruining Norfolk George's day, Carmichael leaned back in his chair and studied the text once again.

Chapter 3

It took Stock and his team all morning to painstakingly gather all the pieces of the unfortunate casualty of the train strike.

'So I take it he was a man?' enquired Cooper as soon as it was clear the pathologist had concluded his work at the scene.

'Yes,' replied Stock as he reached where Cooper and Dalton were standing. 'And he's in a real mess. I'd say he was probably in his forties, but I will know more after I've had a chance to take a closer look at him in the path lab.'

'Did he have any identification on him?' Dalton asked.

'No,' replied Stock with a small shake of his head. 'But he almost certainly died at seven thirty-seven this morning.'

Cooper was suitably impressed by Stock's ability to be so precise. 'How do you know that?' he asked.

'It was the express train to Manchester that hit him. The station master reckons it would have been about that time that it reached here,' Stock responded wryly and, without another word, trundled off in the direction of his car.

'How can anyone enjoy that job?' Cooper asked.

Rachel Dalton shrugged her shoulders. 'God only knows,' she replied, 'but he certainly does love his work.'

*　*　*　*

Carmichael sniggered to himself as he watched Norfolk George stomp over to his car, slam the door shut and screech out of the car park.

7

He looked down at the phone in his hand before turning back to face Sergeant Watson, who was equally as amused as his boss.

'I think he's a tad unhappy,' he remarked sarcastically.

Carmichael stretched out his arm and passed the mobile to Watson.

'Not my problem, Marc,' he said indifferently. 'We need to trace who sent the text message. Get on to it. I want to apprehend this person.'

'It's probably a hoax,' suggested Watson.

'You may be right,' affirmed Carmichael. 'But if it is, it's a sick one, so either way this person needs finding.'

Watson exited the room leaving his boss to look again at the text message on his mobile that Norfolk George had forwarded to him earlier:

Two down ... two to go. 737 strikes again. Have you been down to Alcar this morning? ... There's blood on the tracks. Sorry I made such a mess with this one. The next will be neater, I promise. Catch me if you can.

Carmichael hoped that the message was a hoax, but his gut told him that this was very real.

*   *   *   *

It was 12:25 p.m. when Cooper received the call from Carmichael. He and Rachel Dalton were already in his beaten-up Volvo and just about to head back to Kirkwood Station when Carmichael's name came up on the screen and the mobile emitted the ring tone that confirmed it was the boss.

'Good afternoon, sir,' said Cooper. 'We are just on our way back.'

'So what have you found, Paul?' enquired Carmichael forcefully.

'It's not easy to say yet,' replied Cooper. 'It was a real mess. Stock thinks the dead person is male and his hunch is he's about fortyish, but to be honest that's about all we can tell you at the moment.'

'Any ID on the body?' probed Carmichael.

'No, sir,' responded Cooper. 'The SOCOs didn't find anything.'

Carmichael thought for a moment. 'Is the area still cordoned off?'

Cooper looked quizzically at Rachel, who returned a blank look, having no idea what Carmichael was saying to Cooper.

'It is,' replied Cooper in slight bewilderment. 'But they've taken away all the body parts. Stock's gone back to the path lab to do his autopsy and it looks like the rest of the SOCOs are just about to wrap up.'

'Stop them!' instructed Carmichael firmly. 'This may be a murder rather than just a jumper. There's been a text sent to the local press claiming responsibility.'

'You're joking,' responded Cooper with amazement.

'What's happening?' Rachel mouthed.

'I'm not,' replied Carmichael. 'Marc's just gone to try and see if he can trace who sent the text. It may be a sick prank, but until we are one-hundred-per-cent certain I want the area to remain cordoned off. Tell the SOCOs I need them to do a detailed sweep of the area to look for anything suspicious, particularly where the body first made contact with the train.'

Cooper put his hand over the mobile. 'The boss thinks it may have been murder,' he told Rachel much to her astonishment.

'Also, get some extra plain-clothed officers down there,' continued Carmichael. 'I want Rachel to stay and supervise a full house-to-house in the surrounding area. Can you get her to do that?'

'Yes, no problem,' responded the flabbergasted sergeant.

'I want you to interview the train driver,' continued

Carmichael. 'I want to know what he saw. I am specifically keen to know if the poor man he hit was dead or alive before the train struck him.'

'OK,' replied Cooper. 'I'll get on to it straight away.'

Carmichael checked his watch. 'Let's all get together back here at the station for a debrief at six,' he said. 'I hope neither you nor Rachel had any plans for this evening. It might be a late night for us all.'

Carmichael did not wait for a reply. He pressed the red button on the mobile to end the call.

Cooper put down his mobile and looked towards his bemused young colleague. 'There's been a development on this one,' he said calmly. 'Someone's claiming to have murdered our mystery man, so the boss has given us a few specific tasks to do.'

'Yes,' replied Rachel cautiously, realising that more was to come.

'And he wants us to report our findings at a debrief back at Kirkwood at six.'

Rachel gave a hint of a smile and shrugged her shoulders to further demonstrate her acquiescence. 'So what instructions did he have for me?'

Chapter 4

The large frosted windows that dominated the two sides of the Women's Institute Hall had been completely shrouded by long dark curtains. The bright summer sunshine normally illuminating the hall at that time of day was now obscured and replaced by two dimly lit spotlights that shone down on to the centre of the stage. At the back of the hall a woman in her late fifties, one of the younger of the event organisers, occasionally shone a torch to help latecomers find an available seat. Not that there were many free seats to be found in the dark hall that afternoon.

Despite it still being only one o'clock in the afternoon, the WI hall was almost full and the eager audience waited in anticipation for the celebrated spiritualist to take to the stage.

'It's exciting, isn't it?' remarked the beaming Susan Watson, who had almost had to drag Penny to the event.

Penny shook her head and gazed back in her friend's direction. 'I have no idea what we're doing here, Susan. Steve thought I was going mad when I told him.'

Susan smiled. 'Marc was the same. It may well be all mumbo-jumbo as he says, but it's going to be a laugh.'

Penny looked down at the floor, shook her head again, only more pronounced this time and tried her best to suppress the surge of nervous laughter she felt coming. 'I only hope she doesn't summon one of my dead relatives,' she remarked. 'Especially if it's Steve's Auntie Barbara. I couldn't cope if she's somehow conjured up. She was a real pain in the derrière.'

Both women started to giggle uncontrollably as the absurdity of what they were doing fully kicked in. To conceal their sniggering they bowed their heads low and covered their mouths tightly with their hands.

Suddenly the lights went out and a voice boomed from the speakers located in each of the four corners of the room.

'Ladies and gentlemen, I have great pleasure in introducing the world-renowned medium, Psychic Siobhan.'

In keeping with the sense of theatre, the lights on the stage came back on and in the centre stood the imposing figure of Siobhan Ballentyne, the self-appointed 'Queen of Clairvoyants'.

'Well, you have to give her ten out of ten for her entrance,' remarked Penny, who was still trying her level best to keep her laughter in check.

'Absolutely,' replied Susan, tears rolling down her face. 'I can't wait to see what her impression of Auntie Barbara is like.'

* * * *

Given the potential seriousness of the text message, Carmichael decided to share what little information he had with Chief Inspector Hewitt. Although he still struggled to cope with his self-important boss, nevertheless in the time he'd worked at Kirkwood, Carmichael had come to respect his superior and his counsel was often helpful.

'Is the Chief in?' Carmichael asked Angela, Hewitt's able PA.

'Hello, Steve,' replied Angela with a welcoming smile. 'Yes, he's in and he's free. He has a call with the Super in about twenty minutes, but he's free until then.'

Carmichael returned the smile to Angela before knocking on Hewitt's door.

'Come,' Hewitt bellowed from inside the office.

'I'll see you in twenty minutes then,' said Carmichael with an impish grin. 'Remember mine's white with one sugar.'

He didn't hang around to witness Angela's reaction, but opened the door and burst into Hewitt's office.

'Can you spare me ten minutes?' Angela heard him ask just before the door closed behind him.

* * * *

Rachel had already knocked on about a dozen doors before she arrived at Betty Wilbraham's terraced cottage in the tiny hamlet of Hasslebury.

Hoping that her visitor was Dennis Preston who had called earlier that day to ask if he could drop off yet another abandoned hedgehog, Betty rushed to the door.

'What do you want?' she asked grumpily, her disappointment etched across her face.

'I'm DC Dalton,' replied Rachel with a cheerful smile and her identity card in her hand. 'I wonder if I could ask you a few questions about an incident on the railway line this morning.'

'Incident,' retorted Betty gruffly. 'What sort of incident?'

'A man was killed on the line at around twenty to eight this morning,' continued Rachel. 'I'm just calling on all the houses around here to see if anyone saw anything suspicious or out of the ordinary.'

'Like what?' snapped Betty curtly.

'Well, anything that seemed unusual,' replied Rachel.

Betty thought for a moment then shook her head. 'No, nothing,' she said. 'I haven't seen anyone today, only you, and at that time I would have been in the back garden feeding my babies.'

Rachel's furrowed brow gave a clear indication that she was puzzled by the dishevelled woman's comment.

'I look after sick and abandoned hedgehogs,' announced Betty, to counter her visitor's bewilderment.

'Really!' exclaimed Rachel with genuine curiosity. 'How many do you have?'

Seeing that the DC was clearly interested in her prickly charges, Betty's mood eased. 'I have twelve at the moment, thirteen later today when the RSPCA man brings another one,' she said with pride.

'Wow,' replied Rachel with enthusiasm. 'Could I see them?'

Betty thought for a few seconds then smiled softly. 'Of course you can. Come on in, my dear.'

Excitedly Rachel followed Betty Wilbraham into her messy front room.

*　*　*　*

'In fairness, you've got to admit she's not bad,' whispered Susan as Psychic Siobhan concluded her second conversation with the spirit world.

'It's certainly impressive,' agreed Penny. 'But a bit of research could have got her a lot of that information. I'm not convinced.'

As she spoke, Siobhan raised her arms and in a strong deep voice proclaimed, 'I'm now picking up someone called Barbara.'

Susan and Penny exchanged a horrified look.

'She's here beside me,' continued Siobhan. 'She's asking for someone called P ...' Penny's stomach churned and her palms began to sweat. 'Pauline,' announced the psychic.

A rotund woman with a red face nervously raised her arm.

'That will be me,' she uttered timidly.

Siobhan fixed her attention on the poor frightened lady. 'She says she doesn't blame you for not coming to the party. Does that mean anything to you?'

Pauline squirmed in her chair. 'It's my mum,' she said

14

apprehensively. 'She died in hospital the day after her seventieth birthday. My eldest daughter was ill so I couldn't get to see her that day. I was there when she died but I don't know if she knew I was there as she was unconscious.'

'She did see you, my dear,' replied Siobhan with certainty. 'She says thanks for being there and not to worry about the birthday.'

Pauline, who had now been encouraged to stand by one of Siobhan's assistants, was welling up. 'I'm so relieved,' she confessed. 'I thought she might not have known I was there.'

'She says she did see you and says you must not worry about that,' continued Siobhan.

The now sobbing but happy Pauline replaced her considerable bottom back on its chair.

'She's not gone away yet, my dear,' added Siobhan. 'She's saying that you're a good girl and she loves you, but you need to do the right thing. Do you understand that message?'

Pauline looked puzzled and shook her head slowly.

'She says that you've done something you regret,' said Siobhan. 'It's not clear what it is, but Barbara is saying you must do the right thing. You must face up to what you've done and do the right thing.'

Pauline remained in her seat, but from the expression on her face it looked very much like she knew what her dead mother was saying.

'She says all will be OK as long as you make it right,' added Siobhan. 'She knows that you regret what you did and you've been tormented about this for weeks, but she says you must do the right thing.'

Clearly distressed, Pauline clambered out of her seat, tearfully pushed past the people in her row and, as quickly as she could, exited the hall.

'Sounds like a bit on the side,' remarked Susan out of the corner of her mouth.

'Shh,' replied Penny, who found the whole episode with

15

Pauline distressing but at the same time, to her embarrassment, rather humorous.

* * * *

Hewitt's dark frown as he carefully studied the text message said everything. 'It may be a hoax, but I tend to agree with you: the "catch me if you can" taunt has that eerie feel of reality about it.'

Carmichael raised his eyebrows and nodded his head. 'Watson's checking with the service provider. Hopefully we'll get an answer soon on who sent it.'

Hewitt's eyes continued to scrutinise the message. 'So what does seven three seven mean?' he enquired. 'And two down suggests that there has been another death. Who was the first one?'

'That's what I intend to try and find out this afternoon,' explained Carmichael. 'I've got the team together at six this evening for a debrief. With any luck by then we'll have uncovered a bit more.'

At last Hewitt looked up from the small screen on Carmichael's mobile. 'Keep me in the loop on this one,' he said as he handed the phone back to Carmichael. 'Let me know as soon as you uncover anything.'

Carmichael took the mobile from Hewitt's open hand, placed it into his shirt pocket and rose up from his chair. 'Of course, sir,' he replied.

Carmichael had not yet reached the door when Angela entered Hewitt's office carrying a tray with two mugs of coffee and a plate of chocolate biscuits.

'That was very perceptive of you,' exclaimed Hewitt with surprise in his voice. 'But unfortunately Inspector Carmichael is just leaving.'

'It's OK, Angela,' retorted Carmichael cheekily. 'I'll take mine with me – which is mine?'

16

Angela stood still as Carmichael hovered over the tray. 'It's the mug nearest you,' she calmly replied.

Carmichael lifted the mug from the tray with his left hand. 'I'll pinch a couple of these bickies, too,' he said with a wry smile. 'Chocolate digestives are my favourite.'

Hewitt's PA stood to attention as the Inspector grabbed a handful of biscuits and made his exit from the room.

* * * *

Rachel Dalton had always liked animals and the opportunity to see Betty Wilbraham's hedgehogs was something she was genuinely relishing. As soon as she was inside the large garden shed that housed Betty's charges, Rachel's eyes widened.

'They are so sweet,' she enthused, the pitch of her voice raising an octave as if to emphasise her delight.

Betty was thrilled to find someone who appeared to share her love of the small prickly mammals. 'Do you want to hold one?' she asked.

'Could I?!' exclaimed Rachel, who found it impossible to contain her joy.

* * * *

It took Cooper less than an hour to interview the driver of the train involved in that morning's incident. Having completed his assignment, he headed back to Kirkwood Police Station where he found Carmichael in the incident room.

'What did the driver have to say?' enquired Carmichael.

'Interesting,' replied Cooper. 'He's still in shock, but he maintains that the man hit the front of his train as it emerged from under a bridge. Apparently he'd come down from the bridge and had only just landed on the track as the train hit him.'

'Could he tell whether the man was alive or dead when he landed on the track?' asked Carmichael.

Cooper shook his head. 'No, the driver had only a split second before the train struck the poor guy.'

'But he confirmed it was a man?' added Carmichael.

'Yes he did,' replied Cooper. 'But he said it all happened so quickly he didn't even manage to start to brake until after the collision. He reckons he was doing about 80 miles an hour so it's no wonder the body was such a mess.'

'So how's Rachel doing with the house-to-house?' Carmichael enquired.

Cooper shrugged his shoulders. 'I've no idea. She said she'd get a lift back with the uniformed guys.'

'She knows we are having our debrief at six, doesn't she?'

'Oh yes,' confirmed Cooper. 'She knows. Anyway what's this about you getting a text message claiming it was murder?'

Carmichael handed Cooper his mobile. 'Look at this.' He waited while Cooper read the message, then continued. 'While we're waiting for Rachel and for Marc to join us, I want you to help me try and work out who the hell the other murder victim was and what seven three seven means?'

Cooper's eyes continued to study the text, if anything even more intently than Hewitt had done earlier. 'I don't know who the other murder victim may be, and it may just be a coincidence that it was seven thirty-seven this morning when the accident happened, but do you think that seven three seven could refer to the time of death?'

'I have no idea,' Carmichael replied. 'But it's certainly worth considering. Let's look for other suspicious deaths in the area that occurred at around that time. It seems a reasonable place to start.'

*　　*　　*　　*

Having spent nearly twenty minutes admiring Hedgehog Betty's spiky charges, Rachel finally decided it was time to resume her house-to-house enquiries.

'I will have to go,' she said reluctantly as she handed back the tiny creature to its surrogate mother. 'So are you sure you didn't see or hear anything unusual this morning?'

'No, I'm sorry, dear,' replied Betty. 'I did hear the train's brakes screeching at about seven forty, but other than that, nothing.'

Rachel smiled. 'OK, thank you for your help and for letting me see the hedgehogs. They're beautiful.'

'That's no problem, my dear,' replied the now cheerful Betty. 'You're welcome to come and see them at anytime.'

As Rachel made her way towards the garden gate, she turned back to face Betty. 'Who lives next door?' she asked. 'I knocked before I came here but there was no answer.'

'It's Aiden Davidson,' replied Betty. 'He's an artist. I'm surprised he's not at home. He's usually about at this time.'

'Not to worry,' replied Rachel. 'I'll call back later. It will give me an excuse to come and see the hedgehogs again.'

Betty smiled. 'As I've said, you're more than welcome anytime, my dear.'

As Rachel reached the garden gate she was greeted by a tall, young man in uniform, clutching a small plastic carrying cage.

'Hi, Dennis,' shouted Betty. 'Come through to the garden.'

Rachel smiled and held open the gate for Dennis Preston, the handsome RSPCA officer. 'Some additions to the sanctuary?' she remarked.

'Yes,' replied the RSPCA man. 'Without Betty, God knows what we'd do with these poor things.'

Betty Wilbraham and Dennis Preston watched as Rachel continued down the lane to complete her house to house enquiries.

'Who's she?' Dennis asked.

'She's a police officer,' replied Betty. 'She's investigating the death of a man on the railway line earlier today.'

'She's a pretty girl.'

'And I thought *I* was your only girl,' said Betty with a wry smile before taking the cage from his hands and heading off towards her shed.

'You are,' muttered Preston, who remained stationary, staring down the road until Rachel's shapely silhouette had disappeared out of sight.

* * * *

It was almost 4 p.m. when Penny Carmichael and Susan Watson finally emerged from the hall into the warm summer sunshine.

'Wow, that sun's bright,' Susan cried out as she quickly pulled down her sunglasses over her eyes.

Penny squinted and fumbled about in her handbag for her pair. 'I don't know about you but I'm mighty relieved to get out of there,' she said, head down, as the two ladies strolled slowly into the balmy late afternoon. 'Those chairs get pretty uncomfortable after three hours.'

Susan, who had noticed the unmistakeable figure of Siobhan Ballentyne making a beeline for them, nudged her friend as surreptitiously as she could to prevent Penny saying too much.

'You're not convinced of my powers, ladies,' announced Siobhan in a loud confident voice. 'I can sense when I have doubters in the audience and I can see you are still not sure I'm genuine.'

Having at last located her sunglasses, Penny looked back at the psychic. 'I would not go so far as to say I'm a complete sceptic,' she replied as tactfully as she could. 'But I'm not someone who finds it easy to accept what I can't see or touch.'

'Me too,' added Susan, who was more than happy for Penny to take the lead.

'Psychic Siobhan' smiled in a sneering sort of way. 'Then let me help to convert you, my dear,' she replied eerily.

Penny glanced in Susan's direction with a look of apprehension on her face. As she did, without any warning, Psychic Siobhan gently placed her cold hands on Penny's wrist and closed her eyes. 'I can feel that you have a solid relationship,' she muttered. 'The bond within your family is strong. I see nothing but love and warmth.'

Penny raised her eyes to the heavens, and Susan had to fight hard to stop herself giggling.

With her eyes still closed, 'Psychic Siobhan' continued, 'You need to tell your husband that the message is no hoax. Tell him to take it seriously and to follow his instincts regardless of what others may say.' Siobhan released her grip, opened her eyes and smiled. 'I know that means nothing to you but it will to him,' she said. 'And if he wants me to help him in any way, tell him I will gladly do so.'

Penny and Susan stood motionless with expressions of bewilderment on their faces as 'Psychic Siobhan' turned away, walked a few paces and started to engage a group of elderly ladies who had been waiting patiently for an audience with the great mystic.

'Sounds like a load of twaddle to me,' whispered Susan, as soon as she was confident that Siobhan was out of earshot.

'I imagine that's just what Steve will say when I tell him,' replied Penny, 'but his language will be a little more explicit than yours.'

Chapter 5

The debrief started at precisely 6 p.m. Cooper, Watson and Dalton had worked with Carmichael long enough to know punctuality mattered to him. So when he said 6 p.m. they all knew he meant 6 p.m. and being late, even by a minute, would not be tolerated for any reason.

'Good evening, team,' began Carmichael. 'Who wants to kick off?'

Cooper, Watson and Rachel exchanged furtive glances.

'OK, let me start then,' continued Carmichael, who in truth was only too keen to share what he knew.

Without waiting for the team to reply, he grabbed the marker and strode purposefully towards the whiteboard.

'At around seven thirty-seven this morning, a man was hit by an express train near Alcar station.' As he spoke Carmichael scribbled the time on the whiteboard in his usual untidy handwriting. 'At around ten past eight Norfolk George received a text message from someone claiming responsibility for the death and, more alarmingly, asserting this is the second such murder he or she has committed. For your benefit, Rachel, I've had the message printed out.' Carmichael handed to each of the three officers an A4 sheet of paper which had a draft of the full message. Rachel studied it closely.

'It says there will be two more,' announced Rachel with alarm in her voice. 'And what on earth does seven three seven mean?'

Carmichael smiled. 'That puzzled me too, but Cooper twigged it straight away. Do you want to tell her?'

Cooper, modest as ever, elected to allow the boss to carry on. 'No, sir, you continue,' he muttered.

'It's a time. Seven thirty-seven,' revealed Carmichael enthusiastically. 'It's precisely the time our mystery man was killed. And importantly also the time we think the first murder occurred.'

'I'm impressed,' exclaimed Watson in amazement. 'You've already traced the first murder? That was bloody quick!'

Carmichael squirmed a little. 'We think we have, but let's not jump to any conclusions yet. We need to keep an open mind, but we think he's talking about a hit-and-run close to Alcar from back in June.'

'What – the old tramp who we couldn't name?' remarked Watson.

'Yes,' replied Carmichael. 'If you recall, his body was found at about 8 a.m. and his broken watch had stopped at seven thirty-seven.'

'But there was no text message associated with that one,' remarked Watson. 'Surely, if it was the same person he'd have sent a text that time, too.'

'You've got a good point there,' interjected Rachel.

'As I say, we aren't totally sure it's this murder the text is talking about,' concurred Carmichael. 'However, it's the only unexplained death we've had in the area for months and it happened near Alcar at seven thirty-seven, so we have to follow it up.'

'That's assuming the text Norfolk George received is pukka,' added Cooper.

'Pukka,' Rachel teased. 'Get you, Jamie Oliver!'

'So what else do we know?' Carmichael asked, ignoring Rachel's flippant comment.

'Well, as you know, sir,' Cooper added. 'The driver of the train could not confirm whether the man was dead or alive before the train struck him. He did say, though, that he came down off the bridge and he hit the line just as the train hit him.'

'To be honest, sir,' added Watson. 'If you ask me, the man just jumped. I reckon the tramp is a straight-forward hit-and-run and this text, sick though it is, is just a hoax.'

Carmichael took a deep breath. 'You could be right for once, Marc,' he announced forthrightly. 'But until we find names for the two dead men and the person who sent this text message, we treat this as suspicious. Do you all understand?'

Cooper, Watson and Dalton all nodded; they could see the boss was getting frustrated.

'This "catch me if you can" comment is a bit melo-dramatic,' added Carmichael. 'I'm not sure what to make of it.'

Rachel sniggered. 'It's a movie, sir.'

'Really,' replied Carmichael, who clearly had never heard of it. 'What film is that?'

Even Cooper and Watson looked surprised at Carmichael's ignorance.

'It's got Leonardo DiCaprio and Tom Hanks in it,' Rachel replied. 'It's about a man who evades capture by adopting new identities.'

'It's a Steven Spielberg film,' added Cooper. 'It was quite popular.'

'Was it?' replied Carmichael who could sense that his limited knowledge of recent screen hits had struck his team as curious. 'I'll have to have a look at it.'

'It's really good,' remarked Rachel. 'I've seen it a few times.'

'Anyway, what have you two discovered?' continued Carmichael, turning his attention to Watson and Rachel, now keen to change the subject.

'Nothing from the house-to-house,' replied Rachel

diffidently. 'We've a few houses we need to get back to tomorrow, but the people we did speak to said they neither saw nor heard anything other than the train brakes screeching at about seven thirty-seven.'

'What about you, Marc?' Carmichael asked, although he knew full well that if Marc had discovered something he'd have already made sure the team knew.

As Carmichael had expected, Watson shook his head. 'Still waiting on the service provider to get back to me,' he replied awkwardly. 'They've had system issues today with their computer and they say they can't get me a name until tomorrow morning at the earliest.'

'Sodding computers,' said Carmichael, his dismay clear to everyone. 'You'd think they'd have some sort of bloody backup.'

Watson shrugged his shoulders. 'It's a sign of the times, boss,' he argued. 'We can't survive without them these days.'

Carmichael shook his head to confirm his irritation, not that anyone in the room needed any additional evidence. 'So what else have you been doing, Marc?' he asked pointedly. 'You've surely been doing something constructive this afternoon.'

'I've been clearing up paperwork on a few other cases I'm working on,' replied Watson, who could feel his boss's wrath heading in his direction.

'Well, tomorrow,' snapped Carmichael irritably, 'I want this whiteboard to have more than just "seven thirty-seven" written on it.'

The three officers could feel that Carmichael was less than pleased with their progress.

'I want you, Marc, to get on to the service provider and get me that damn name. I also want you to get Stock's autopsy report. I don't want you to do anything other than focus on this case. Do I make myself clear?'

'Crystal, sir,' replied Watson.

Carmichael then turned to Rachel. 'Let the uniformed guys finish the house-to-house,' he said resolutely but with a little less aggression. 'I want you to go through the case notes of the hit-and-run. If need be, go back out and re-interview any of the people we spoke to before. I want to know if the cases are linked.'

'Right you are, sir,' replied Rachel, who had no desire to say anything that would make Carmichael any angrier than he was already.

'What about me?' asked Cooper.

'I want you round at my house at eight sharp,' announced Carmichael firmly. 'I want to have a look at the scene myself, especially the bridge he came down from.'

Chapter 6

Carmichael's journey home that evening was quick and uneventful, in stark contrast to his journey to work in the morning. However, this did little to improve his frame of mind, and Carmichael was still very tense and annoyed when he entered the hallway.

'Hi, how was your day?' Penny enquired as her husband made his way through to the kitchen.

'Terrible,' he replied with no attempt to contain his frustration. 'Sometimes those three just beggar belief,' he ranted. 'We've a dead man, who as yet is unidentified, and then some other person is texting to say he's responsible for not just that death but another. You'd think that my team would be one-hundred-per-cent focused on finding the text messenger and discovering the name of the dead man, but in our briefing they could offer nothing. Not one bloody thing. I tell you sometimes I swear …'

Penny put her arm around her husband's waist. 'I think you need to sit down, calm down and have a glass of wine,' she interjected. 'Then let's talk about it.'

Carmichael puffed out his cheeks and sat down as he'd been told.

Penny removed the stopper from the half-full bottle of Pinotage they had opened the day before, poured Carmichael a large glass and handed it over to him. 'Now, tell me again,' she said in a firm but composed tone. 'But this time, try not to get so wound up.'

Carmichael clasped the glass and took a large gulp of the blood-red liquid. 'OK,' he said as calmly as he could, 'it's like this.'

* * * *

Norfolk George had spent most of the day debating whether he should run the story. His weekly paper was due out the following day and he was desperate to include this scoop. He'd always enjoyed a great relationship with Carmichael, which he was keen to preserve, and he knew that if he went against Carmichael's instruction there would certainly be consequences. However, after much soul-searching, George decided that he'd not only run the story, but would also talk to one of his old chums who worked on a national red-top. His plan was simple, give his friend a little snippet of information, just enough to get a small story printed the next day, then go to town on the story himself on the front page of this week's *Observer*.

By 8 p.m. that evening, with his plan now executed, Norfolk George signed off the paper to the printers and poured himself a large scotch. He was certain he'd made the right decision, but was also anxious about what Carmichael would say when he found out. For a fleeting moment Norfolk George did consider texting Carmichael to at least give him some forewarning but, after a few more gulps of whisky, discounted any such idea.

* * * *

Having successfully managed to get her husband to calm down and explain the day's events in a composed and lucid manner, Penny sat back in her chair to consider the implications of what Siobhan Ballentyne had said to her outside the WI hall.

'Aren't you going to ask me about my day?' she enquired.

Carmichael looked up into his wife's eyes. 'Of course,' he replied. 'Tell me about your day. How did it go with Mystic Meg?'

Penny smiled. 'It's Psychic Siobhan,' she replied sternly. 'And it was interesting.'

'She didn't take you in?' said Carmichael, the derision palpable in his voice. 'Tell me that you don't believe there's any substance to all that drivel?'

'No,' replied Penny resolutely, 'I'm not converted, but I'm not as sceptical as I was.'

'I can't believe it!' exclaimed Carmichael teasingly. 'She's suckered you in.'

'No, she hasn't,' Penny retorted firmly. 'But she did come up to Susan and me afterwards and gave me a message for you. At the time it meant nothing, but after what you've just told me, you need to know.'

Carmichael frowned as he listened to what Penny was saying. 'So, what pearls of wisdom did she bestow on you?' he asked a tad sneeringly.

Penny took a deep breath. 'Well, she took hold of my wrists like so.' Penny took hold of Carmichael's arms just above the wrist. 'She then said I needed to tell you that the message was no hoax. She told me to tell you to take it seriously and to follow your instincts regardless of what others might say.'

Carmichael was stunned. 'How did she come to say that?' he asked.

'Search me,' replied Penny. 'It just sounded like total nonsense until you told me about the text message. It is creepy, though, isn't it?'

Carmichael thought for a moment. 'It's got to be some sort of trick,' he declared. 'Those people are all charlatans. For sure, they're good at what they do and I have no idea how they do it, but it's all a con.'

Penny shrugged her shoulders. 'You may be right, Steve,'

she confessed, 'but you've got to admit it's all a bit spooky and it's too close to the truth to be a lucky guess, or just a coincidence.'

Carmichael drained his wine glass.

'It's really good stuff,' he remarked as he took hold of the wine bottle. 'I think I'll have another. Do you want one?'

Penny shook her head. 'One's enough for me.'.

As he poured himself another large glass of red wine, Carmichael looked earnestly into Penny's eyes. 'I may go and have a chat with this mystic woman tomorrow,' he remarked offhandedly. 'I guess I need to leave no stone unturned, including voices from beyond the grave.'

Penny smiled. 'I'll get her details; they're in the programme,' she replied smugly. 'I'm glad and impressed that you're being so open-minded about all this.'

As his wife left the kitchen, Carmichael puffed out his cheeks and shook his head gently. 'God only knows what Hewitt will say if I tell him I've been talking to some batty old spiritualist,' he muttered. 'He'll think I've gone soft in my old age. Or, worse still, he'll think I'm losing the plot.'

Chapter 7

At precisely 8 a.m., Cooper's battered old Volvo pulled up outside Carmichael's house.

'I'm off now,' Carmichael shouted as he spied the car from the front-room window. 'I've no idea when I'll be back.'

'OK,' replied Penny from the kitchen, 'have a nice ...'

She didn't manage to get the end of the sentence out of her mouth before the front door slammed and Carmichael was away.

'... day,' she eventually muttered to herself.

It was another beautiful day. The birds were singing and the sweet aroma of lavender and roses filled Carmichael's nostrils as he strode purposefully down his driveway.

'Morning, sir,' said Cooper, his greeting as warm and genuine as the summer morning.

Carmichael carefully clambered into the passenger seat. 'Morning, Paul,' he replied, although not as cordially. 'Are you sure this thing will get us to Alcar?' he remarked mockingly.

'No problem,' replied the smiling Cooper, who had every faith in his trusty old Volvo. 'She's done over one hundred and eighty thousand miles so far and has never broken down. The Swedes certainly know how to make cars. This beauty will run for a good few years, no problem.'

Carmichael belted up. 'Right, let's go then,' he instructed. 'I want to see where it all happened.'

31

Cooper slammed the gear lever into first and with a slight jerk (which suggested to Carmichael that all may not be well with the trusty car's gear box) pulled away.

'Right you are, sir,' remarked Cooper cheerily. 'It should take us no more than fifteen minutes, assuming there's no major hold-ups.'

* * * *

Rachel Dalton placed the plastic coffee cup she'd bought from the drive-in McDonald's on her desk, rested her handbag on her chair and slipped off her jacket.

'Morning, Marc,' she said cheerily. 'You're in early.'

Watson grimaced. 'I want to make sure his lordship has nothing to moan about later. I thought he was way over the top yesterday.'

Rachel nodded. 'You're right, but I think he was a bit stressed,' she added. 'But I'm with you. I'm going to go through those records with a fine-tooth comb.'

'Yeah, that was a strange one,' remarked Watson as he cast his mind back a few months. 'I was on that case and we spent ages trying to identify the man but drew a complete blank.'

'Well, it would appear I've got less than a day to achieve what you couldn't in weeks,' she replied. 'Wish me luck.'

Watson glanced at his watch and then picked up the telephone receiver. 'I'd better call the service provider to see if they've had any joy discovering who owns that damn mobile.'

* * * *

Cooper parked his car a few metres away from the tiny bridge that spanned the main line railway line.

'Here we are,' he said as if it was a major achievement.

Carmichael didn't reply. He was keen to take a look at where the man had jumped, or had maybe been thrown.

'It's really quiet around here,' he finally remarked as they strode on to the raised hump. 'If someone wanted to drag a body up here and launch it over, he'd probably be able to do so without worrying too much about being seen.'

'It would still be a bit risky in my view,' remarked Cooper. 'At that time in the morning you'd have thought there may be at least a few cars driving through here.'

'Where does this go to?' Carmichael asked, looking down the road away from Cooper's car.

'It winds through the countryside for about three miles before hitting the main road from Southport to Kirkwood.'

Carmichael looked around. 'Well, it's eight twenty now, so not too much later than when the accident happened yesterday and, as far as I can remember, we didn't pass anything as we drove down here and nothing has come by since we got out of the car. No, I think our killer, if indeed there was one, would have been pretty unlucky if he'd been spotted.'

Cooper found it hard to argue against this logic. 'But I suggest we still get some uniformed officers down here tomorrow morning to stop and speak with any passing vehicles,' he said.

Carmichael nodded. 'You're right, Paul,' he said. 'We shouldn't assume anything.'

Carmichael stood on his tiptoes and peered over the side of the bridge and down on to the railway line. 'It's a hell of a drop down,' he remarked. 'It's got to be twelve to fifteen metres.'

Cooper, who was a good few inches taller than his boss, gazed over as well. 'Yes, I think the fall on to the track would probably kill you.'

'Did the SOCOs come up here yesterday?' Carmichael asked.

'Yes,' replied Cooper, 'they were very thorough.'

Carmichael stepped back from the side of the bridge. 'So, did he jump or was he pushed?' he enquired rhetorically.

Before Cooper could comment, Carmichael's mobile began to ring in his pocket.

'It's Marc,' announced Carmichael as he looked at the incoming number. 'Maybe he's at long last got us the name of the mystery texter.'

Carmichael remained quiet as he listened to Marc provide the information he had been keen to obtain.

'We'll meet you there,' he replied before ending the call.

Cooper waited patiently to learn the name of the texter.

'Where's Hasslebury?' enquired Carmichael eagerly.

'It's a tiny hamlet about thirty or forty metres down the road,' replied Cooper. 'It's about two minutes walk from here.'

'Well, that's where our texter lives,' announced Carmichael excitedly. 'His name's Aiden Davidson and he lives at number 10, Ivy Cottages.'

Chapter 8

Hasslebury was made up of just twelve terraced houses, six facing east called Rose Cottages and, a few hundred yards away, a further six facing west called Ivy Cottages. They had been built in the mid-nineteenth century to house the local farmer's workers. In more recent times they had been acquired either by young couples as first-time houses or by people who enjoyed an isolated existence.

Aiden Davidson fell into the second category. His house was the next-to-last one facing west.

'Shall we wait for backup?' enquired Cooper as they arrived close to the house.

Carmichael nodded. 'Yes, we need to cover the back in case he tries to make a run for it. We can't risk him getting away.'

The two officers walked slowly past the house and, once out of sight, hid behind a large sandstone wall.

'Did you manage to see anybody through the window as we passed?' Carmichael enquired.

'No,' replied Cooper. 'To be honest the place looked deserted. Maybe he's at work.'

'Go and see if you can get around the back,' instructed Carmichael. 'I'll wait here for Marc.'

Cooper nodded and carefully picked his way through the long grass and brambles that led to the back of the terraced houses.

Within a few minutes Cooper was out of Carmichael's eye-line and within five more minutes Watson arrived in a marked police car with two uniformed officers.

'You two get yourselves round the back,' whispered Carmichael to the uniformed officers. 'Cooper's already there. We'll give you two minutes then we're going to go through the front.'

Without a word the two uniformed officers did as they were instructed.

'Do we know anything about this Davidson character?' Carmichael asked.

'Not much,' replied Watson. 'Rachel said she tried his house yesterday when she was making enquiries, but there wasn't anyone in. The lady next door said he was an artist of some sort and Rachel seems to think he lives alone.'

Carmichael looked at his watch. 'They should be in position now – let's go.'

The two officers marched up the driveway and banged loudly on the front door.

'Open up, Mr Davidson,' Watson shouted. 'It's the police.'

They waited a few seconds. When there was no response, Watson hammered loudly on the door for a second time, but for a good few seconds.

Slowly the door started to open and as soon as Watson saw this he pushed hard against it, sending Cooper recoiling backwards.

'Hold on,' Cooper shouted, holding his knee which had taken the brunt of Watson's power. 'It's me.'

'I take it he's not here?' Carmichael enquired.

Cooper, still clutching his knee, shook his head. 'I don't think so. The back door wasn't locked, so we just came in. The uniformed lads are checking upstairs, but we've found a mobile. It's clear for all to see on the kitchen table.'

Carmichael pushed past Cooper, indifferent to his obvious pain, and entered the kitchen.

36

'Sorry, Paul,' said Watson apologetically as he followed his boss into the kitchen.

'Do you have that mobile number, Marc?' Carmichael asked.

Watson nodded. 'Then call it. I want to be sure this is the offending phone.'

Watson took out his mobile and dialled the eleven digits. Seconds later the mobile resting on the table started to let out a buzzing noise.

'Well, that's the mobile,' proclaimed Carmichael. 'Now let's find its owner.'

The two uniformed officers entered the kitchen. 'He's not upstairs, but we found this on his bed,' announced one of the PCs, who held out a sealed white envelope in his hand.

Gingerly, with his thumb and forefinger, Carmichael took hold of the envelope from the PC.

'Be careful,' he said scornfully, 'this may be evidence.'

The envelope was hand-addressed in block capitals to:

THE CHIEF POLICE OFFICER.

'I guess that's me,' said Carmichael, who took hold of a kitchen knife from a rack mounted on the wall. Gently, he slit open the envelope and pulled out a folded piece of paper.

'What does it say?' Cooper asked.

Carmichael read the note then calmly placed it face up on the table. 'It tells us where to find Aiden Davidson,' replied Carmichael.

'Where's that?' enquired Watson.

'In the mortuary in little bits,' Carmichael responded. 'If this note is correct, he's the poor sod that got hit by the train yesterday.'

Chapter 9

Rachel Dalton was so engrossed in the case notes from the hit-and-run in early June that she failed to notice Chief Inspector Hewitt as he entered the incident room.

'Where's Carmichael?' he barked, his face almost purple with rage.

'They've found the owner of the mobile that sent the text yesterday,' replied Rachel apprehensively. 'They're in Hasslebury.'

Hewitt slammed a copy of that morning's *Sun* newspaper and the *Observer* on to Rachel's desk. 'He told me the papers were not going to print anything,' continued Hewitt. 'I've had the Super on the phone already this morning asking me what the hell's going on. Tell Carmichael to call me urgently.'

Hewitt didn't wait for a response, turning sharply on his heels and stomping out of the room like a petulant child.

Rachel was irritated by the way that Hewitt had behaved. 'Why can't you call him?' she muttered out loud. 'You've his mobile number just like the rest of us.'

She cast her eyes down at the headline on the front of the local newspaper:

OBSERVER ALERTS POLICE TO POSSIBLE DOUBLE MURDER.

'Carmichael's going to go ape when he sees this,' she mumbled to herself.

*   *   *   *

The SOCOs were just arriving at Davidson's house when Carmichael took Rachel's call.

'Bloody marvellous,' he replied sarcastically when Rachel had finished telling him the bad news. 'I'm just about to leave here. I'll pick up a copy on my way and call Hewitt from the car.'

'Do you want me to tell Hewitt you'll be calling him?' enquired Rachel, half expecting to still be required to act as the messenger between the two senior officers.

'No,' replied Carmichael. 'I'll be calling him within the hour so there's no need. Anyway, have you made any progress with the other case?'

'Not really,' replied Rachel. 'He seems to be a real mystery man. There's nothing to go on at all.'

Carmichael sighed deeply. 'Put that on hold for a while and get the pathology report from Dr Stock on the one from yesterday. We think it was Aiden Davidson.'

'What!' exclaimed Rachel. 'The guy whose mobile sent the text?'

'Yes,' replied Carmichael. 'It looks like his killer came back to the house after he'd dropped the body on the railway line. He then sent us the text and also wrote us a little note. He left the mobile on Davidson's kitchen table and the note on his bed.'

'What did the note say?' enquired Rachel.

'It was really short,' replied Carmichael. 'It just said you'll find Aiden on the railway line. Two down, two to go.'

'That's sick,' replied Rachel, 'and pretty brazen, too.'

'The killer's certainly not afraid to take risks,' added Carmichael, 'and I know it's pretty isolated out here, but still I'd expect someone to have noticed something.'

'Yes, I agree,' concurred Rachel.

Carmichael thought for a moment. 'I'm going to leave

Watson here to see if he can get any leads from the neighbours.'

'Worth a try,' remarked Rachel, 'but if someone did see something you'd have thought they'd have told me or one of the other officers yesterday when we were down there. Mind you, there were a few houses where we got no answer. Maybe the occupants of one of those saw something.'

As Rachel was talking, Carmichael noticed the net curtains of the house next door twitching.

'I'm going to have to go,' he said abruptly. 'Let Marc know which houses you didn't have any luck with yesterday and get on to Stock for that autopsy report. I'll see you back in the office later this afternoon.'

As he placed his mobile in his jacket pocket, Carmichael noticed Watson walking towards him.

'Come and have a look in the garage,' he said with a bewildered look on his face. 'I think you should come and see what we've found in there.'

*   *   *   *

Betty had been watching the toing and froing next door all morning through a small chink in her curtains. She thought her spying would go unnoticed, so was alarmed when Carmichael looked in her direction. She immediately realised she'd been observed by his reaction when he ended his call. His piercing blue eyes seemed to pinpoint her like a laser beam, which made her let go of the curtains and recoil backwards in fright. Betty scurried into the kitchen at the back of the house and hoped they'd leave her alone.

*   *   *   *

Davidson's rickety old garage, with double doors facing the house, was at the end of his long unkempt garden. From the outside it looked in need of some urgent attention, with the paint on the doors flaking away and the boarded-up windows cracked and thick with dirt.

'Strange place to have a garage,' remarked Carmichael. 'There's no access to the road from here.'

Watson smiled wryly. 'It's not used for a car, that's for sure,' he replied mysteriously.

Carmichael, now extremely curious about what he was about to discover, opened up the creaky wooden door and marched in.

'My God,' he exclaimed as he looked about him. 'You'd never have guessed this was here.'

Although it was the width of a normal suburban garage, it had been extended back for a good ten metres and had been converted into a bright, clean and comfortable studio. There were dozens and dozens of canvasses, some finished some partially finished, some on easels, and some resting up against the walls.

At the far end of the room there was an area which Carmichael assumed was where Davidson's subjects would sit as he painted them. It had a couple of wooden chairs and a bright-red chaise longue.

'Blimey,' remarked Carmichael, 'it's a proper artist's studio.'

Watson nodded. 'Yes, but I'm not sure about the artwork.'

Carmichael looked at a few of the paintings which were, in the main, a series of brightly coloured lines crisscrossing over one another surrounded either by splashes of paint or just blank white canvas.

'Not my taste either,' replied Carmichael.

After spending a few moments gazing around the room, Carmichael decided it was time to move on.

'I want you to stay here, Marc,' he ordered. 'Make sure that SOCO don't miss any clues. Take a look through Davidson's papers and see if you can find any details of his movements in the last few days and any names of friends and acquaintances. Then make sure the residents from all the houses in Hasslebury are interviewed. Speak with Rachel – she can tell you which ones she wasn't able to talk to yesterday.'

'OK,' replied Watson. 'What about Stock's pathology report – you asked me to follow that through today?'

'Rachel's doing that,' Carmichael confirmed. 'You focus your efforts here today, Marc. Don't worry about the house that side, though,' continued Carmichael, who gestured to the end house of the row. 'I'll speak with her on my way out.'

'Fine,' replied Watson who, for once, was happy with his assignment.

Carmichael left Watson in the garage and strode back into the house. 'Come on,' he shouted in Cooper's direction. 'Marc's going to manage things here; we've other things to be getting on with.'

Cooper put back the pile of letters and papers that he had pulled out from a drawer in the kitchen and dutifully followed Carmichael out of the front door.

*   *   *   *

Stock's autopsy report was emailed over to Rachel within minutes of their telephone conversation ending. It indicated, as he'd told her, that Aiden Davidson had been alive when he'd been hit by the train, but his system had so much Etorphine in it that he'd have been completely unconscious and would probably have felt nothing.

Rachel had never heard of Etorphine, but in his customary style Dr Stock had elaborated further. 'It's related to morphine, but much stronger. In the UK it's used by zoos and vets to anaesthetise large animals.'

'So would a normal vets' practice use it?' Rachel had asked.

'Yes,' he'd replied, 'especially if they deal with large animals like horses.'

Rachel decided to use her initiative and locate all the vets' practices in a five-mile radius of Hasslebury. She felt sure Carmichael would make this a priority for the team once he knew about the Etorphine, and she wanted to be ahead of the game.

* * * *

'Let's have a quick chat with the neighbour,' Carmichael said as he walked down the drive to Betty Wilbraham's door. 'We've got a lot to get through today, but I want to speak to the old dear here first. She was peeking through the curtains earlier, so with a bit of luck we may have found the village nosey-parker, which is like a gift from the heavens in cases like this. My bet is she knows what happened here or at least she'll have seen something that's important.'

'I hope you're right, sir,' responded Cooper, who had to break into a trot to arrive at Betty's green door before Carmichael started to rap loudly on it.

Betty took her time to answer. She pulled back the door a few inches and peered out.

'Can I help you?' she enquired as if she had a couple of door-to-door salesmen on her step.

Carmichael smiled and held out his identity card. 'Hello, we are from the police; we'd like to ask you some questions.'

'More questions!' exclaimed Betty agitatedly. 'I told Rachel all I know yesterday.'

Carmichael was a little surprised to discover the old woman was on first-name terms with a member of his team, but carried on as if it was of no consequence.

'We need to ask you some questions about your next-door neighbour, Aiden Davidson,' added Cooper.

Betty pulled open the door. 'You'd better come in then,' she grudgingly suggested.

43

Carmichael and Cooper walked through into the small front room, which was a mirror image of the house next door and equally as untidy.

'I'm sorry, I didn't ask you your name,' remarked Carmichael as he looked around for an empty chair.

'My name's Betty Wilbraham,' she replied as she reluctantly removed a few newspapers and crumpled garments from her settee. 'You can sit here,' she grumbled, pointing at the worn old couch.

Cooper and Carmichael lowered themselves tentatively on to the aged sofa.

'My name's Carmichael, and this is Sergeant Cooper,' said Carmichael. 'We'd like to know more about your neighbour, Mr Davidson.'

Betty sat herself down on an armchair facing the two officers. 'Was it him that was killed on the track yesterday?' she asked with little sign of emotion in her voice.

Carmichael decided there was nothing to be gained by being evasive. 'We think so,' he replied. 'How long had you known him?'

'He moved in about eight year ago,' replied Betty. 'It was old Mrs Wilson's house before.'

'And did you know him well?' enquired Cooper, who had his pocket book and pen at the ready to take notes.

Betty shook her head. 'Not really,' she replied. 'We spoke now and then, but he kept himself to himself really.'

'He was an artist, I believe,' Carmichael added. 'Was that his main occupation?'

Betty shrugged her shoulders. 'Yes, that's correct,' she replied. 'His paintings were not to my taste – a bit too modern for me.'

Carmichael smiled. 'That's what we think too, Mrs Wilbraham,' he conceded.

'Did you ever go into his studio?' Carmichael asked.

'Only once,' replied Betty thoughtfully. 'And he wasn't best pleased neither,' she added with a hint of anger in her voice. 'He told me to get out and swore at me, he did.'

'When was that?' asked Cooper, who was busily scribbling in his pocket book.

'It was about a year or so after he moved in,' replied Betty. 'I had a parcel for him that the postman had left with me. I'd not seen him for days, so when I saw the light on in his shed I went down to give it to him. He did apologise later, but he was really angry. His young model was OK about it, but he was very angry at the time.'

'Did he often have models posing for him?' enquired Carmichael.

Betty shrugged her shoulders again. 'Oh yes,' she replied. 'Not so many recently, but still I'd say one or two a month.'

'But none of the paintings I saw had people in them,' remarked Cooper. 'Are you sure he had models visit him?'

Betty screwed up her face and, for the third time, shrugged her shoulders. 'That's what I assumed they were,' she replied. 'Either that or he has lots of young nieces coming to call.'

Carmichael sniggered quietly to himself. 'When did you last see Mr Davidson?' he asked.

Betty thought for a few moments. 'The day before yesterday,' she replied, after due consideration. 'It would have been at about four in the afternoon. He was walking down the drive back to his house. He was on a mobile phone talking to someone. Actually, I think they were arguing about something. I didn't hear what they were saying, but his voice was raised.'

Carmichael looked at Cooper. 'We need to check all his recent calls,' he whispered.

'One last question,' Carmichael said as he stood up from the sofa. 'Did you know if Mr Davidson had any friends or family?'

Betty once again looked back blankly. 'No,' she responded. 'As I said, I didn't really know him that well. He did like his drink though and he often walked down to The Drunken Duck in Alcar, so you might want to ask some questions there. They will probably be better help to you than I.'

'Thank you, Mrs Wilbraham,' replied Carmichael. 'We'll do that.'

Once safely outside and out of earshot, Carmichael turned to face Cooper. 'What do you make of her?' he enquired.

'Batty but harmless, I'd say,' replied Cooper. 'Do you want me to check out The Drunken Duck?'

'Yes,' replied Carmichael. 'Drop me off home and then go and talk to the landlord.'

'What are you planning to do, sir?' Cooper asked.

Carmichael grimaced. 'I need to speak to Hewitt. According to Rachel he's not a happy man. I also need to get a copy of today's *Sun* and this week's *Mid Lancs Observer*, which I'm reliably informed are the source of Hewitt's irritation. After that I'm going to give Norfolk George the biggest rocket of his life and then I'm going to visit Mystic Meg.'

'Right,' replied Cooper with a confounded look on his face. 'Are we having a debrief at the office later today?' he added, not knowing what else to say.

Carmichael looked at his watch. 'Yes, we'll start at four thirty,' he replied. 'Tell the other two to make sure they're there on time.'

Chapter 10

Cooper dropped Carmichael outside his house at 10.45.

'See you at Kirkwood later,' Carmichael said before closing the door behind him.

Instead of getting straight into his car, Carmichael opted to stroll over to the newsagents to buy the two newspapers that, according to Rachel, had caused Hewitt so much angst.

A simple glance at the headline and the first few lines of the *Observer* was enough to help Carmichael understand what had so riled his boss.

'He's even named me,' muttered Carmichael to himself as he read the story while crossing the road. 'The rotten, miserable, scheming old bugger!'

With his blood pressure rising, Carmichael climbed into the driving seat of his BMW and started the engine. The screen on the centre consul showed him that his mobile had been successfully patched into the car. 'Here goes,' he said out loud as he dialled Hewitt's office line.

Angela picked up the call. 'Chief Inspector Hewitt's office,' she said in her best diction.

'Hi, Angela, it's me,' announced Carmichael, who knew that she would instantly recognise his southern accent. 'Is Hewitt around?'

'Hello, Steve,' replied Angela. 'I'm sorry, but he's gone out. He won't be back until late this afternoon.'

'Oh dear,' he replied. 'He asked Rachel to get me to call

him. Can you tell him I tried and I'll brief him later today on the case. I'm due to be in the office at four thirty.'

'No problem, Steve,' replied Angela. 'I'll let him know.'

Carmichael pressed the red button on the screen to end the call.

'Result!' he exclaimed, the smile as broad as his face would allow. 'Now it's time to pay my chum Norfolk George a visit,' he muttered to himself as he headed off in the direction of the *Mid Lancs Observer* headquarters, which in reality was a tiny office above the bookmaker's on Moulton Bank's high street. 'He'll regret ignoring my instructions.'

* * * *

Rachel was feeling very pleased with herself. She'd managed to establish that there were two veterinary practices within the five-mile radius she'd drawn around Hasslebury.

With the time just after eleven, she figured that she'd easily be able to speak to both before the briefing at four thirty. She grabbed her coat and headed off to the nearest of the two.

* * * *

The look of guilt on Norfolk George's face was plain for all to see.

'You've got to look at it from my shoes,' stuttered the reporter, who often mixed his metaphors when he was flustered. 'I have a duty to my readers to print the facts and this story is in the public's interest.'

'Rubbish,' shouted Carmichael. 'This is a murder case and by publishing the story you may jeopardise our enquiries.'

'How?' retorted George firmly. 'The killer is blatantly flaunting his actions – what possible harm has my publishing the facts done to your investigation?'

'He wants the notoriety,' snapped Carmichael, 'and you've

just delivered it to him on a plate.' To emphasise his fury, Carmichael threw down his copy of the *Observer* on to George's desk. 'And', he continued, his irritation now palpable in his voice, 'you've also sold it to the bloody nationals.' Carmichael angrily chucked the copy of that morning's *Sun*, folded back to reveal the offending article, into George's midriff. 'How much did they pay you for that?' he snarled.

George was clearly embarrassed, but remained resolute. 'I thought long and hard about this, Steve,' he said, as calmly as he could. 'I've done nothing wrong; I'm just doing my job.'

Carmichael stared angrily at the local hack. 'I won't forget this, George,' he exclaimed, before turning his back on the uncomfortable-looking reporter and making a hasty exit, slamming the door behind him to emphasise his displeasure.

* * * *

The Park Road Veterinary Practice was a small surgery located midway between Alcar and Moulton Bank. By the time DC Dalton arrived it was eleven thirty. She could see from the prominent notice on the door that the practice was not yet open to the public. She rang the bell and, after a short wait, was greeted by a young woman in a baggy blue uniform whom she took to be a nurse.

'I'm from the police,' Rachel announced. 'Can I speak to the practice manager?'

The young woman let Rachel in and asked her to take a seat in the waiting room while she fetched the manager. Rachel remained alone for fifteen minutes before a lady, also dressed in blue overalls, entered the room.

'Good morning,' she said cheerily. 'My name's Joan Henderson. How can I help you?'

Rachel stood up and extended her right arm to shake hands.

'Hang on a minute,' Joan Henderson remarked with a

smile. 'Let me take off these gloves. I've just finished extracting some teeth from an old greyhound, so I'm not sure you'd want to shake my hand at the moment.'

Rachel laughed. 'Thanks,' she replied as she watched the vet remove the gloves and discard them into a robust-looking metal bin. 'I'm from Kirkwood CID and was wondering if you could help me with a case we are working on.'

'Of course,' remarked Joan. 'Do you want to come through?'

'No,' said Rachel, 'I can see you are busy and this will only take a few moments.'

The two women sat down. 'I'd like to ask you about the drug Etorphine,' said Rachel. 'Do you use it here?'

'Yes,' replied Joan, 'we use it occasionally to anaesthetise large animals before we operate. I've not used it for quite a while, though.'

'What sort of regulations are there governing its use and its storage?' Rachel enquired.

Joan Henderson raised her eyebrows. 'Very stringent ones,' she replied. 'Only fully trained anaesthetists can administer the drug and we have to account for every last drop of it. It's always kept locked up and we have a log to make sure that we can account for how it's been administered.'

Rachel listened intently. 'So if any went missing, you'd spot it fairly quickly?' she enquired.

'Absolutely,' replied the vet. 'Why, what's the issue?'

'I can't tell you, I'm afraid,' replied Rachel. 'But I would like you to double-check your stocks. If you find there's any missing, I'd appreciate you letting me know.'

Rachel took a card from her pocket and handed it to Joan. 'My number's on the card.'

The vet took the card placed it in her own pocket and proceeded to open the door to allow Rachel to depart. 'I'll check our stocks,' she remarked. 'But I can assure you there will be none unaccounted for.'

Rachel smiled and walked out into the warm sunshine.

She had always liked animals, but was relieved to be in the open air and away from the distinctive and not so pleasant smell of the vets' waiting room. 'One down, one to go,' she mumbled to herself before unlocking her car door and clambering in.

*   *   *   *

As soon as he left Norfolk George's office, Carmichael called Siobhan Ballentyne's telephone number, which Penny had taken from her programme. At 1 p.m. precisely, as they had agreed, Carmichael arrived at Siobhan's grand detached house. 'There's clearly money to be made being a psychic,' he mumbled to himself as he strode up the gravel drive.

Carmichael had never met a clairvoyant before, so on his short journey to her house he'd tried to imagine what she would look like. He'd concluded that she'd be a frumpy-looking, middle-aged woman with big hair and psychedelic clothing that harked back to the sixties.

I must be psychic myself, he thought as she opened the door and got his first glimpse of Siobhan Ballentyne.

'Good afternoon, Inspector Carmichael,' said Siobhan, her greeting loud and gushing. 'I'm so pleased to meet you.'

As she spoke, Siobhan took hold of Carmichael's forearms and held them tightly. 'I can feel a strong aura from you, Inspector,' she added, much to Carmichael's disquiet.

Siobhan released her grip and ushered Carmichael into the house.

'Please go through to the lounge,' instructed the psychic as she pointed to the first door to Carmichael's right.

Carmichael did as he was told and, once inside the room, sat down on one of the two expensive-looking antique settees.

As he was making himself comfortable, Carmichael suddenly became aware of a tiny pair of eyes behind a clump of long golden hairs, staring at him from the centre of the sofa directly opposite.

'That's Mr Swaffie,' remarked Siobhan blithely, as she gently moved the diminutive frame of her small dog to one side and carefully sat herself down on his sofa.

'He's a Cairn terrier,' continued Siobhan. 'Mr Swaffie's getting on a bit now, poor chap; but he's clearly very interested in you.'

'It was good of you to see me at such short notice,' remarked Carmichael, who had no intention of entering into any small talk with the psychic regarding her scrawny-looking dog. 'I am here to talk to you about the conversation you had yesterday with my wife.'

'Yes, I know,' replied Siobhan unnervingly. 'She's a delightful lady and still very much in love with you, Inspector.'

Carmichael's perplexed expression clearly indicated that he'd been taken aback by her comments.

Siobhan smiled as if to reassure him. 'I held her arms just as I did with you and I could feel the love,' she remarked.

'Really?' replied Carmichael, who was quite noticeably sceptical.

Siobhan smiled. 'I see you are not altogether sure about my powers,' she stated candidly. 'Your wife wasn't either, but I think she's probably less of a cynic than she was twenty-four hours ago.'

Carmichael decided it was time to take control. 'Whether I believe is not the issue, Ms Ballentyne,' he remarked. 'I'm here to find out what you meant by your comments to her yesterday and how you came by that information.'

Siobhan smiled and nodded with a sagacious air. 'I have powers, Inspector Carmichael,' she stated with calm assuredness. 'I am a fourth-generation intuitive. I hear voices from the spirit world, I can read the Tarot, I practise psychometrics and I have a guardian angel that remains with me wherever I am. His name is Guthrie; he's a monk from the twelfth century.'

Carmichael listened in silence, although he refused to believe a single word that Siobhan was saying.

'My speciality, if that's the right word,' she continued, 'is relationship issues. I find them easy and, although I'm not infallible, my success rate is approaching ninety per cent.'

'I'm not sure how that answers my question,' retorted Carmichael, who was getting a little frustrated by the baloney he was hearing.

Siobhan remained calm throughout. 'I'm used to being ridiculed, Inspector,' she added. 'I've been called a fraud and a freak and been asked to prove myself on more occasions than I care to remember. So your cynicism does not worry me. In fact, I see it as a challenge to help you change your mind.'

Carmichael, who by now was very agitated, stood up from the settee. 'If you aren't prepared to answer my question, I'll be going,' he remarked curtly. 'I've a murder enquiry to attend to. I've no time to waste being converted to believe in the supernatural.'

'But I have not had a chance to answer your question,' replied Siobhan, still calm and composed. 'Please remain, Inspector, as I truly believe that I can help you.'

Carmichael returned to the settee. 'I'll give you ten minutes,' he conceded.

Siobhan nodded. 'The message I had for you was to follow your instincts and that the message was no hoax,' she said. 'I assume from your presence here what I said was true?'

Carmichael shrugged his shoulders. 'There was a message and we now believe that it wasn't a practical joke, so in that respect, yes, what you said was true,' he conceded. 'But I need to know where you got your information.'

'From Guthrie, of course,' replied Siobhan with amazement in her voice. 'It was Guthrie who told me.'

Carmichael shook his head. 'I'm sorry, but this is just nonsense,' he remarked caustically. 'Your ten minutes are up – I'm going.'

Carmichael stood up and walked briskly towards the door.

'I think you are foolish to ignore my powers,' Siobhan added. 'I can help you with your investigation, if you'll allow me.'

Carmichael was just a few strides from the door when Siobhan spoke again. 'I will tell you two things that I know, Inspector,' she said serenely. 'Firstly, I see a woman who cares more for animals than people. You need to talk with her again. And, secondly, you need to face your own demon. You have a guilty secret that haunts you.'

Carmichael turned around to face the spiritualist. 'What demon are you talking about?' he enquired, with a puzzled expression on his face.

Siobhan looked directly into his eyes. 'Her name begins with L,' she replied. 'I think it's Lucy.'

An unsettling shiver shot down Carmichael's spine. 'Nonsense,' he responded angrily, but also with a feeling of uneasiness. 'I'm wasting my time here.'

*   *   *   *

Trinity Pet Hospital was Rachel's second and final port of call that afternoon. Unlike Park Road, this was a large and very busy practice, complete with beaming young receptionist with long bleached blonde hair and expensively manicured fingernails.

'Can I help you?' the receptionist enquired in her broad Lancashire dialect.

'Can I speak to the practice manager?' Rachel asked.

'Do you have an appointment?'

'No,' replied Rachel, who pulled out her identity card and thrust it under the young woman's nose. 'I'm from

Kirkwood Police Station. It's very important that I speak with him today.'

The receptionist studied the identity card carefully. 'I'm sorry, Mr Romney is in surgery at the moment,' she replied. 'He'll not come out for anything. He could be some time, too, as I know he has a difficult operation to perform.'

Rachel puffed out her cheeks. 'Do you have any idea how long he'll be?'

The young woman, her teeth gleaming out of her forced smile, shook her head. 'It could easily be an hour or two,' she replied unhelpfully. 'It's on a King Charles Spaniel with acute Chiari. It's really time-consuming.'

Rachel looked back at the receptionist, her irritation written across her face. 'Can you ask him to call me today, please?' she said as she handed over her business card. 'My number's on here.'

'No problem,' she replied, her artificial-looking grin remaining faultless as she spoke.

Rachel glared at her for a few seconds before turning on her heels and walking away towards the exit. As she did, she could feel the receptionist's eyes burning holes in her back.

Chapter 11

There was no way that Watson, Cooper or Rachel Dalton were going to be late for the 4:30 debriefing. None of Carmichael's team was about to provide their boss with another opportunity to have a go at them, as he had the previous evening.

So when, true to form, Carmichael entered the incident room at 4:29, his three lieutenants were already in position. In preparation for the debrief they had each updated the whiteboard with notes based upon their actions that day.

Carmichael was suitably impressed.

'Looks good, team,' he remarked as he studied their various contributions. 'Why don't you start, Marc?'

Watson walked over to the board. 'We've completed a thorough house-to-house around Davidson's place,' he commented. 'The only person who heard anything untoward was a young woman in the house at the opposite end of Ivy Cottages. She has a young child and she's fairly sure she saw someone dragging something behind the houses at about seven thirty yesterday morning.'

'Why was this not picked up when you were supervising the house-to-house interviews?' Carmichael pointedly asked Rachel Dalton.

'This was one of the houses where there was no answer when we knocked,' replied Rachel.

'Yes, the woman told us she'd been away visiting her mother here in Kirkwood all of yesterday,' added Watson in support. 'She left home at about eight thirty and didn't get back until about six yesterday evening.'

'So what exactly did she see?' Carmichael enquired.

Watson lifted up his shoulders and scrunched up his face. 'To be honest, she wasn't very helpful,' he reluctantly had to concede. 'She was attending to her new-born baby at the time in the bathroom upstairs. She says she only glanced out for a few moments, but is adamant she saw someone in the field behind the houses dragging something through the long grass towards the railway bridge.'

'Does this woman have a name?' asked Cooper casually.

'Lorraine Morrison,' replied Watson, pointing to the name he'd scribbled on the whiteboard.

'And was Lorraine able to give you a description of the person she saw, or help you identify what was being dragged?' Carmichael asked.

Watson shook his head. 'No,' he replied. 'But SOCO did check out the field and they did find evidence of a large object, possibly a body, being dragged through the grass in the last few days.'

Carmichael thought for a second. 'What about the other houses?'

Watson shook his head again. 'Nothing at all,' he replied downheartedly.

Carmichael again took a few seconds to think. 'You've written photographs on the board under Davidson's name,' he added quizzically. 'What is that all about?'

'I wrote that,' replied Cooper. 'It's based upon a comment from the landlord at The Drunken Duck.'

'Which was?' enquired Carmichael.

'In fairness, he did say that it may just be malicious gossip,' continued Cooper a little awkwardly. 'But he told me that Aiden Davidson was rumoured to do a little bit of photography of an adult nature.'

'What, glamour photos?' enquired Rachel.

'From what the landlord was saying, it was a bit more adult than that, if you get my drift,' continued Cooper.

Carmichael looked surprised. 'It would stack up with what the old lady next door told us,' he said, referring to the comment that Betty Wilbraham had made regarding the number of female visitors to Aiden Davidson's house.

'Well, we didn't find any mucky photos,' remarked Watson, who sounded disappointed. 'We searched the house and his studio from top to bottom. There were no photographs and I can't even remember seeing a camera, if I'm honest.'

'Let's check it out again,' ordered Carmichael. 'If it's true, it may provide us with a motive.'

His three officers nodded in unison.

'That's one for you tomorrow, Marc,' added Carmichael.

Watson smiled. 'OK, boss,' he replied gratefully.

'Anyway, Marc, what else did you find when you searched the house?' said Carmichael, trying to get the debrief back on track.

'In the studio, just paintings, canvasses, paint and brushes,' replied Watson. 'There were loads of them … must have been thirty or forty finished paintings and at least twice as many unfinished.'

'What about in the house?'

'Some letters and statements from a gallery in Southport,' continued Watson. 'It must have been where he sold some of his work. The SOCOs have taken away his computer to look at, but outside of that, nothing.'

'So did they find any signs of violence or a struggle?' Carmichael enquired with a hint of frustration in his voice.

Watson shook his head. 'They dusted for fingerprints, but as yet there are no signs of there being a struggle,' he grudgingly replied.

'I think I should tell you all something that Dr Stock has found,' interrupted Rachel. 'He reckons that Davidson was alive but certainly unconscious when he was hit by the train.'

'Really?' replied Carmichael enthusiastically. 'And I assume the anaesthetic used was Etorphine?' he added, pointing to the name Rachel had already scribbled on the whiteboard.

Rachel nodded excitedly. 'Correct,' she replied. 'It's mainly used by vets to sedate large animals before operations.'

'Not used on humans then?'

'No,' replied Rachel confidently. 'I've already checked out the only two veterinary practices in the Hasslebury area,' she added smugly.

'Really?' remarked Carmichael, who was impressed with Rachel's enterprise. 'And what did they tell you?'

'The first one I visited was called Park Road Veterinary Practice,' continued Rachel. 'It's a small practice run by a lady called Joan Henderson. She told me that they use Etorphine but only on rare occasions. According to Mrs Henderson, the regulations governing the storage of the drug are very stringent.'

'Have they had any go missing?' Cooper asked.

'She said not,' replied Rachel. 'But she did say she'd check and get back to me.'

'What about the other vet?' Carmichael asked.

'They are called Trinity Pet Hospital,' said Rachel, still very smug about her afternoon's work. 'I've just come off the phone to the proprietor. He's a man called Harvey Romney. He maintains they frequently use the drug, but again he's sure all their stocks are accounted for. He also said that he'd double-check and get back to me.'

'Good work, Rachel,' remarked Carmichael. 'Make sure both vets are thorough in their checks. If either of them cannot account for all their stocks, then we need to crawl all over them.'

Rachel nodded. 'I'll get on to it first thing in the morning.'

Carmichael studied the whiteboard for a few moments.

'OK, let's focus on what we know,' he said as he grabbed the marker. 'We have two deaths, both male and both suspicious.' As he spoke, he started to record what he was saying.

'Both happened at seven thirty-seven in the morning,' he continued. 'The first death was on ...'

'The fourth of June,' interrupted Rachel, who could see that Carmichael was looking for an exact date.

Carmichael wrote '4th June' on the board.

'We have no idea who he was,' said Carmichael, 'but he was killed outright by a car that did not stop. No witnesses have come forward and, in spite of concerted efforts, we have nothing at all to go on to help us with his identification. So far so good?'

Cooper, Watson and Dalton all nodded.

With his back to the team, Carmichael continued to record his statements on the whiteboard. 'Then, on 15th July, Aiden Davidson is anaesthetised with a drug that's used by vets, presumably in his house and is dragged to the railway bridge. He's then hoisted over the side and dropped into the path of the express train at precisely seven thirty-seven.'

Carmichael turned around to face his team. 'Have I missed anything so far?' he enquired.

'No,' Cooper replied calmly, as if he were speaking for the entire team.

'Apart from a vague sighting by Lorraine Morrison,' Carmichael continued, 'we've not much to go on to help us identify this mystery man, if indeed it is a man.'

'What I'm struggling with', interjected Cooper, 'is any link between the two deaths. Apart from them both being male, both being killed by fast-moving modes of transport and them both being killed at seven thirty-seven, it's not easy to link them at all.'

'Maybe we should be keeping an eye on a boat or plane for the next one,' remarked Watson flippantly.

'What I don't get', remarked Rachel slowly, 'is why we didn't get a text after the first killing and why did he only start bragging about what he'd done after the second death?'

'Good questions,' replied Carmichael. 'I agree – you'd have expected him to be consistent and to claim the first death at the time.'

'Maybe he did send a message but it was never passed on,' suggested Cooper.

'Possibly,' remarked Carmichael. 'It's a factor we need to consider.'

Rachel grabbed the nearest marker and wrote her observation on the board.

'How did your afternoon go?' enquired Cooper.

Carmichael sighed. 'I spoke with Siobhan Ballentyne,' he said somewhat uneasily. 'She's the psychic that Susan and Penny talked with yesterday,' he continued, looking directly at Watson.

'Surely, you don't believe all that claptrap?' remarked Watson, who was clearly amazed. 'Susan told me about it and I just dismissed it as complete hogwash.'

'I tend to agree,' replied Carmichael. 'However, we need to explore all avenues and what she said was uncanny enough that I wanted to talk to her.'

'Who is this woman?' enquired Rachel. 'And what did she say?'

'She purports to be a psychic,' replied Carmichael calmly. 'Susan and Penny, for some bizarre reason only known to them, went to one of her spiritualist meetings yesterday afternoon. After the meeting had finished she told Penny that I needed to take "the message" seriously and that I should follow my instinct. As this was before anyone knew about the text message we received, it did seem a strange thing to say.'

'Wow,' replied Rachel with astonishment. 'That *is* uncanny. How did she know about the message?'

'That's exactly what I thought,' continued Carmichael. 'And that's why I went to see her.'

'So, what did she say?' Rachel eagerly enquired.

'It was as I expected,' replied Carmichael coolly. 'In fact, it was a bit of a let-down. She maintains the message came to her from some personal spirit that protects her. She also believes we need to talk again to a woman who cares more for animals than people. God knows who that is.'

Rachel's pupils enlarged. 'Oh my God!' she exclaimed. 'That will be Betty Wilbraham. She's obsessed with hedgehogs. It must be her she's talking about.'

Marc Watson raised his eyes skyward. 'It's all nonsense,' he bellowed in frustration. 'Surely we're not taking her weird predictions seriously?'

'You're right, Marc,' said Carmichael firmly, wishing to cut short any further discussion about Siobhan Ballentyne. 'Having met her, I'm certain that she's a fraud and we needn't waste any more time on her.'

The incident room went silent for a few moments until Watson spoke. 'The murders both seem to share one other common theme ...'

'And what's that?' enquired Carmichael, expecting to hear another of Watson's classic witticisms.

'They're both seemingly motiveless,' he remarked profoundly.

*　*　*　*

Joan Henderson checked then double-checked the stock of Etorphine. Alarmed at what she had discovered, she considered what she should do next.

Rachel Dalton's card sat in front of her on the desk. She took a few more seconds to consider her options before she picked up the phone.

*　*　*　*

After the debrief had finished, Carmichael sat alone in the incident room. Although he hadn't told them that they'd done well, inwardly he was delighted with the progress the team had made, which was especially pleasing given their poor display the previous day.

As he gazed out of the window, his thoughts went back to the conversation he'd had with Siobhan Ballentyne and her mention of his own demons. He didn't hear Rachel re-enter the room until she was stood next to him.

'I thought you might like a coffee,' Rachel said as she placed a steaming mug on the desk beside him.

Seeing Carmichael so preoccupied with his thoughts, she gently enquired. 'Are you OK, sir?'

'I'm fine, Lucy,' he replied as he turned back and smiled at the young DC.

'Lucy!' repeated Rachel who was totally flummoxed by her boss's inability to remember her name. 'She left three years ago, sir,' she added. 'I'm Rachel.'

Totally embarrassed by his faux pas, Carmichael quickly tried to recover the situation. 'Sorry, Rachel,' he said. 'It's been a long day, I'm exhausted.'

Rachel smiled. 'I thought it was just my dad who couldn't remember my name,' she joked. 'He's forever calling me Janet. That's my elder sister's name.'

Carmichael laughed. 'Get yourself off home and spend some time with Gregor,' he said. 'You showed a great deal of initiative today tracking down the two vets. Good job.'

'Thanks, sir,' replied Rachel. 'I'm just about to go.'

She started to walk slowly towards the door, but before she reached it she turned back to face Carmichael.

'What did Chief Inspector Hewitt say?' she enquired. 'He was really agitated when he came down here this morning.'

Carmichael rolled his eyes and puffed out his cheeks. 'I haven't managed to hook up with him yet,' he replied gloomily. 'I'll have to pop up to see him before I get off home.'

Rachel smiled. 'Good luck with that,' she remarked cheekily.

'Thanks,' Carmichael replied, his stare now focused at something out of the window. 'I'll need it.'

'Actually, sir,' said Rachel nervously. 'It's not that important and I haven't told the others but, just so you are aware, Gregor and I have split up.'

Carmichael looked back towards the young DC. 'Oh, I'm sorry to hear that, Rachel,' he said with genuine concern. 'Are you OK?'

Rachel smiled. 'Yes, I'm fine,' she replied. 'It was my decision really. He's a nice guy but it wasn't working. He moved out last week and, as far as I know, he's returned to Estonia.'

Carmichael forced a smile. 'As long as you're OK,' he said considerately. 'But I appreciate you letting me know.'

'Thanks, sir,' replied Rachel. 'I know it's a private matter, but I just wanted you to know.'

Rachel turned once more and started to walk out of the office.

'Have a good evening, Rachel,' Carmichael called after her before turning his head to gaze once more out of the window. 'I'll see you in the morning. Don't be late.'

Chapter 12

Rachel Dalton arrived back at her neat and tidy cottage on the outskirts of Newbridge at around 6:20 p.m., which was unusually early for her.

It was a warm evening and the sun, although now fairly low in the sky, was large and still intense. As soon as she had closed the door behind her, Rachel kicked off her shoes, took out a glass from the cupboard, pulled out a half-empty bottle of Pinot Grigio from the fridge and walked out into her small back garden. She sat quietly for a few moments at her tiny garden table and breathed in the gorgeous sounds and smells of that perfect English summer evening.

After several sips of cold white wine she started to fiddle with her mobile. She checked her recent photos, the last one being of Gregor two weeks earlier when they'd had a nice day out in the Lake District, probably the only day in the last month when they had not argued. She smiled as she looked at it, then, as if to make a statement to herself, she deleted it.

Having drained her glass, Rachel walked back into the kitchen, placed a frozen meal for one in the microwave and returned to the garden. She was halfway through her third glass of wine when she realised that her mobile was still on silent.

One of Carmichael's many pet hates was mobile phones interrupting his debriefings. To avoid irritating her boss, Rachel always made sure her mobile was on silent when she attended these meetings. She normally remembered to switch the volume back up after the meeting was over, but on this occasion she'd forgotten.

'Damn,' she muttered as she spotted a missed call.

She dialled 121 and listened to the voice message Joan Henderson had left an hour earlier.

*　*　*　*

Carmichael's meeting with Hewitt was short and to the point. Hewitt was keen to get to the golf club, so his attention span was even shorter than usual. He'd also had time to calm down after his hormonal display earlier in the day with Rachel and, once Carmichael had explained that he'd marked Norfolk George's card and that they were making good progress, Hewitt seemed relatively happy.

'Great, Steve,' he remarked as Carmichael updated him on where the team's focus would be the next day. 'You seem to have it all under control, but for God's sake apprehend this man before he murders again,' was his parting sentence as he rushed out of his office and down the passageway.

'He's playing nine holes with the Deputy Commissioner tonight at seven thirty,' remarked Angela as they watched the Chief disappear down the long corridor.

'Well it's good to see he has his priorities in the right place,' remarked Carmichael with a sarcastic smirk.

*　*　*　*

Carmichael was almost home when Rachel's name came up on his screen as the incoming caller.

'Hi, Rachel,' he said nonchalantly. 'Are you missing me already?'

Rachel laughed. 'No,' she said. 'I just wanted to update you on a voicemail that Joan Henderson has left me. She says she's checked her stocks of Etorphine and they're missing a bottle.'

'Really?' replied Carmichael. 'Have you called her back?'

'I've tried,' she confirmed, 'but the out-of-office message is on at the practice. They've finished for the day.'

'That's fine, Rachel,' Carmichael replied just as his car came to a halt in his driveway. 'It can wait until tomorrow, but get to the practice first thing and interview the staff. I want to know who took that bottle. Ask Cooper to go with you.'

'Right, sir,' said Rachel. 'I'll call Paul now.'

Carmichael ended the call, switched off the engine and clambered out of the car.

By the time he reached the front door it was open and Penny was waiting for him, a glass of Chardonnay in hand.

'Now that's what I call service!' he proclaimed just before he took hold of the wine glass and simultaneously kissed his wife on the lips.

'My aim is to please,' Penny replied with mock servility. 'Actually I was in the front room when I saw you pull up. This was supposed to be mine,' she remarked, looking at the now partially drained glass in her husband's hand.

'Oh, sorry,' he replied, a little embarrassed. 'Let me pour you one in that case.'

Carmichael sauntered through to the kitchen, took a clean glass out of the dishwasher and filled it as high as he could with the crisp, clear liquid. 'How's that?' he remarked as he passed it over to Penny.

Penny's eyes bulged out of their sockets. 'Thanks,' she said. 'This will last me all night.'

* * * *

The golden rule in the Carmichael household was never to discuss an active case in front of the children. Even with them all getting older, Penny and Steve still stuck firmly to the rule. So over dinner the conversation remained on other subjects, although Steve did see this as an ideal opportunity to delve a little more into one area of the case.

'Has anyone seen the film *Catch Me If You Can?*'

'Yes,' replied his three children almost in unison.

'I've got the DVD,' added Jemma. 'You can borrow it if you like.'

'Thanks, I will,' replied her father. 'I've heard it's a good film. I thought I might have a look at it.'

Penny remained silent but was immediately suspicious of her husband's motives. He rarely watched movies and one starring Leonardo DiCaprio was certainly not something she would expect Steve to want to see.

It was nearly 9:30 p.m. before their three children had departed to their bedrooms and Penny at last had a chance to talk to her husband about the day's developments.

'*Catch Me If You Can?*!' she said quizzically. 'Why on earth do you want to watch that?'

Carmichael laughed. 'It's research into the case. That's how the text message Norfolk George received ended. I just want to make sure it's not connected to the film.'

'Mr Thorough,' replied Penny sarcastically.

'In Hewitt's eyes it will be Mr Pillock if I didn't and it contains something pertinent to the case,' Carmichael continued.

It was now Penny's turn to smile. 'So did you talk to Siobhan?' she enquired.

'Yes,' replied Carmichael in a dismissive fashion.

'And?' probed Penny excitedly.

'Well, I was pretty disappointed with her, if you want to know,' remarked Carmichael. 'I still think she's a fraud.'

Penny wasn't surprised to learn that her husband had avoided becoming a convert, but she had expected him to be more forthcoming about his discussion with the mystic.

'So what did she say?' she asked firmly. 'If Siobhan was anything like the person I met yesterday, I'm sure she would

68

have had more interesting things to tell you direct from the spirit world.'

Carmichael shuffled uneasily around on his seat and, no matter how hard he tried, he could not manage to look directly at Penny. 'Well, she also told me that we should talk again to the old lady that prefers animals to people.'

'And do you know who that might be?' Penny asked.

'We think it may be the next-door neighbour of the man killed yesterday on the railway,' confirmed Carmichael. 'She runs some sort of volunteer hedgehog sanctuary from her house,' he added. 'We're going to talk with her again, but I'm certain Psychic Siobhan is a con artist, so we're not going to spend any more time on her. We've enough genuine avenues of enquiry to pursue without adding to them with her spirit-world claptrap.'

Penny could see that her husband was in no mood to discuss the psychic any further, so she decided to drop the subject. However, she couldn't help feeling that Steve was not telling her everything. After twenty-three years together she knew Steve well enough to tell when he was hiding something from her. And, in her opinion, that was certainly what he was doing now, although she couldn't work out why.

*　　*　　*　　*

It was a humid night and to stay cool Joan Henderson had only a thin cotton sheet on the bed. Her bedroom window was open wide, just like almost every other window in the street, in the unlikely event that, if a small breeze were to enter, it would bring some cool refreshing air to ease her discomfort.

Even if it had been less sticky, it's debatable whether she'd have got much rest, as all she could think about was the missing bottle of Etorphine.

'This is ridiculous,' she grumbled when at last she decided

to get up and get herself a cold drink. Joan put on her thin cotton dressing gown and carefully descended the staircase. She wandered into her kitchen gazing up at the clock on the kitchen wall; it was 2:25 a.m.

As Joan poured herself a drink she heard a noise behind her. Turning quickly to see what it was, she was struck hard in the face and, oblivious to the identity of her attacker, fell pole-axed on to the tiled floor.

Chapter 13

Thursday 17th July

Lou Henderson, a larger-than-life character, was holding court at breakfast in the Marriott hotel, York when he received a text message. The distinctive ring tone of 'Three Times a Lady' by Lionel Richie told him the message was from his wife.

He made a quick apology to the three young executives who had, up until that moment, hung upon his every word, and gazed down at the screen on his mobile. As he read, his three colleagues could see his expression change from its normal open friendly state to one of great concern.

'What's up, Lou?' enquired one of his minions.

Henderson didn't answer at first; he was too busy rereading the message.

'I don't know,' he replied anxiously in his recognisable Carolina accent. 'It's from Joan's mobile, but I don't think it's from her. I need to call her.'

He got up quickly from the table and dashed out of the breakfast room.

*   *   *   *

It was 8:30 a.m. when Carmichael was informed about the message from Joan Henderson's phone, and it was a further twenty minutes before he arrived at Henderson's house.

'What have you found?' he enquired of Watson, who had arrived just five minutes earlier.

'She's dead,' replied Watson. 'She's been tied up, but it looks like it was a massive blow to the head that did for her.'

Carmichael ducked under the police cordon, scurried up the drive and into the house.

The unmistakable figure of Stock was the first person Carmichael saw as he entered the kitchen. He was crouched over the limp body of a woman in yellow pyjamas who had been bound tightly to one of the kitchen chairs.

'So what have you gathered so far, Harry?' he asked without bothering to exchange any normal pleasantries.

'Morning, Carmichael,' replied Stock caustically. 'Another day, another murder!'

Carmichael walked over to take a look at the body. 'How did she die?'

'She's had a heavy blow to her head,' Stock said, pointing to the large indent on the dead woman's temple. 'I'm not sure that's what killed her, but it would have certainly rendered her unconscious.'

'So what killed her?' enquired Carmichael.

'By the colour of her lips, I'd say a substantial dose of some form of immobilising drug,' replied Stock.

'Etorphine,' suggested Carmichael.

'That would be my best guess,' replied Stock. 'That's if I were prone to guesswork, which, of course, I'm not.'

'And the time of death?'

Stock considered the question carefully. 'She's not been dead long. I'd say between one and four hours.'

'So she could have been killed at seven thirty-seven?' interjected Watson.

Stock looked at his watch. 'Yes, that's possible.'

Carmichael pulled Watson to one side. 'The husband,' he said quietly, 'when is he expected to be here?'

72

'He's driving down from York,' replied Watson. 'I suspect he'll be here in about thirty to forty minutes.'

'OK, we'll wait for him,' replied Carmichael. 'I want to know exactly what that text message said. But while we're waiting, let's make ourselves useful by looking around to see if we can find her mobile. If our killer is following the same pattern, it's bound to be around here somewhere.'

* * * *

Rachel and Cooper had just arrived at the Park Road Veterinary Practice when Watson called them to relay the news of Joan Henderson's death.

'We need to interview all the staff,' announced Cooper as they sat in the car in the small visitors' car park. 'Let's not mention her death until the end of their interview.'

Rachel nodded. 'Do you want to split up to conduct the interviews?'

'No,' replied Cooper. 'There's only a handful of them so we can probably get through them all in a couple of hours. Let's just focus on the missing Etorphine and also check their movements earlier today and on the morning Davidson died.'

The two officers climbed out of the car and strode up to the main entrance of the veterinary practice.

* * * *

Lou Henderson's large black Audi screeched up outside the police cordon at 9:45 a.m. He leapt out of the car and, having advised one of the uniformed officers of his identity, was ushered up the drive to where Carmichael was standing.

'This is Mr Henderson,' said the PC.

Carmichael looked sympathetically at the clearly worried man. 'I'm terribly sorry, Mr Henderson,' he said as compassionately as he could. 'But I'm afraid we believe your wife's been murdered.'

Henderson's shoulders drooped and he nervously ran his fingers through what little hair he had. 'Oh my God,' he cried. 'It can't be true. Who would do that to Joan?'

Carmichael pointed over to a low wall a few yards from where they were standing. 'Why don't we sit down over there?' he suggested.

'But I want to see her,' protested Henderson, his strong American accent more pronounced as he spoke.

'We must allow the scene-of-crime people to finish their work first,' replied Carmichael placidly. 'Once they're through, you can see your wife, but please bear with us for a short while.'

Henderson nodded and wandered in a state of bewilderment to the wall and quietly sat down.

*　*　*　*

The Park Road Veterinary Practice employed fourteen people. There were three vets; Joan Henderson and Adam Charles, who worked full time, and Malcolm Page, who was semi-retired and worked about sixteen hours a week. In addition, five qualified nurses worked at the practice together with six unqualified assistants. That morning ten of the fourteen were on duty.

They had been offered a tiny office to conduct their interviews, and once the two police officers had made themselves suitably comfortable they made a start.

Having established that Adam Charles was the most senior of the staff on duty, Cooper and Dalton elected to speak with him first.

Adam Charles was a tall, imposing man in his early thirties, with a friendly open face and welcoming smile.

'How can I be of help?' he enquired, his slight Scottish

74

accent suggesting his origins were closer to Edinburgh than Glasgow.

'We need to ask you a few questions to help us with some ongoing enquiries,' replied Cooper, trying hard to keep the mood calm and friendly.

'I'll help as much as I can,' remarked Charles, who seemed genuine enough. 'Joan is the practice manager, so she will most probably be able to help you more than I, but I'll help as much as I can.'

'Thank you,' replied Cooper. 'My colleague spoke with Mrs Henderson yesterday, and following that conversation Mrs Henderson called to inform us that a quantity of Etorphine was missing and was unaccounted for. We're trying to establish how that could have happened.'

Adam Charles looked surprised. 'I was not on duty yesterday. I haven't spoken to Joan for a few days and I certainly wasn't aware any drugs had gone missing.'

'When did you last speak to Mrs Henderson?' enquired Rachel.

Charles thought for a moment. 'It must have been Monday,' he remarked. 'We were both on duty that day. It would have been when the practice closed at around eight that evening.'

'So what days do you work late?' Rachel asked, curious that when she'd called Joan Henderson back on the previous evening she had been put through to the answer machine.

'We are open seven days a week,' replied Charles. 'On Mondays, Tuesdays, Thursdays and Fridays we stay open until eight; we close at five on all other days. Joan has Tuesdays off and I have Wednesdays off, so we don't normally see each other from when we close on Monday until Thursday morning.'

'I see,' said Rachel, who was satisfied with the vet's explanation. 'So the last time you saw Joan was on Monday 14th July?'

'As I indicated before,' continued Cooper, 'the reason why we came here today is to follow up with Mrs Henderson about the missing Etorphine.'

Charles shrugged his shoulders. 'I'm sorry, Joan isn't around,' he remarked with a hint of embarrassment in his voice. 'She's normally here by now. I have no idea why she's late. It's really not like her.'

Rachel glanced uneasily at Cooper. 'Can we ask you some questions about the procedures here for keeping drugs like Etorphine?' she said, trying hard not to deliberately mislead the vet.

Charles nodded. 'Of course, what would you like to know?'

'First of all, who within the practice has access to the drugs?' Cooper asked.

'That would be just Joan, Malcolm and I,' replied Charles. 'Once we are in theatre and the drug is being used, I guess in theory the nurses could also have access to it, but normally it's kept in a locked cabinet with the other drugs and only one of the three vets has a key to that cupboard.'

'So if a bottle went missing, it could only be one of you three that could have taken it?' continued Cooper who, as he spoke, stared directly at Charles.

'I suppose so, yes,' he replied rather uncomfortably. 'But Joan and Malcolm are professionals. They wouldn't take any drugs and I can assure you I certainly didn't.'

'Which begs the obvious question,' remarked Cooper. 'Who did?'

*   *   *   *

Lou Henderson's distress was clear for all to see. He sat on the low wall in stunned silence for several minutes before he said anything.

'So how was Joan killed?' he enquired, his tone of voice suggesting a fear for what he was about to be told.

'We've still to establish all the details,' replied Carmichael as tactfully as he could. 'But it appears she was killed earlier this morning.'

'But who'd want to kill Joan?' remarked Henderson, his face showing just how baffling this was to him.

Carmichael shrugged his shoulders. 'We're not sure,' he admitted. 'But I can assure you, Mr Henderson, we'll catch whoever did this.'

'Where I come from,' announced Henderson through gritted teeth, 'they execute people like that. You're too liberal over here, Inspector. I expect, even if you catch him, he'll just get twenty years and be out in ten.'

Carmichael sat next to Henderson on the wall. 'Can you think of anyone who had a grudge against Joan?' he enquired.

Henderson shook his head. 'Nobody. She was everyone's friend.'

'Does the name Aiden Davidson mean anything to you?'

'Aiden!' exclaimed Henderson with surprise. 'He wouldn't kill Joan. We are drinking buddies at The Drunken Duck. He's never met Joan. Why do you think he's involved?'

Carmichael cleared his throat. 'No, I'm afraid you have misunderstood me, Mr Henderson,' Carmichael added. 'Aiden's been murdered, too, and we think there's a connection.'

*　*　*　*

Adam Charles sat for a few moments frozen with shock upon hearing about the death of Joan Henderson.

'Murdered!' he muttered. 'You say she's been murdered. I can't believe it.'

'I'm sorry,' Rachel said sympathetically. 'I'm afraid it's true.'

'And was her death to do with the missing Etorphine?'

'We're not sure,' replied Cooper honestly. 'We do think it may be connected to the death of a man earlier this week.'

'Who was that?'

'A man called Aiden Davidson,' said Cooper. 'Did you know him?'

Adam Charles shook his head. 'No,' he replied quietly. 'I've never heard of him.'

* * * *

Carmichael and Henderson sat together on the low wall for almost twenty minutes.

'Can I see the text message you received from your wife's mobile?'

Henderson pulled out his phone and opened up the message. Once it was visible on the screen, he handed the mobile to Carmichael.

Sorry Henderson but she had to pay. 737 strikes again. Catch me if you can.

'Does any of this mean anything to you?' asked Carmichael.

'Not a goddamn thing,' snapped Henderson, his Carolina accent as strong as ever.

'I'll need to keep the phone for the time being I'm afraid. I hope you understand.'

'No problem. If it helps find the person who did this you can keep it for as long as you want.'

'Thanks. Why don't you go with one of my officers to the station,' he continued. 'If you are willing, I'd like you to make a statement about when you last saw or spoke to your wife. It would also help if you could share with us details of all your joint friends and her colleagues; also anything you can tell us about Aiden Davidson and, if you do think of anyone who

78

held any sort of grudge against Joan, that would really help us, too.'

'Of course. But before we go am I allowed to go upstairs and collect a few things? I expect I'll need to stay elsewhere for a few days so it would be good to just grab some clothes.'

'I suppose so. But please just go upstairs, at the moment we need to keep the kitchen sealed off.'

Henderson stood up. 'Is that where she died?' he asked, his misery palpable in his voice.

Carmichael beckoned a uniformed officer over. 'Can you accompany Mr Henderson upstairs. He needs to pick up a few things.'

As Henderson and the uniformed officer walked slowly towards the house, Watson emerged and strode over to the low wall where Carmichael was still seated. 'Is that the husband?' he asked.

'Yes,' replied Carmichael. 'He's distraught.'

They both watched as Henderson disappeared into the house.

'Any joy finding her mobile?' Carmichael asked.

Watson shook his head. 'Not so far, but I've only really had a chance to look downstairs. It's a big house and there's a lot of drawers to check.'

'OK,' continued Carmichael. 'You can stop looking for now as I've another job I need you to do. When he comes out I want you to take Mr Henderson back to the station. He tells me he used to drink with Aiden Davidson in The Drunken Duck.'

'Really,' remarked Watson. 'A link at last. Do you think that's significant?'

Carmichael raised his eyebrows. 'I've no idea, but as you say there's clearly a link and we need to find out from Mr Henderson as much we can about his wife, her friends, colleagues … You know the drill.'

Watson nodded. 'OK, leave it with me. I'll drag as much

79

out of him as I can. I'll also check his movements for the times the other two were killed.'

'Thanks, Marc,' said Carmichael. 'Take it easy on him though, as he's clearly still in shock.'

Watson nodded. 'What about the formal ID of her body?'

'I'll get Stock to get her body down to the path lab and ask him to call you when he's ready to allow Henderson to carry out the identification,' responded Carmichael. 'I suspect you'll be able to do it early this afternoon.'

At that moment Henderson appeared at the front door clutching a small sports bag.

'I'll leave you to it,' remarked Carmichael as he gestured for Watson to go over to the murdered woman's distraught husband. 'Let me know if you uncover anything you feel is important.'

Watson walked over to Henderson and respectfully ushered him down the drive towards his car.

Chapter 14

Penny had endured a busy but thankless morning.

Her first job had been to act as taxi driver and ferry Natalie, her youngest daughter, ten miles to the stables. As she had done so, she had listened to Natalie argue her case for getting a dog.

'I'm sorry, my dear,' Penny had said as she eventually managed to jettison her pleading daughter at the stables. 'There is no way your dad will allow you to have a dog. You know how he hates animals.'

Natalie's disconsolate expression cut no ice with Penny, who left her teenage daughter without the slightest pang of guilt, given she'd been forced to endure this persistent argument off and on for the past three weeks.

Upon her return home Penny had spent the following twenty minutes trying desperately to get her eldest daughter to stop moping around and telling her how bored she was and how she hated living in Moulton Bank.

Eventually, with her patience tested to its limits, she snapped. 'Well, if you're really bored to death, you could consider helping me!' she yelled at Jemma. 'I've got washing to do, I've got the beds to change and in the next few minutes someone is going to be saying what's for lunch. If you want to make yourself useful, you could give me a bit of a hand.'

Jemma's screwed-up face said it all. 'Excuse me,' she replied, her hands firmly on her hips. 'I do my own washing and ironing. You should get Robbie and Natalie to do theirs. That would ease your workload.'

Penny glared angrily in Jemma's direction. 'You're twenty years old,' she reminded her. 'Natalie's five years younger than you.'

'But Robbie's not! *He* doesn't do his own washing.'

'No, that's true,' Penny acknowledged. 'But he will once he goes to university in September, and I'd like to remind you that he's the only one of you three that has bothered to get a summer job. He even gives me a bit of housekeeping money.'

'Very reluctantly,' observed Jemma. 'As I recall it, Dad had to almost physically extract that twenty quid out of him.'

'At first, yes,' conceded Penny. 'But now Robbie gives it to me every Friday without any problems.'

With a great sense of theatre, Jemma rolled her large brown eyes and exhaled loudly and with feeling. 'OK,' she conceded. 'Give me the shopping list, I'll go to that excuse of a supermarket over the road and get whatever you need.'

'Thanks, dear,' replied Penny, who was astounded to have got such a positive result and fully intended to take advantage of this rare offer of assistance. 'The list's in the kitchen on the fridge, I'll get you some money.'

As soon as Jemma had departed, Penny decided to have a break. She was desperate for a coffee and thankful for a few minutes' peace and quiet.

As she sat in the front room sipping her coffee her thoughts went back to her tête-à-tête with Natalie earlier. Secretly, she too wanted a dog but she knew there was no way Steve would agree.

Having pushed that thought out of her head, Penny cast her mind back to the conversation she'd had the evening before with Steve. She was still confused by the way he had acted and the more she thought about it, the more she was certain he was keeping something from her. She wasn't sure how she would manage it, but she fully intended to find out what it was.

As soon as Lou Henderson was away from the house, Carmichael decided to go back inside to talk to Dr Stock. He found the pathologist exactly where he'd left him more than thirty minutes earlier.

'Have you discovered anything else?' he asked.

Stock nodded enthusiastically. 'Yes, I have. I've found traces of what appears to be the adhesive from a sticking plaster around her lips, her cheeks and in her hair. I think she may have been gagged by a length of plaster wrapped around her head.'

'Really? So does that suggest she came around after she received that initial blow?'

Stock again nodded, but this time less vigorously. 'That would seem likely. My guess is that she was concussed with a blow to her head here,' Stock pointed to the bruise on her temple. 'I think she was then tied up on the chair and, to prevent her cries being heard, the killer wrapped a length of sticking plaster around her mouth.'

'And he then injected her with Etorphine?' suggested Carmichael.

'That would be my hypothesis from the evidence we have here,' added Stock. 'However, I'll not know for sure until I've carried out an autopsy.'

Carmichael shook his head. 'If she was conscious when the Etorphine was administered, she would have been terrified … What an awful way to die!'

Stock looked up at Carmichael with a perplexed expression. 'In my experience,' he remarked profoundly, 'there aren't many *pleasant* ways to be murdered.'

Carmichael smiled. 'Point taken.'

Having completed their interviews with the staff at the Park Road Veterinary Practice, Cooper and Dalton headed off to find and interview the three people who had not been on duty.

'So, what do you think?' Rachel enquired.

Cooper thought for a moment. 'I thought Adam Charles was genuine enough. But I suppose we have to consider him and Malcolm Page as suspects, as they had the keys to the drugs cabinet.'

Rachel sighed. 'I agree, but their processes are so inadequate that pretty much anyone could have taken the Etorphine. It doesn't sound like they were that fussy about who had the keys when they were busy.'

'Certainly, the nurses seem to have been given easy access.'

'So where does that lead us?' Rachel asked despondently.

'Nowhere,' replied Cooper. 'We need to interview the rest of the staff pretty quickly, but at this stage I'm not sure any of the ones we spoke to today stand out as being our killer.'

Much as she hated to admit it, Rachel fully agreed with what Cooper was saying.

*   *   *   *

It was almost midday by the time Carmichael eventually made his exit from the Henderson house. He was just about to start the car engine when one of the uniformed PCs rushed down the path.

Carmichael wound down his window. 'Why all the excitement?' he enquired.

'We've found a mobile,' he announced elatedly. 'It was in a drawer in one of the upstairs bedrooms.'

Carmichael was delighted. 'OK, get it checked out,' he ordered. 'I want to know whose fingerprints are on it and I want details of all the people she communicated with in the last twenty-four hours.'

'I'll get on to it right away,' the PC replied fervently.

Carmichael started to close his window, but stopped when it was halfway. 'Was there a note with it?'

The PC shook his head. 'No, we haven't found one.'

'Keep looking,' Carmichael instructed. 'If this guy's true to form he will have probably left one somewhere.'

Carmichael finished closing the car window and sped off in the direction of Kirkwood Police Station.

Chapter 15

Carmichael had intended to go straight back to Kirkwood Police Station, but as he neared the junction he saw the signpost stating that it was only ten miles to Hasslebury, so he changed his mind and hurriedly indicated to turn left.

He thought he'd have another look at Davidson's house and, although he wouldn't have dreamt of admitting it, he also thought there might be something in what Siobhan Ballentyne had told him the day before, so he intended to talk again to the hedgehog lady. Carmichael was a matter of minutes away from Ivy Cottages when his mobile rang.

'Hi, Paul,' he said when he saw Cooper's name flashing up on the screen.

'Actually, it's Rachel,' replied the familiar voice of the young DC. 'I can't get a signal on my phone and, as Cooper's driving, he said I could borrow his mobile.'

'Oh really?' said Carmichael, who was really not in the slightest bit interested in hearing why she was using Cooper's phone. 'How did you get on at Park Road?'

'They were all shocked to hear about Joan Henderson,' Rachel remarked. 'But the bad news is that their security with drugs is so lax that any one of them could have taken the missing Etorphine.'

Carmichael wasn't pleased at hearing that piece of news. 'So, in your view, was anyone you interviewed a candidate to be our killer?' he enquired in hope rather than expectation.

'Possibly,' replied Rachel unconvincingly. 'But none of

them jumped out as serious contenders. Mind you, we've still three of the staff to interview. Maybe one of them may be a better candidate.'

'Where are you now?' asked Carmichael abruptly.

'We're on the A49 heading towards Moulton Bank.'

'Well, make a detour over to Hasslebury,' Carmichael instructed. 'I'm on my way to talk with Betty Wilbraham. It may help if you're there, too, given you seem to have built a bit of a rapport with her. I'm sure Cooper can manage the remaining interviews by himself.'

Rachel removed the mobile from her ear and put her hand over the mouth piece. 'The boss wants you to drop me off at Hasslebury,' she whispered to Cooper.

'That's fine,' he replied calmly. 'It's not far out of our way. Tell him we'll be there in about fifteen minutes.'

Rachel put the phone back against her head. 'We'll be there in fifteen minutes,' she said, almost parrot-fashion.

*   *   *   *

Including their car journey to Kirkwood Police Station, Marc Watson had spent almost an hour with Lou Henderson. Although it was patently obvious that Henderson was finding it hard to keep himself together, to his credit he was able to provide a clear statement to Watson about his last conversation with his wife, and was able to elaborate in more detail about his acquaintance with Aiden Davidson. They also found time to talk about his work as a sales director with a large private health-care provider and also to discuss his hometown in North Carolina.

Watson liked Henderson's warmth and easy manner and could not help thinking that the American certainly would, in normal circumstances, be great company. But, of course, the situation wasn't normal and Watson was conscious he needed to treat Henderson not only as a grieving relative, which he unquestionably was, but also as a potential suspect, albeit in his heart Watson doubted the American was involved.

Remembering one of Carmichael's instructions was for him to arrange for Henderson to formally identify Joan's body. Watson excused himself and left the room so he could talk privately with Stock. When he returned just a few minutes later, he could see that Henderson's eyes were red and moist, and his need to sniff frequently and habitually pinch shut his nostrils with his thumb and forefinger suggested the grieving husband was fighting hard to hold back his tears.

'I have arranged for us to carry out the formal identification of your wife at one thirty,' he remarked as tactfully as he could. 'Are you feeling up to doing this today, Lou?'

'If the truth was known, no,' Henderson replied candidly, before sniffing once more. 'But it needs doing, so the sooner I do it the better I suppose.'

*   *   *   *

Carmichael arrived a few minutes before the others. He parked his car outside Davidson's house and waited in the warm afternoon's sunshine for Rachel to arrive. He didn't notice the curtains in Betty Wilbraham's bedroom twitch as the curious neighbour observed him in silence.

It took a good ten minutes before Cooper's beaten-up Volvo car came into view, which gave Carmichael a little time to attempt to consider the three deaths. The case held two significant dilemmas for him. Firstly, he struggled to understand a motive for any of the murders and secondly, and even more perplexing, was the absence of any significant link between the three events. Given the murderer had mentioned there would be four murders, Carmichael was worried their lack of progress in answering these two important questions might mean that some other poor soul would die.

As Cooper's car was nearing Ivy Cottages, Carmichael gazed briefly towards Betty Wilbraham's house. Although Betty recoiled back away from the window as soon as she saw Carmichael's head turn towards her, she was not quick enough and on this occasion Carmichael spotted the curtains move. As he turned to face away again, he sniggered to himself. In his experience, nosey individuals like Betty invariably knew everything about their neighbourhoods. Much as he hated to admit it, he was sure Siobhan Ballentyne was correct and the hedgehog lady could help much more than she had to date.

*　*　*　*

There were a number of things that Watson disliked about being a policeman. He had an aversion to paperwork, he loathed being told what to do, and he detested autopsies, but, without question, his biggest hate was supervising when family members were required to identify murder victims. He found these events awkward and excruciatingly difficult to manage with the due dignity required. Unless instructed specifically to oversee such proceedings, he tried to avoid them at all costs. When he was forced to be involved, he found himself either being struck dumb or, even worse, making ridiculous small talk to try and relieve the uneasy atmosphere. On this occasion his body selected the silent option.

Watson and Henderson stood patiently behind the glass window as the mortuary assistant, clad completely in white, carefully and sensitively rolled down the shroud to reveal the pale face of the motionless body.

Watson glanced sideways to see how Lou Henderson was coping with this painful ordeal. At first the dejected American didn't flinch, but after a few seconds Henderson turned and stared at Watson, his eyes wide open and his face turning dark purple.

'What the hell's going on?' he shouted angrily. 'Do you fellas think this is some sort of joke? This isn't my wife!'

Chapter 16

Penny was determined to find out more about her husband's conversation with Siobhan Ballentyne the previous day. She knew Steve well enough to know it was highly unlikely he would tell her himself, so she decided to take a more direct approach.

'Oh hello,' she said as she heard the familiar voice of the psychic on the other end of the telephone. 'This is Penny Carmichael here,' she continued in as friendly a voice as she could summon up. 'We met on Tuesday at the WI.'

'Oh hi,' replied Siobhan. 'I remember you very well.'

'I was wondering if I could make an appointment for a reading later today?' Penny asked, her voice shaking a little as she spoke.

'I'm sure that could be arranged,' replied Siobhan. 'I'm certainly free for an hour at four if you'd like to come over.'

'That would be perfect. I'll see you then.'

As she replaced the receiver, Penny could feel her heart beating inside her chest. She wasn't sure how she was going to manoeuvre her conversation with Siobhan to discover what she had said to Steve, but she was certainly going to try her hardest to get some answers.

* * * *

'So, what's the plan?' asked Rachel chirpily as she climbed out of the car.

'I want to talk to Betty again,' Carmichael replied, his eyes moving in the direction of the hedgehog lady's cottage. 'You can take the lead as you seem to have built up a rapport with her. Then, when we're through with her, we can have another look inside Davidson's house.'

Rachel smiled. 'That's fine with me, sir,' she replied obediently. 'Is there anything in particular you want me to focus on?'

Carmichael nodded. 'Yes, I want to know more about Davidson and these female visitors he was getting. I'm sure she knows more than she's telling us. Also, you need to ask her if she knew either Joan Henderson or the identity of the first victim.'

'Understood.'

'I'll get off and interview the three employees from Park Road,' added Cooper, who had remained in the car with his engine running and window down.

'Thanks, Paul,' replied Carmichael. 'Let's regroup back at Kirkwood Station at four thirty. Can you let Marc know?'

'No problem,' replied Cooper, who pushed the gear lever into first and drove away.

From behind her bedroom window, Betty Wilbraham had been straining her ears to try and hear what was being said. Although she didn't pick up everything, she heard enough to understand what was about to happen.

*　*　*　*

In the ten minutes that had elapsed since the disastrous episode in the morgue, Marc Watson must have apologised ten times to Lou Henderson for the embarrassing mix-up. Not that Henderson was listening.

'So where the hell's my wife?' he kept saying angrily. 'And what are you all doing to find her.'

Watson eventually managed to usher Henderson into a

small empty office where he left him with a coffee and another abject apology before he retreated into the car park to call Carmichael.

*　*　*　*

Carmichael's finger was a matter of inches from Betty Wilbraham's door knocker when his mobile rang. He extracted the offending item from his jacket pocket.

'It's Marc,' he sighed with some irritation. 'I'll just take it.'

Carmichael pushed the green button and walked a few paces down the path.

'Hi, Marc,' he whispered. 'Is it important? We're just about to talk again with Davidson's next-door neighbour.'

Rachel patiently looked on as her boss stood motionless listening to Watson. Although he said nothing, his expression indicated that it wasn't good news.

'I'm on my way,' was all Carmichael said before ending the call.

'Bad news?' remarked Rachel apprehensively.

With his index finger, Carmichael beckoned her over to join him.

'The body we found this morning isn't Joan Henderson,' he told her in a hushed voice. 'Understandably, Henderson is going mad so I'm going to have to get back to the station.'

'What?!' exclaimed Rachel, louder than ideally she would have wanted. 'So who's the woman we found at her house? And where's Joan?'

'Good questions, Rachel,' replied Carmichael calmly, 'but ones Marc couldn't answer.'

'Do you want me to come with you?'

Carmichael shook his head. 'No, you talk with Betty again. Put some pressure on her.'

'OK. ... Do you want me to take another look around Davidson's house?'

93

Carmichael considered her question for a moment. 'No,' he concluded. 'Once you're done with Betty, get yourself back to Kirkwood. We may need as many bodies as we can to identify who we found at Henderson's house. You can leave Davidson's house for now.'

Rachel watched as her boss strode purposefully away, climbed into his car and screeched off down the narrow country road.

'How am I getting back to the station?' Rachel muttered to herself when it dawned upon her that she had no car. Then, with a quick shake of her head and a deep intake of breath, she turned back and walked up to Betty Wilbraham's green front door.

Chapter 17

On the way back to Kirkwood Police Station Carmichael received another call on his mobile. This one was from one of the scene-of-crime officers, who believed he had found something that might be important on Davidson's computer. Carmichael listened intently as the officer meticulously outlined his important findings.

'So how many images are there?' Carmichael enquired.

'Dozens.'

'And all of young women?'

'Yes. It's hard to tell from the photographs, but I'd say that most are from the Middle East or Southern Europe.'

'How do you make that out?'

'Their skin. There are some with fair skin and blonde hair, but I'd say that the majority are of Middle Eastern extraction.'

'Call Rachel Dalton and tell her exactly what you've just told me. It's critical she knows *now*,' he stressed. 'It may help the interview she's currently conducting.'

As the call finished, Carmichael noticed a white Citroën van heading straight for him. 'Bugger!' he shouted as he braked hard, turned the wheel sharply and came to rest on the grass verge.

The white vehicle shot past him, its driver apparently oblivious to the evasive action Carmichael had been forced to take. Carmichael noticed a blue logo on the side but couldn't make out what it said. However, through his rear-view mirror he could clearly see the rear number plate as it disappeared down the lane.

'RV55EMU,' he muttered to himself over and over again as he searched to find a pen and scrap of paper. 'I'll be seeing to you later.'

* * * *

Paul Cooper had already interviewed the two nurses and had now reached Malcolm Page's imposing detached house. Totally unaware of the developments elsewhere, he sat back in the comfortable armchair in Malcolm Page's large study as he waited for the elderly vet to return with the tea he'd been offered.

Scattered on every available horizontal surface were photographs, which Cooper took to be of Page's children.

'Here you go,' remarked Page as he entered the room carrying two mugs. 'I'll set yours down here,' he continued as he carefully placed Cooper's tea on the small table beside him.

'Are these your children?' Cooper enquired, pointing to a recent-looking picture of him, in which he was flanked by a couple of women in their late twenties.

'Yes,' replied Page as he proudly lifted up the photograph. 'This one's Sarah,' he said, pointing to the woman to his right. 'She's a vet, too,' he said proudly. 'She's working in a zoo in Holland at the moment.'

'And your other daughter?' enquired Cooper.

'That's Victoria,' replied Page. 'She works as a receptionist for Harvey Romney at Trinity Pet Hospital nearby. She studied to be a veterinary nurse at college, but was never that keen. She worked at Park Road with me at first, but moved over to Harvey's place about a year ago. The pay's better there.'

'They're both pretty girls,' remarked Cooper flatteringly.

'Yes,' remarked Page with a clear sense of pride. 'Their

mother died many years ago, so they've been the centre of my world ever since. But of course, like all pretty birds, they fledge eventually – Sarah a few years ago, and Victoria, I suspect, won't be much longer here with me.'

'So she still lives here?' enquired Cooper.

Page laughed. 'In theory,' he replied, 'but she's usually out with friends so I can go days without seeing her.'

Page replaced the photograph on the sideboard. 'Anyway, Sergeant,' he remarked. 'I'm sure you're not here to talk about my daughters.'

* * * *

Rachel sat on the edge of Betty Wilbraham's worn and dusty settee. 'We need to know more about Aiden Davidson,' she said. 'We also need to know a little more about his female visitors. Inspector Carmichael said that you told him there were quite a few.'

Betty raised her eyes skyward as if to imply disapproval. 'I'm not going to suggest I knew exactly what was going on,' she said openly. 'However, they were all young things, they only ever seemed to come once, and they would be here for about thirty minutes and then they were away. What would you make of that?'

Rachel smiled. She'd already been briefed by the scene-of-crime officer, so she knew something was going on, but was keen to find out what Betty had seen. 'So when did these visits start and how many girls did you see going into Aiden's?'

Betty considered the question for a few seconds. 'It started about a year ago. And I'd say in the last six months I saw at least twenty or thirty different women in total.'

'And they were always alone and you never saw any of them more than once?'

Betty frowned. 'Actually, there was *one* that came more than once. I suspect she was one he liked the most.'

Rachel chuckled to herself. 'Could you describe her?'

Betty nodded. 'She was in her thirties, very pretty, had shortish mousey hair and looked quite normal. She was married, too.'

'How do you know she was married?' enquired Rachel.

'Because she wore a wedding ring on her finger,' replied Betty with surprise in her voice.

'That's very observant of you,' said Rachel in a complimentary tone of voice.

Betty ignored Rachel's remark. 'I suppose married women do that sort of thing, too,' she added with a faint shrug of her shoulders, 'but she didn't look the type to me.'

'So what sort of man was Aiden Davidson?' Rachel asked.

'As I told your Inspector, he kept himself to himself,' replied Betty. 'I hardly knew him really.'

As she finished her sentence, there was a loud knock on the door.

Betty stood up, shuffled over and carefully opened the wooden door. 'Oh it's you, Dennis,' she said, clearly pleased to see her visitor. 'Do come through.'

In walked the tall figure of Dennis Preston, the local RSPCA man. 'Oh, hello,' he said cheerily as soon as he saw Rachel perched on the edge of the settee. 'Am I interrupting anything?'

'No,' responded Betty almost immediately. 'I am just giving Rachel some information on poor Aiden Davidson who lived next door.'

By Rachel's sober expression Preston could see he was disturbing them and his presence was not welcomed, at least not by the pretty police officer. 'I'll go through to the garden,' he said tactfully. 'I was passing and thought I'd pop in to see how the new charge is faring.'

'Thanks,' replied Rachel, who smiled to illustrate her appreciation. 'We'll just be a few more minutes.'

* * * *

Cooper took another sip of his tea. 'A quantity of Etorphine is missing from the Park Road Practice and we are trying to find out where it went,' he said as diplomatically as he could.

'Missing!' exclaimed Page. 'Is that a police euphemism for stolen?'

Cooper smiled. 'Yes,' he conceded. 'We believe it was stolen. We also believe it was used to sedate a man who was later murdered, and possibly involved in another suspicious death earlier today.'

Malcolm Page looked surprised. 'Oh I see. Well, I've no idea who would have taken any Etorphine from the practice, but procedures are fairly lax so it could be any one of the employees.'

Cooper nodded. 'Yes, we've already established that.'

'You mentioned some murders? Are these people connected to the practice?'

Cooper considered the question for a few seconds. 'The first was a man from Hasslebury called Aiden Davidson. Do you know of him?'

Malcolm Page shifted backwards in his armchair. 'Yes, I do, He painted that beautiful picture for me.' As he spoke, Page pointed to a large oil painting of his two daughters which was hanging over the fireplace. 'I'm so shocked to hear about his death.'

Cooper leaned forward. 'Did you know him well?'

Page shook his head. 'No, not really. He painted the picture about two years ago. He was recommended to me by a colleague at work.'

'Who was that?'

'Joan Henderson,' responded the now ashen-faced, elderly vet. 'He was a friend of her husband's, as I recall.'

'And when did you see him last?'

Page thought for a moment. 'Not for over a year.'

There was a short pause, while Cooper considered whether it was the right time for him to disclose the identity of the other victim.

'I'm afraid I've some more disturbing news for you,' Cooper announced, as calmly as he could. 'I'm afraid to say that the identity of the other murder victim I mentioned is Joan Henderson.'

'What!' exclaimed Page. 'When did she die?'

Cooper remained composed. 'She appears to have been killed in her own home last night or, more likely, in the early hours of this morning.'

Malcolm Page put his cup down on the floor in front of him and brought his hands up to his face. 'What about Vicky?' he asked, his eyes showing clear signs of distress. 'Is Vicky all right?'

Cooper gazed quizzically back at the vet. 'I'm sorry, I don't understand what you mean.'

'Vicky was staying over at Joan's house last night,' Page said, his voice faltering as he spoke. 'Is she all right?'

* * * *

As soon as the RSPCA man was out of earshot, Rachel resumed her questioning. 'Do you know a lady called Joan Henderson?'

Betty Wilbraham shook her head. 'No,' she responded firmly and convincingly. 'I don't believe I do. Who is she?'

'What about the man who was run over down the road back in June? Did you have any idea who he was?'

'No.'

Although Betty's reply was clear and delivered without any hesitation, it wasn't anywhere near as forthright as her response regarding Joan Henderson, which caused Rachael to question whether the hedgehog lady was being truthful in this latest denial.

'Are you certain? You don't sound so sure to me.'

Betty broke eye contact. 'I'm sure,' she said steadfastly. 'If I knew him, I'd have told you.'

Rachel wasn't convinced and was deciding how she should continue the conversation when Dennis Preston reappeared.

'I'm sorry to interrupt,' he said apologetically. 'I need to be on my way. I've got to get to Kirkwood. I just popped in to see the hedgehog.'

'Oh, do stay a while,' pleaded Betty, who seemed genuinely upset that he was about to go. 'We've finished anyway!'

Preston smiled. 'No, I'm sorry. I really can't stay. I do have to get off.'

As he headed towards the door, Rachel quickly rose from her chair. 'You said you're going to Kirkwood,' she said as affably as she could and with the sort of smile she had used many times over the years to ingratiate herself to her father. 'Could I possibly cadge a lift with you? I need to be back at the Police Station and, unfortunately, I've no transport.'

Dennis Preston smiled. 'Absolutely. That's no trouble at all and, as I'll be driving right past the police station, it's not even out of my way.'

Betty Wilbraham stared irately out of the window, as the RSPCA van, with Rachel Dalton in the passenger seat, sped off in the direction of Kirkwood. As soon as they were out of sight she traipsed over to her old sideboard, extracted a brown faded envelope from the top drawer and, with a pained expression on her face, stared intently at its contents.

Chapter 18

Carmichael's first thought when he arrived at Kirkwood Police Station was to find Watson, who he finally discovered sitting alone in the canteen.

'So, what happened?' Carmichael enquired as he placed two plastic cups of coffee on the table and sat down opposite the beleaguered sergeant.

Watson, still pale and a little shaken by the fiasco at the morgue, took a sip of coffee. 'It's not his wife,' he said quietly. 'What's more he's gone apoplectic and is threatening us with all sorts.'

Carmichael could see that Watson was still stunned by the whole ordeal. 'Look,' he replied reassuringly, 'it's just one of those things. He gets a weird text from Mrs Henderson's mobile, he reports it to us, we find a dead woman in her night attire in their house – it's not surprising we thought it was his wife. Anyway, you'd think he'd be relieved that she's not dead.'

Watson looked back at his boss. 'I think he is, but he keeps asking when we're going to find her.'

Carmichael put the coffee cup to his lips and took a large swallow. 'Yes, that's a reasonable question, but equally I'd like to know who the hell that dead woman is and why was she in her pyjamas in someone else's house.'

'Me too,' replied Watson. 'Henderson swears he doesn't know who she was.'

'Do you believe him?'

Watson nodded. 'If he does, then he's a good actor, that's all I can say.'

'Where have you put him? I suppose I should talk to him.'

'I took a full statement from him before we went to the morgue. Then we talked again for almost an hour after the identification. In the end I suggested he book himself into a hotel and try to get some rest. To be fair to him, he looked totally exhausted.'

Carmichael nodded approval. 'That makes sense. So which one is he at?'

'The Lindley. PC Tyler took him there about twenty minutes ago.'

Carmichael stood up and looked at his watch. 'We've our debrief in thirty minutes,' he added. 'If you want to remain here until then, that's fine with me.'

'Thanks,' replied Watson. 'I'm grateful but I'd rather keep focused on the case. I'll call Stock to see if he's found anything else.'

Carmichael was pleased with his sergeant's response. 'That's fine,' he replied with a kindly smile. 'You could also call Rachel and Cooper to make certain they're here. Tell Cooper about the body not being Joan. Rachel was with me when you called, so she knows, but I haven't had time to tell Cooper.'

'Will do, sir,' replied Watson obediently.

'We may also need to order in some food,' added Carmichael. 'I think this briefing may be a long one.'

Watson forced a smile. 'What are you going to be doing?'

'Mine is the short straw,' replied Carmichael ponderously. 'I'm going to have to brief Chief Inspector Hewitt.'

* * * *

To say Dennis Preston's driving was erratic would be a mammoth understatement. For the first mile or two Rachel

103

managed to maintain her composure and made no comment. However, when the RSPCA van narrowly missed colliding with an oncoming car as it overtook a refuse lorry on a blind bend, and then within seconds clipped the kerb sending it back out towards the centre of the road, Rachel felt she could not remain silent any longer.

'Do you always drive like this?' she asked anxiously.

'Am I going too fast?' replied Preston his eyes focused entirely on Rachel rather than on the winding country road in front of him.

'Among other major traffic offences, yes!' exclaimed Rachel, her left hand clutching tightly to the armrest.

Preston broke hard, making Rachel lurch forward in her seat and causing the contents of her bag to spew out into the foot well.

'Is this better?' he asked, his eyes still concentrating on Rachel rather than the road ahead.

'Can you pull up somewhere?' snapped Rachel. 'All my stuff's going under the seat.'

Dennis Preston broke hard again and guided the van into the driveway of a large house. 'Sorry,' he said once the van had stopped. 'I'm not used to having passengers, apart from cats, dogs and the odd hedgehog.'

Rachel scrambled out of the car and started to collect her belongings from the foot well and from under her seat, thrusting them haphazardly into her bag.

'Who taught you to drive?' she remarked angrily and with no attempt to demonstrate any tact. 'You're a total menace!'

Preston looked stunned by her comments. 'It did take me five attempts to pass,' he conceded. 'But I've had a full licence for five years now and had no accidents at all.'

'I bet you've caused a fair few though,' muttered Rachel under her breath as she finished retrieving her possessions.

'Sorry,' replied Preston, who looked genuinely apologetic. 'I'll be more careful for the rest of the journey, I promise.'

Rachel clambered back into the van and clicked her seat belt in place. 'I damn well hope so,' she remarked.

* * * *

Cooper had just got back into his car when Marc Watson called him on his mobile.

'Hi Marc,' Cooper said. 'How's it going with you?'

'Terrible,' Watson remarked. 'The boss asked me to call you. He wants to make sure you're here for the debrief at four thirty and you need to know that the body we found at Henderson's house isn't Joan.'

'Really?' replied Cooper. 'In that case, I might know who it is.'

'Who?' exclaimed Watson, shocked by Cooper's announcement.

'Victoria Page. I've just spoken to her father. He's one of the vets at Park Road. He told me his daughter was staying at the Hendersons' house last night. She's not been home since.'

Watson was astonished at what he was hearing. 'I suggest you go and talk to him again. Prepare him for some bad news, and get him down to the morgue to do an ID. Hopefully we'll get it right this time.'

'Hopefully for you, Marc,' remarked Cooper coolly. 'Somehow I doubt Malcolm Page would share those sentiments.'

* * * *

Hewitt listened intently as Carmichael outlined where they were with the investigation and explained that they were yet to identify the woman's body they'd found at Henderson's house.

'So, where is Joan Henderson?' Hewitt asked.

Carmichael shrugged his shoulders. 'We don't know.'

'Do you think she's another victim?'

Carmichael nodded. 'I'm afraid that's a distinct possibility,' he added, rising up from his chair. 'I'm meeting with the team later so I'll update you then. I just thought you needed to know the state of play.'

'Do you think we need to make an announcement to the TV and press?' Hewitt asked.

Carmichael shook his head. 'I don't think so at this stage, sir,' he replied. 'I'm not sure that would do us any good and it may cause some anxiety in the area. Let's keep this all in house for the next day or so.'

Hewitt nodded. 'Very well, but for God's sake find this nutcase before he or she kills again.'

As Carmichael was leaving Hewitt's office, he noticed a familiar white van enter the police car park. He retrieved the scrap of paper from his pocket and read the registration number, RV55EMU. To his amazement, the registration he'd written down a few hours earlier was the same as the one on the van. He was even more astonished when he saw DC Dalton clamber out of the vehicle and then appear to engage in conversation with the driver.

*　*　*　*

'Sorry about my driving,' said Preston with a smile. 'I did get you here safe and sound, though.'

Rachel leaned down to look through the open passenger window. 'Well, I suppose that's true. But I wouldn't like to risk it again.'

Preston's smile broadened. 'So, does that mean I can't take you out for a drink one evening?'

Rachel was a little taken aback by his suggestion. 'I don't think so. Thanks for the lift and also thanks for the offer, but I'll pass if you don't mind.'

Preston showed no sign of disappointment; in fact, he looked as though he fully expected this to be her reply.

'Maybe I could call you?' he shouted as Rachel headed over to the rear entrance of the police station.

Rachel did not turn around or respond – she just kept walking.

'At least I've got your number now,' muttered Preston to himself, clutching the business card he'd picked up from the foot well earlier when Rachel was collecting her bits and pieces.

Chapter 19

At four o'clock precisely Penny Carmichael sat down in Siobhan Ballentyne's ornate sitting room.

'How can I help you?' enquired the psychic, her unnerving, piercing stare like a laser beam.

'I'd like to have a reading,' replied Penny as she spotted Siobhan's tiny dog out of the corner of her eye. 'What a lovely little dog!' she added. 'What breed is he?'

'He's a Cairn terrier,' replied Siobhan who lovingly stroked the diminutive animal. 'Aren't you, Mr Swaffie?'

'Oh, he's lovely,' continued Penny, her attention now totally focused on the cute creature.

'He's already met your husband. I think they hit it off.'

'Really?' replied Penny in astonishment. 'Steve's not normally that keen on dogs.'

'So what exactly is it that's troubling you?' the psychic asked.

Penny moved her eye-line to engage with Siobhan Ballentyne. 'I'm not really sure,' she replied feebly. 'I suppose I just want to understand a bit more about what the future holds for me.'

Siobhan smiled. 'First of all, you need to realise that I'm not an oracle. I don't know everything and may not have the answers you are looking for. However, I'm willing to help you as much as I can.'

'Thank you,' Penny heard herself saying, although she wasn't quite sure why.

'Bring your chair closer to me,' Siobhan instructed. 'I'd like to examine your chakras.'

Penny moved her chair closer. 'What are my chakras?'

Siobhan pulled her chair forward too, so near their knees were almost touching and their noses were no more than a foot apart. 'Your chakras are energy points in your body. There are seven main ones, starting at the base of your spine and working up to the top of your head.'

As she spoke, she pulled out a crystal pendulum, which she proceeded to hold close to Penny's knees. 'Your chakras are emitting and receiving energy constantly. If they are aligned, then my pendulum will rotate equally and will signify harmony and calm. If one or more are not aligned, then this may account for you feeling sluggish or having negative emotional and even physical symptoms.'

Penny sat still as the pendulum whirled around. She was just thankful Steve could not see her. She shuddered to think what he would make of all this.

*　　*　　*　　*

When the morgue assistant carefully rolled down the white shroud to reveal the face of the dead woman, Watson's hopes of a positive ID were realised and Malcolm Page's heart was broken.

'Yes, that's Vicky,' Page replied, his eyes moistening as he spoke.

Cooper placed a reassuring arm around his shoulder and led the distraught father out of the viewing area.

'I'm so sorry,' he said with genuine sensitivity.

Malcolm Page stared aimlessly ahead, his face expressionless. 'I need to call Sarah,' he said eventually. 'God knows how I'm going to tell her.'

*　　*　　*　　*

'So how are my chakras?' Penny enquired as soon as Siobhan had finished checking out the seventh one at the top of her head.

Siobhan carefully placed the pendulum on the table by her side. 'Your spine, chest, throat, third eye and the top of your head are all nicely balanced,' she remarked. 'But I sense some misalignment in your lower pelvis and above the naval.'

Penny was genuinely fascinated with what Siobhan was saying but still very perplexed about the whole experience. 'So what does that mean exactly?'

'Each of the major chakras is associated with a colour. The ones where I've identified a misalignment are yellow and orange. It would certainly help if you wore more of those colours and included more yellow and orange foods in your diet.'

Penny, who was wearing blue jeans and a pink-and-blue top, nodded gently. She was certain that if Steve were there he'd either be dragging her away shouting 'Charlatan!' or, more likely, rolling about on the floor in a heap.

'I see,' replied Penny. 'Will that really help me?'

'Without question! You have a strong aura and I sense a huge amount of love in you and surrounding you, but there is some pain, too. Not a physical pain and I don't think it's the pain of grief either,' she added, as she softly rested her hands against Penny's forearms. 'It's a worry within a relationship. It's something that you don't talk about to anyone and a feeling you try to mask, but it's a major pain and one that's become stronger quite recently. Am I correct?'

* * * *

When he learned that Cooper was taking Malcolm Page to identify the body, Carmichael decided to delay the debrief by an hour to allow Cooper time to get back from the morgue. During that extra hour, Watson had helpfully added photographs to the whiteboard of the hit-and-run victim, Aiden Davidson, and the body that had just been identified as Vicky Page.

∗ ∗ ∗ ∗

'How much do I owe you?' Penny asked as soon as the session was over.

'Forty-five pounds, please,' replied Siobhan with her usual expansive smile.

Penny rifled through her handbag, extracted her purse and handed over the fee.

'Has our session helped you?'

'I think so,' replied Penny rather unconvincingly.

Siobhan's smile remained on her face. 'Sometimes it's good to confront your fears head on,' she added. 'However, in some instances it's better to accept that what has happened is history and move on. I don't know exactly what the circumstances are, Mrs Carmichael, but you may want to let sleeping dogs lie.'

Penny thought carefully about what Siobhan was saying.

'Maybe you're right,' she replied as her attention moved back to Mr Swaffie and patted him gently on the head.

Siobhan nodded and smiled sympathetically. 'All I can do is to repeat to you is what I've said already. You have a strong aura and you are surrounded by love. I'd try not to worry if I were you. I think your fears may be unnecessary.'

Penny forced a faint smile. 'My husband also came to see you the other day,' she said, trying hard to make her comment sound as flippant as she could. 'Did you give him any advice?'

Siobhan smiled back and her forced smile was altogether more distinctive than Penny's had been. 'Oh, as I'm sure he told you, his visit was purely in connection with his current investigation. And of course, even if he had asked for a

111

reading, I'd not be able to share the details of that conversation, even with his wife. That would be totally unethical.'

Penny shook the mystic's hand and went to make her exit, none the wiser for her consultation and forty-five pounds poorer.

'I'm not sure it's totally suitable for you,' announced Siobhan as Penny reached the door. 'But every Friday I do hold a session with a small group of ladies in the village which helps many of them come to terms with their various concerns and fears. You're more than welcome to join us if you like.'

Penny turned and, by the bewildered expression on her face, it was clear to the mystic that she wasn't interested. 'I may pass on that if you don't mind,' she replied as tactfully as she could.

'Of course,' replied Siobhan. 'It may not be for you, but the offer's open if you change your mind. We hold the sessions here starting at eight in the evening. Let me give you a leaflet.'

Siobhan walked over to the bookcase and extracted a small printed flyer, which she handed to Penny.

Penny looked at the heading, which read 'The White Vixens Group', folded the leaflet, placed it in her handbag and departed.

* * * *

At five thirty prompt, the four officers gathered in the incident room at Kirkwood Police Station.

'God knows where we start,' remarked Carmichael. 'All I know is that this debriefing may take us some time, so I hope you've no plans for this evening.'

The three officers all shook their heads.

'Let's begin with the first murder,' said Carmichael,

pointing at the photograph of the hit-and-run victim. 'Why don't you talk about him, Marc, as you were one of the investigating officers?'

Watson ran his fingers nervously through his hair. 'The victim was a white male, aged about sixty years old, scruffy appearance but not thought to be living rough,' he said.

'Remind me, why don't we think he was living rough?' enquired Carmichael.

'He was clean as if he'd had a shower that morning,' Watson replied.

'Just so we are all clear,' added Carmichael. 'Outline exactly when and how he died.'

Watson looked at his notes. 'He was hit by a white vehicle on 4th June in Back Lane, a small country lane only a couple of miles from Hasslebury. We know it was a white car because of the paint fragments found on his clothing. He had nothing on his person to identify him and, as yet, nobody's come forward either to offer any idea of who he was or to provide information about his death.'

'I drew a complete blank when I tried to find out anything about him, too,' Rachel added.

'But we have a time of death at 7:37 a.m.,' added Carmichael. 'That's correct, isn't it?'

'Based upon the evidence of Dr Stock and the fact his watch had been broken at seven thirty-seven, that's what the coroner concluded,' replied Watson.

Carmichael scratched his head. 'Who found the body?'

Watson rifled through his notes. 'It was a man called Adam Charles.'

'Really?!' exclaimed Rachel. 'He works at Park Road Veterinary Practice. He's one of the vets. Paul and I interviewed him earlier today.'

'So how come you didn't make the link with the vet before now?' Carmichael asked. 'You went through the notes, didn't you?'

Rachel looked nervous. 'I didn't look at *all* the case notes. I was focused on trying to find his identity,' she replied awkwardly.

'OK,' continued Carmichael. 'At least we have a connection now. Do we know if this Adam Charles character knew Aiden Davidson or Vicky Page?'

'He'll have known Vicky Page,' replied Cooper. 'Her father told me earlier that Vicky had worked at Park Road before moving to her current job.'

'But what about Davidson?' Carmichael asked once more.

'He denied knowing him when we asked this morning,' responded Cooper with a shrug of his shoulders.

'Rachel, I want you to check that out again tomorrow,' instructed Carmichael.

'Do you think he's a possible suspect?' Watson asked.

'I've no idea,' replied Carmichael. 'But he's certainly someone that we need to question. Rachel, you'll also need to check out his whereabouts on Tuesday morning and also this morning, too. Let's see if he has a decent alibi for either Davidson's or Vicky Page's murder.'

Rachel smiled. 'Will do, sir,' she replied dutifully.

'Let's move on to the second suspicious death,' Carmichael announced. 'Why don't you walk us through this one Paul as you were one of the first officers at the scene on Tuesday?'

Cooper picked up his notes and started to outline the facts.

'The victim's name was Aiden Davidson,' he began. 'He was killed by the express train heading north on Tuesday 15th July, also at seven thirty-seven. He is known to have been alive when he was struck by the train but was anaesthetised by the drug Etorphine. Based upon evidence at the scene, we believe that he was drugged at his house and then dragged to the nearby bridge where he was dropped, just as the train came through. His murder and the connection between his death and the hit-and-run were suggested by a person, as yet unknown, who used Davidson's mobile to text the *Observer*

114

newspaper. However, as yet we can find no link between the two men other than the timing of the deaths and of course the fact that they died in suspicious circumstances and within close proximity.'

'Good summary,' remarked Carmichael. 'Have we any information on other calls made or received on Davidson's mobile before his death?'

'His most recent statement shows he'd received numerous calls from Trinity Vet's practice in the last month,' replied Cooper. 'The last one being on Monday at three fifty-five in the afternoon.'

'Presumably from Victoria Page?' suggested Carmichael.

'That would be my guess,' replied Cooper, 'but in fairness, it could have been anyone working there.'

Carmichael thought for a moment. 'Betty Wilbraham said she'd heard Davidson arguing with someone on his mobile at that time. Maybe it was Vicky.'

'But if it was her,' added Cooper, 'we may never know what they were talking about.'

Carmichael nodded. 'You're probably right,' he reluctantly conceded. 'Does anyone want to add anything more?' he added, conscious that they still had a lot of ground to cover.

'Only that we now seem to have an explanation for the numerous visits he had at home from young women,' said Rachel, referring to the call she had received earlier from the scene-of-crime officer.

'Do we?' remarked Cooper, who had yet to be briefed on the findings on Davidson's computer.

'Yes, we do,' quipped Carmichael with a wry smile. 'But it's not what you'd think.'

'So, what is it?' Cooper asked his curiosity palpable.

'Mr Davidson had evidence on his computer of dozens of what the SOCOs believe to be fake passports and driving licences,' Carmichael explained. 'It looks like our murder victim was a forger.'

'Really?' replied Cooper. 'So do you think that may be the reason he was killed?'

'Possibly,' replied Carmichael. 'We need to understand more about what he was up to and who he was working for. My guess is that he was not the mastermind behind the deception. That's what I want you to investigate tomorrow.'

Cooper was clearly pleased with his assignment. 'No problem!'

'So what else do we know about Davidson?' Carmichael enquired.

'We know he knew Lou Henderson,' Watson said. 'Henderson told us that they drank together.'

'Which the landlord of The Drunken Duck confirmed,' added Cooper. 'And we also know that Davidson was known to Malcolm and Vicky Page, as he'd been commissioned by Malcolm to paint a portrait of his two daughters. He told me earlier today. In fact, I saw the painting.'

'*Two* daughters?' remarked Carmichael.

'Yes, there's an older daughter called Sarah,' replied Cooper. 'She lives in Holland.'

'We've already discussed whether Adam Charles knew Davidson,' remarked Carmichael. 'What about anyone else at Park Road? If we assume that the Etorphine used to anaesthetise him came from there, is there a link between him and anyone else at the practice?'

Cooper nodded enthusiastically. 'Yes,' he replied. 'He knew Joan Henderson too. It was Joan Henderson who recommended Davidson to Page.'

'Really?' replied Carmichael with similar fervour. 'Now that's very interesting, as when I spoke with Lou Henderson earlier today he told me his wife hadn't met Davidson.'

* * * *

Penny arrived back at the house in a despondent mood. She'd gained precious little from her consultation with Siobhan Ballentyne and, to compound her malaise, she discovered that Steve had left a text message telling her he'd be very late home that evening.

'Brilliant,' she muttered to herself as she closed the front door behind her.

She took the half-empty bottle of chardonnay from inside the fridge door, poured herself a large glass and plonked herself down on the comfy armchair in the corner of her kitchen.

After a few sips of cold wine, Penny suddenly remembered the handout that Siobhan had given her. She extracted it from her bag and read it intently.

'White Vixens,' she muttered derisively to herself before throwing the flier contemptuously on to the kitchen table. 'What a load of twaddle.'

* * * *

'So, I guess we need to discuss this morning's fiasco,' pronounced Carmichael uncomfortably. 'Let me take the lead on that one.'

Cooper, Watson and Dalton looked on, awaiting his summary of events with eager anticipation.

'Lou Henderson, who is away at a hotel in York, gets a text message from his wife's mobile which concerns him. He calls the police and we get to his house within the hour. We find the body of a woman who we assume is his wife, but it now appears to be Vicky Page, the receptionist at another vets' practice and daughter of Malcolm Page, a vet at Park Road.'

Carmichael stared towards the three detectives. 'So far so good?'

'Yes,' replied Watson disconcertedly. 'And what's more we have an irate husband demanding to know what we're going to do to find his wife and, of course, we've no idea where Joan Henderson is.'

'What if she's our killer?' suggested Cooper.

'I don't buy that,' replied Rachel with a slight shake of her head. 'If she was, why would she have called me last night to tell me that she'd discovered that her practice could not account for all of its Etorphine? Surely she'd have tried to hide it. Also, why would she text her husband and then leave her mobile at home?'

'Both fair arguments,' conceded Carmichael pensively. 'However, until we locate her she's got to be a suspect.'

'What I can't understand,' added Watson, 'is why Vicky Page was at Joan's house last night?'

'That's easy,' remarked Cooper. 'According to Malcolm Page, Vicky was a good friend of Joan and last night Joan called her and invited her around as her husband was away. Apparently, it's not the first time they've had a girls' night in when Lou is away on business.'

Carmichael looked baffled. 'Given that Vicky had worked at Park Road and given that she appears to have been a frequent visitor to Joan's house, I can't understand how Lou Henderson could not have known her,' he said with incredulity. 'Marc, you need to focus on finding Joan. Get onto Lou Henderson again and find out where she might have gone. Also, push him hard about Vicky Page. I'm convinced he must have known her.'

Watson nodded, although inwardly his heart had sunk once he realised he was going to have to spend another day with the distressed and infuriated American.

Carmichael preceded his next sentence with a long and pronounced exhalation of air, as if to give it extra kudos. 'Let's have a short break and then start to think in more detail about links between the deaths, motives and suspects.' He looked up at the clock. 'Take fifteen minutes,' he said as if he had just granted them all a generous bequest. 'Be back here at seven.'

* * * *

Carmichael remained in the room trying to make some sense of the murders. As he sat pondering in silence his mobile rang. It was Harry Stock, the pathologist.

'I thought I'd try and catch you before you clocked off for the evening,' said Stock mockingly. 'I've found a couple of things that you may find interesting.'

'Really?' replied Carmichael who sat up straight as he spoke. 'What sort of things?'

'I can confirm that the woman we found this morning was killed by a massive heart attack,' he replied.

'Heart attack!' exclaimed Carmichael. 'What about the wound on her head?'

'That blow would have concussed her,' agreed Stock. 'It probably allowed time for someone to then tie her to the chair. But it was a heart attack that killed her.'

Not for the first time in the last twenty-four hours, Carmichael was perplexed. 'I don't understand. Are you suggesting that she died of natural causes?'

'Not at all,' continued Stock, whose glee at leading Carmichael on was palpable in his voice. 'It was murder all right. Someone pumped enough Etorphine into her to give a five-ton bull elephant a heart attack. This poor woman weighed under ten stones – she stood no chance.'

Carmichael took a few seconds to digest the information. 'You said you had a couple of things to tell me. What else do you have?'

'This is the interesting one,' replied Stock. 'When we analysed the blood we found on the kitchen floor we identified two blood types, A positive which belonged to the dead woman, but also significant quantities of O positive.'

'So what are you saying?' enquired Carmichael.

'Well, it's your job to make some sense of the information I give you,' retorted Stock rather pompously. 'But what I can

119

tell you for sure is that there was a second person in that kitchen, in the early hours of this morning, who sustained an injury.'

'That has to be Joan Henderson,' replied Carmichael out loud, although he was really just articulating his thoughts. 'What about the time of death?' he asked.

Stock considered the question. 'It's not easy to be precise. However, I'd say it was between two and four this morning.'

'Are you sure? Our killer seems to favour killing his victims at seven thirty-seven.'

'No,' replied Stock firmly. 'It couldn't have been that late. I'd accept five at a push, but I'd stake my reputation on it being no later than that.'

Chapter 20

Having ended the call with Dr Stock, Carmichael spent the next few minutes considering how to make the best use of the briefing session when the meeting reconvened. With so many unanswered questions, it would be easy for the team to waste time wandering down blind alleys. He decided to keep it simple and focus what remained of the briefing on four key areas. He hurriedly scribbled four headings on the now increasingly populated whiteboard.

'Blood type, links, motives and suspects,' announced Watson loudly as the three junior officers returned to the incident room.

'Glad your expensive education at Kirkwood Comprehensive wasn't all wasted,' remarked Carmichael with a wry, derisive smile.

'I learnt a lot more than reading at my school,' replied Watson with an impish grin in Rachel's direction.

'Spare us the details, Marc,' remarked Rachel with a look of distain on her face.

'OK, let's crack on,' added Carmichael, who knew at the most he had no more than an hour or so before fatigue would kick in and they would have to call it a day.

'While you were out there's been a development,' he announced. 'Stock called and informed me that there were two blood types found in the kitchen, one which is a match with Vicky Page, the other which could well prove to be a match with Joan Henderson.'

'What type was that?' enquired Cooper.

'O positive,' said Carmichael.

'I'll check that out with her husband in the morning,' added Watson.

'So what does this tell us?' enquired Rachel with a puzzled look on her face.

'That either the two women were both attacked this morning,' responded Watson, 'or that Joan Henderson and Vicky Page had a fight which resulted in Vicky's death and Joan being injured.'

'That leads me on to something else Stock just told me,' continued Carmichael. 'He's adamant that Vicky died before seven thirty-seven this morning. He reckons it was probably much earlier, at least two and a half hours before. If that's the case, and if we assume the three deaths are linked, our killer has changed his timing for this one.'

'Maybe they weren't carried out by the same person?' said Rachel. 'Seems unlikely I know, but maybe they aren't linked.'

Carmichael shook his head. 'No, I'm sure they are. Stock confirmed that Vicky died of a massive heart attack brought on by being injected with a huge dose of Etorphine and remember, Lou Henderson received a text about the murder just like Norfolk George did when Aiden Davidson was killed.'

'That's where the seven thirty-seven might come in,' remarked Cooper calmly. 'I bet if we check Lou Henderson's mobile we'll find that the text he received this morning from his wife's phone was sent at seven thirty-seven.'

'You may well be right,' replied Carmichael, who not for the first time was impressed by Cooper's ability to make such a sound hypothesis. 'Why don't you get on to SOCO and check it out? Actually, while you're at it, find out if they got any prints off Joan's mobile, and I need the breakdown of her last calls too. I already asked the young PC who found it to ask them to do that, but I've not heard anything yet.'

'Which PC was that?' enquired Cooper.

Carmichael returned a blank look and shrugged his shoulders. 'I don't know his name,' he remarked brusquely. 'He's the one that looks about twelve and is always smiling.'

'It will be PC Wainwright,' replied Rachel, instantly recognising who Carmichael was talking about. 'I think he was at the Henderson house earlier.'

'Yes,' added Watson with a smirk. 'He was there this afternoon so I'm sure it will be him.'

Cooper nodded dutifully then started to make a call on his mobile. As he was talking, Rachel turned to face Watson.

'I don't buy your second version of events,' she remarked. 'I don't see Joan and Vicky having a fight. I think it's far more likely that they were both attacked by the same person.'

'Why?' replied Watson. 'If they had been attacked, surely we would have found two bodies.'

'That's a good point,' conceded Rachel, 'but I think it's more likely that they were both attacked and either Joan managed to escape, albeit maybe badly injured, or more likely she's been taken somewhere.'

'The bottom line is that we just don't know,' remarked Carmichael frustratedly. 'But I think there are several questions here we need to consider.'

'What are they?' enquired Watson.

'Firstly,' continued Carmichael. 'Why did the killer text Lou Henderson on Joan's mobile when it was Vicky's body he left in the house? It suggests to me that our killer didn't know either woman that well.'

'Maybe he just wants us to think that,' remarked Rachel.

'Possibly,' concurred Watson. 'But I agree it does seem peculiar.'

'The second thing that's puzzling me is why we didn't notice there was a second person in the house that night. And where are Vicky's possessions. If she was staying over at Joan's, where are her mobile, her clothes, her handbag? I assume, too, she drove there, so where's her car?'

'Good questions,' remarked Watson. 'We didn't find any of her belongings at the house, and there were no cars in the drive.'

'Which brings me on to my third question,' continued Carmichael who was becoming more and more frustrated. 'Where was Vicky sleeping that night? As far as I remember, only Joan's bed looked like it had been slept in.'

'Maybe they were sleeping in the same bed?' Watson suggested.

'It's possible, I suppose,' Rachel concurred, the inference of Watson's suggestion all too evident to her.

As Rachel Dalton spoke, Cooper ended his call.

'It was as I thought,' he remarked enthusiastically. 'Lou Henderson was sent the text at seven thirty-seven. So there's still that time link with all three deaths.'

'What about Joan's mobile?' Carmichael asked. 'Have they checked that for prints and do they have a breakdown of her last calls?'

'Not yet,' replied Cooper. 'But they promised to get on to that first thing in the morning.'

'Good,' Carmichael remarked. 'Now get back on to them again and ask them to get back to the house and check where Vicky was sleeping. I want them to do it tonight. I need to know whether she was in Joan's room or one of the spare bedrooms.'

* * * *

Malcolm Page sat alone in his front room staring at the photographs of Vicky smiling back at him from happy holidays when she was a child. He could not believe that she was dead and, having broken the dreadful news to his eldest daughter, Sarah, he had sat for the last hour thinking long and hard about who might have done such a terrible thing. He concluded that it could only have been one of two people. He then considered what he should do about it.

*　*　*　*

As Carmichael had predicted, the team's ability to logically analyse the deaths started to diminish dramatically after an hour had elapsed.

'So, let's recap where we are,' he said in an attempt to ensure all four of them were on the same page. 'The only link we have between the three deaths is the time of seven thirty-seven in the morning. We have a strong link between Aiden Davidson's and Vicky Page's deaths in that both were caused after the victims had Etorphine administered to them. They were also known to each other and to various other people connected to the Park Road Veterinary Practice. The last two deaths were also linked by subsequent text messages being sent mentioning seven thirty-seven. Is that a fair summary?'

Through various gestures and positive expressions Watson, Cooper and Dalton all indicated that they agreed.

'We have no strong suspects at present and no clear motives either,' Carmichael continued. 'However, we cannot exclude any of the people we've interviewed so far from our suspicions.'

'I also think we need to consider that there may be more than one person involved,' added Cooper. 'To drag Davidson across the field and throw him over the side of the railway bridge would have been a big effort for one person.'

'Paul may well be right,' concurred Watson. 'It would also explain how both Vicky Page's and Joan Henderson's cars could have been driven away from the house this morning.'

'You both make good points,' said Carmichael. 'We should certainly keep an open mind on whether it was a single killer or two.'

Carmichael looked around at his team to see if they had any more comments to make before proceeding.

'So, Rachel, you are focusing on Adam Charles tomorrow,' he said to the weary young officer. 'He's got to be high on our list of possible suspects. But, before you go home tonight, I need you to get the uniformed guys to start looking for Vicky's possessions and Joan's and Vicky's cars.'

Rachel nodded.

'Marc,' Carmichael continued. 'Your main task is to find Joan. Before you leave tonight make sure her photo and the details of her car, when we know it, are circulated to all other forces. I want all ports to be on the lookout for her as well. And tomorrow, as we discussed earlier, get under Lou Henderson's skin a little. We've been too nice to him so far. I know he's clearly concerned about his wife's disappearance, but he's a suspect like everyone else and I'm not convinced he's telling us the truth about Vicky Page. I'm sure he must have known her.'

'Yes, boss,' replied Watson. 'I'll turn up the heat.'

'Also, can you follow up with the SOCO about where Vicky was sleeping. I think that may well prove crucial to this case.'

Watson nodded. 'Will do, sir.'

'In addition, I want to know if SOCO find any fingerprints on Joan's phone and I want a breakdown of all the calls she made or received in the last twenty-four hours.'

'Will do,' replied Watson once again.

'That leaves you, Paul, to focus on Aiden Davidson,' continued Carmichael as he looked in Cooper's direction. 'I want to know who Aiden Davidson was working for and whether the forgeries had anything to do with his death. Rip down his house if you need to, but get to the bottom of it.'

Cooper nodded gently to indicate his acknowledgement, but said nothing.

'What are you doing tomorrow, boss?' Watson asked.

'I'm doing two things,' replied Carmichael. 'I'm going to go to Vicky Page's place of work and talk to her colleagues. They may have something that will help us. I'm also going to try and find out the name of the first man that died. Until we have his identity it will be hard to understand what it is that links him with the other two deaths.'

As soon as the briefing was over, Cooper and Watson left as quickly as they could. Rachel however, remained in the incident room to take a few more moments looking at the various notes and photographs that had been posted on the whiteboard.

'This is a complicated case,' she remarked.

'Yes, it's that all right,' remarked Carmichael as he started to make his exit. 'Anyway, how did you get on with Betty Wilbraham today?'

'OK,' replied Rachel. 'I'm not sure she's being totally honest with us. I think I'd have got more out of her, too, if it hadn't been for the RSPCA man interrupting us. When he's around, she goes all cow-eyed.'

Carmichael smiled. 'Is that who gave you the lift here earlier?'

'Yes. He was passing this way so I got him to drop me off.'

'Rather you than me. That pillock nearly ran me off the road earlier. He's an awful driver.'

'Tell me about it,' said Rachel with a wry smile. 'I'll not be getting into a car with him again. Not unless my life depends on it.'

*   *   *   *

Carmichael's working day ended with a twenty-minute interrogation by Chief Inspector Hewitt, who was predictably none too pleased with the lack of progress being made.

'We need more urgency on this one, Inspector,' he concluded at the end of their discussion. 'We need to find Joan Henderson. Alive or dead, I want her found!'

'I understand,' replied Carmichael as he made a hasty exit. 'I can assure you that we are doing all we can to find her.'

Carmichael didn't appreciate the extra pressure his

superior was placing on his shoulders, but he knew full well the importance of finding Joan, hopefully alive.

As he drove home that evening, Carmichael questioned his earlier decision to ask Marc Watson to focus on finding the missing woman. Maybe it would have been wiser to ask Rachel or Cooper, he thought. By the time he'd arrived home, stressed out and exhausted, Carmichael had concluded that he'd keep a close eye on Watson's progress the following day and, if need be, take that assignment away from him.

Chapter 21

It was just after 9.40 p.m. when Carmichael finally came through the front door. 'I'm home,' he shouted loudly, half hoping to be greeted with a warm smile and more optimistically a large stiff drink.

He received neither.

'Hello,' he shouted even louder.

'In here,' came the undeniable albeit slightly intoxicated reply of Penny's voice from somewhere at the rear of the house. 'I'm in the garden.'

The sun was already setting, so Carmichael was surprised to find his wife sitting on one of their wrought-iron garden chairs in the back garden. She was more than a little tipsy, too, having consumed not only the remainder of the wine she'd found earlier in the fridge, but also the best part of a second bottle, which now rested within easy reach on the garden table.

'Looks like you've been busy,' he remarked as he sat down beside her. 'Where are the children?'

Penny, knowing she was a little worse for wear, tried her hardest to appear in control, an assignment which she failed miserably.

'Jemma and Robbie are out somewhere and Natalie's in her room watching a DVD,' she replied, her eyes bleary and speech slightly slurred.

Penny rarely drank excessively so Carmichael knew that something was amiss. 'Are you OK?' he enquired.

'Fine,' she replied rather too quickly and directly to be convincing.

'So, what have you been up to today?' continued Carmichael, hoping this question would help him work out why Penny had been drinking a few too many glasses of wine.

'I went to see the mystic again,' retorted Penny. 'She checked out my chakras.'

'What?' replied Carmichael, his brow furrowed to emphasise his bewilderment. 'What the hell are chakras?'

'They are ...' Penny paused for a minute while she tried to think of words to describe this new phenomenon. 'It's something to do with your various parts of the body being in synch,' she slurred, although she knew that her words weren't doing the mystic art of reading chakras any great favours.

'Why on earth did you do that?' remarked Carmichael, pouring himself a large glass of wine.

'God knows,' replied Penny, her eyes rolling to the heavens. 'And before you say anything, you're totally right – she's a fraud. She charged me forty-five pounds for the session and told me diddly squat. She then had the audacity to try and rope me into an intimate circle of no doubt desperate women for some team healing, which if I attended – which I won't – would no doubt also cost me a further twenty or thirty quid.' Penny propelled the leaflet that Siobhan had given her earlier in her husband's general direction.

Carmichael took a sip of wine and started to read the leaflet. 'You're sure you're not going, aren't you?'

'No chance,' replied Penny categorically.

Carmichael grinned widely, kissed his wife gently on the forehead and placed the flyer on the wrought-iron garden table.

'I'm starving,' he announced. 'Have you eaten yet?'

As he spoke, his mobile started to ring. Carmichael extracted the phone from his pocket and looked at the name on the screen.

'It's Marc,' he said forlornly before putting the mobile to his ear.

Penny looked up at her husband as he listened intently to what his sergeant was saying.

'I'll be right there,' was all he said before ending the call.

'Bad news?' enquired Penny, who had seen the serious look on her husband's face numerous times before.

'They've found Joan Henderson,' he replied as he kissed her again, this time full on the lips. 'I'm going to have to go, I'm afraid. I'm not sure when I'll be back, but if it's late don't wait up.'

Penny smiled up at him. 'OK, but who's Joan Henderson?' she said with a combination of resignation and bewilderment in her voice.

'It's a complicated story,' he replied as he made a dash for the back door.

'Drive carefully and make sure you eat something when you're out,' Penny remarked, as her husband disappeared back into the house.

'I'll take a banana,' was the last thing Penny heard before the front door slammed shut and once more Penny was left alone with only her wine glass for company.

Chapter 22

It took Carmichael no time at all to travel the short distance from his house to Carroll Street where Joan Henderson's blue Saab 2000 had been found. As his car approached, Carmichael could see that the street had already been cordoned off. A large blue tent and strong arc lights pinpointed exactly where the car was located.

Recognising who was approaching, two uniformed officers positioned at the end of the street lifted up the blue-and-white tape to allow Carmichael to drive through.

Carmichael brought his BMW to a halt a few metres away from the tent and clambered out of the car.

'So what's the story, Marc?' he asked Watson as he joined him.

Watson shook his head. 'It's definitely Joan Henderson this time,' he announced. 'She's in the boot.'

Carmichael followed his sergeant into the tented area where he was met by Stock, who was leaning into the car boot looking at the dead body.

'What's the verdict?' Carmichael asked.

Stock extracted his head from out of the boot of the car. 'White woman, aged mid-to-late thirties, slightly built and most definitely deceased.'

'Any signs of how or when she died?' enquired Carmichael.

'Difficult to say for sure,' replied Stock predictably. 'I'd say she's been dead for between twelve and twenty-four hours. I'll be able to be more definite once I carry out a postmortem, but I'm sure it will be within that sort of time frame.'

'And the cause of death?' Carmichael probed, more in hope than expectation.

Stock gently shook his head. 'The wound to her head may have contributed,' he remarked, while pointing to the blackened blood stained area on Joan's temple. 'But my guess is that the former contents of that empty syringe may have been ultimately responsible for the poor woman's death …' He shone his flash light on to the needle and empty medicine bottle that lay by Joan's lifeless body.

'Etorphine,' read Carmichael as the torch illuminated the wording on the bottle.

'Glad your reading is up to scratch,' remarked Stock sarcastically.

'I want the whole area photographed meticulously,' ordered Carmichael. 'Don't move anything before that's done. And make sure we dust everywhere for prints, especially the syringe and the Etorphine bottle.'

'Be assured, Carmichael, we'll be as thorough as always,' replied Stock in his customary haughty tone.

Carmichael remained within the tent for a few moments before dragging Watson outside.

'Who found the car?'

'It was one of the local traffic lads,' replied Watson. 'They found it within half an hour of us circulating the details.'

'Impressive,' remarked Carmichael with genuine admiration.

'What about her husband? Shall we tell him tonight?'

Carmichael looked at his watch. It was 10:40 p.m. 'No. We can do it first thing in the morning. I'll meet you at his hotel at seven thirty. We can do it together then.'

Watson, somewhat relieved his boss was going to join him when the news was broken, nodded approvingly. 'I'll make sure Stock's team have her ready for him to formally identify at around eight thirty.'

'Good,' replied Carmichael. 'And make sure all those here tonight keep their mouths shut before we speak with Lou Henderson. I don't want this leaking out until he's done the formal identification. After the fiasco earlier today, I don't want any mistakes with this one.'

Watson nodded. 'Absolutely,' he replied, 'but what about Rachel and Cooper? We should let them know we've found Joan.'

Carmichael nodded. 'I'll do that on my way home,' he remarked before striding off towards his car.

* * * *

Carmichael managed to speak with Cooper and update him about the discovery of Joan Henderson's body in her car in Carroll Street. However, he was unable to get hold of Rachel on her mobile.

Tired and still a little down after splitting up with Gregor, the young DC had decided to switch off her mobile and have an early night. Tucked up in bed, she was unaware of either the voice message left by Carmichael informing her of the developments in Carroll Street, or the text message she'd received from her new admirer.

Chapter 23

Friday 18th July

The unforgiving alarm clock shrieked out its early-morning call.

'What time is it?' Penny asked as she pulled the duvet tight around her ears.

Carmichael's right arm shot out and, in one quick movement, silenced the merciless timepiece.

'Ten past six,' he replied before a sudden spurt of athleticism pitched his legs out of bed and propelled him to a sitting position, although he was still blurry-eyed and yawning. 'I've an early start this morning.'

Penny had wisely elected to stop drinking any more wine after her husband had gone back to the station and had retired well before he'd returned home.

'What time did you get to bed last night?' she enquired.

'About eleven thirty,' replied Carmichael, which wasn't totally correct. It was true he'd arrived home from Carroll Street at about 11:30 p.m., but he'd then sat quietly in his favourite armchair thinking about the day's events while downing a couple of large whiskies. The reality was he'd only finally gone to bed at about 1:00 a.m.

'I must have just missed you then,' replied Penny from under the duvet. 'It was about a quarter past eleven when I turned in.'

Carmichael didn't answer. He wanted to be at the hotel for

135

7:30 a.m. which meant he'd need to be out of the house by 7 a.m. at the latest. This gave him just forty-five minutes to shower, shave, get dressed and get some breakfast, and didn't afford him any time to continue his conversation with Penny. With as much haste as his sleepy body could muster, Carmichael made his way towards the bathroom and a warm shower.

As soon as he'd left the bedroom, Penny grabbed as much of the duvet as she could hold in her small hands and pulled it around her to make a cosy cocoon. 'Have a nice day,' she muttered before descending into a deep sleep.

* * * *

Marc Watson had switched off his alarm and gone back to sleep. So when his wife nudged him at 7:15 a.m. he realised he was in trouble.

'Bugger it!' he yelled as he stumbled out of bed. 'Carmichael will go ballistic if I'm not there at seven thirty.'

'You've no chance,' replied Susan with an all-knowing shake of her head. 'If you get there for eight it will be a miracle.'

As he fumbled around in his wardrobe, Watson decided that he'd have to call the boss to let him know he was going to be late. He'd do that from the car, he thought. At least then Carmichael would know he was en route.

* * * *

Rachel had showered and was eating her breakfast when she eventually switched on her mobile.

She could see that she had a voicemail and a text message. She was just about to look at the text message when a new text message landed on her mobile. Rachel did not recognise either of the numbers of her two text messages, but something in her gut told her to read the newest one first, which she did.

* * * *

It was 7:45 a.m. and Carmichael was sitting in his car outside the hotel, waiting for his errant sergeant to arrive when he received Rachel's call.

'Morning, Rachel,' he said. 'What's happened to prompt a call so early?'

'I've just received a text message from the killer,' she announced excitedly. 'He's telling us where to find Joan's body. And he sent it at seven thirty-seven.'

'What did it say?'

Rachel knew he would ask so had deliberately used her home land line to call Carmichael, which then enabled her to refer to her text message.

'This is what it says,' replied Rachel and then read out the message.

> You're taking your time finding Joan Henderson. Look in the back of her car. It's parked just around the corner.
> That's all four done and dusted ... Seven three seven!

'Get on to the station right away, Rachel,' replied Carmichael. 'Get them to trace whose mobile sent the message!'

'But what about finding the car?' asked the perplexed DC.

'Didn't you get my voice message?' snapped Carmichael. 'We found her last night. Unfortunately she's dead. She was in the boot of her car which was parked a few streets away.'

'Oh no,' replied Rachel sheepishly. 'I've not checked my voice messages yet this morning.'

Carmichael's frustrated sigh came through loud and clear at Rachel's end of the phone.

'Can you get on to the trace right now,' repeated Carmichael. 'Before you do anything else today I want to try and identify who it is sending these damn messages.'

Carmichael pressed the red button to end the call. He didn't wait for Rachel's reply.

Carmichael remained seated in his car, seething at being left waiting by Watson and that Rachel had not bothered to check her messages. As he sat there, he spotted the rather ample frame of Lou Henderson emerging from behind the hotel. Dressed in tight shorts and an equally tight-fitting T shirt, the sweating puffed-out figure came lumbering towards the front of the building and stopped, presumably to draw in some much-needed air. Henderson, who had not seen Carmichael, slowly and with signs of some fatigue, clambered up the short steps that led to the hotel reception.

As he watched Lou Henderson disappear into the hotel lobby, Carmichael could not help thinking about the devastating impact the news he was shortly about to hear would have on the portly and evidently unfit American. Henderson was not stupid, so Carmichael knew he'd have considered it highly likely his wife was dead, but in Carmichael's experience it was one thing preparing for bad news, it was a totally different matter coping with it.

The passenger door in Carmichael's car suddenly opened, which gave him a start. He'd been so engrossed in his thoughts he hadn't noticed Watson draw up and nervously rush over to his car.

'I'm really sorry, sir,' announced Watson, who was genuinely worried about what sort of reception he would be getting from his boss. 'No excuses, sir, I just overslept.'

'Get in, Marc,' replied Carmichael calmly. 'You're lucky. As it happens, we wouldn't have managed to see him even if you were on time. He's just arrived back from his early-morning run. I suggest we give him another fifteen minutes to get himself showered before we hit him with the bad news.'

'Oh right,' replied Watson who was extremely relieved that his being half an hour late appeared to have been forgiven by his normally punctilious boss.

After sitting for a few moments in silence, Carmichael realised that he'd not shared the news Rachel had given him earlier.

'Rachel called to say that at seven thirty-seven this morning she received a text message from the killer telling us where to find Joan's body,' Carmichael announced.

'Really!' replied Watson excitedly. 'So that means the killer is someone Rachel must have interviewed.'

Up until that point Carmichael had not even considered how the killer had got Rachel's mobile number.

'Yes,' he responded slowly. 'Well deduced, Marc. I think you may be on to something. We should get in there and give Lou the bad news, but once we've finished with Henderson we need to call Rachel and get her to list everyone connected to the case who has her number.'

Pleased that his deduction was appreciated, Watson nodded. 'I'll text her now,' he said confidently. 'It'll give her some time to think about it before we call her.'

'OK,' replied Carmichael as he opened up the car door. 'As long as you can text and walk at the same time that's fine with me,' he remarked with a wry smile.

Chapter 24

As instructed, Rachel rang Kirkwood Station as soon as the call with Carmichael was over and put the wheels in motion to trace the owner of the mobile that had sent her the text. She then listened to Carmichael's voice message from the previous evening to ensure that she was au fait with everything that he'd told her. There was no way she wanted to be accused of being remiss the next time they spoke.

Having carried out both these tasks, Rachel then proceeded to look at the other text she'd received. It was from Dennis Preston the RSPCA man, apologising for his bad driving and asking her if she fancied a drink on Saturday.

'How did he get my number?' Rachel muttered to herself. She was about to send a polite but definite refusal, when she received another text message. It was from Marc Watson.

Carmichael told me about the text you received. He's asked me to get you to list all the people you've given your mobile to in connection with the case. We think there's a good chance it will be one of them who sent you the text. We'll call you when we're through with Henderson.

Rachel looked at her watch. It was already after eight and she desperately wanted to get on her way to talk with Adam Charles. She decided she wouldn't send a reply to Dennis Preston's text for now and figured that she could think about who she'd given her mobile number to while she was driving.

Rachel put on her jacket, placed her mobile in her pocket, then grabbed her handbag and headed off towards her front door.

* * * *

Lou Henderson had just come out of the shower when the phone in his room rang and the receptionist advised him there were two police officers in the hotel lobby who wished to talk to him. He'd had barely enough time to get dressed when, ten minutes later, there was a knock on his bedroom door.

* * * *

Cooper arrived at Aiden Davidson's house at 8:10 a.m., where he met the two uniformed officers he'd requested to help him go through every nook and cranny in the house.

As the three police officers marched purposely down the dead man's drive, Betty Wilbraham watched intently through the chink of light she had created in the otherwise tightly drawn bedroom curtains.

'I don't care how long it takes,' she heard Cooper say. 'The main thing is that we are thorough. We can take as long as we need but let's make sure we miss nothing.'

* * * *

It took just a few seconds for the bad news Carmichael had given Lou Henderson to register.

'Are you a hundred-per-cent sure this time?' Henderson asked without malice or sarcasm, only a true desire for clarity.

'We'll need you to formally identify your wife, Lou,' replied Carmichael solemnly. 'But we are sure this time, I'm sorry to say.'

'How did she die?' enquired Henderson.

'We're still looking into that,' replied Carmichael. 'However, it's likely that it was in the same way that Victoria Page was killed. An empty bottle of Etorphine was found by her body.'

'You say she was in her car?' added Henderson, his broad American accent incredulous at the thought.

'Yes,' replied Carmichael calmly. 'She was in a Saab 2000 just a few streets away from your house. We've checked it out and it is her car.'

'So, was she killed at the same time as Vicky Page?'

'We're not sure,' Carmichael responded. 'However, that's what it looks like.'

Clearly still shocked by the news, Henderson stared aimlessly at the floor. 'What happens now?'

'When you're ready,' replied Carmichael, 'Sergeant Watson will take you to carry out the formal identification. After that I'd like you to spend some time with Marc. We have strong reason to believe that your wife's murder is connected to not just the murders of Vicky Page and Aiden Davidson, but also to the death of another man who was killed in June.'

'Four murders!' exclaimed Henderson. 'You think this is the work of a serial killer?'

'We're not certain,' replied Carmichael choosing his words carefully. 'However, it would help us enormously if you could first tell Marc about anyone you know who might have wanted to hurt Joan. We would also like to go over the details of your movements back in early June and during the last few days.'

Henderson looked up into Carmichael's eyes. 'Am I a suspect?' he enquired with disbelief.

'It's just procedure,' remarked Carmichael reassuringly. 'We have to check out everyone's movements. You're not a suspect.'

Henderson did not argue, he just nodded gently before rising to his feet. 'Let's get on with it then, Sergeant. I'll help as much as I can, but Joan didn't have an enemy in the world, so I've no idea who would do such a terrible thing to her.'

*   *   *   *

By the time Rachel arrived at the Park Road Veterinary Practice, she had in her head a list of around twenty people to whom she'd given her mobile details in the last two or three days. First of all there were the various residents of Hasslebury she'd interviewed about Aiden Davidson's death, then there was, of course, Joan Henderson and Vicky Page, whom she'd met at their respective practices, then lastly there were all the other employees at the Park Veterinary Practice whom she and Cooper had interviewed the day before.

When her car had safely come to rest outside the practice, Rachel pulled out her notepad and scribbled down the names of everyone she could remember, then, having finished her list, climbed out of the car and walked towards the door of the practice.

*   *   *   *

Carmichael had absolutely no desire to accompany Lou Henderson and Watson to conduct the formal ID at the mortuary. Having grabbed a few moments with his sergeant in private and reminded him to give Henderson a thorough grilling, to chase SOCO for their report on Joan's mobile, and to discover exactly where Vicky Page had been sleeping the previous evening, Carmichael left the hotel and headed off towards the Trinity Veterinary Practice to talk to Vicky's boss.

As his car glided along the quiet country roads, Carmichael couldn't help thinking how much he preferred living in the countryside when the weather was good. In winter it was a different matter. When it was wet and freezing cold he much

143

preferred his old more familiar life in London, but in summer Lancashire was a much more appealing place to live. Not that he would ever admit that to Penny. That would be far too much for him to concede.

*   *   *   *

Adam Charles sat motionless in his chair as Rachel Dalton told him that both Joan Henderson and Vicky Page had been murdered. When Rachel proceeded to ask him about his movements on Tuesday and Thursday morning, his demeanour was noticeably different from the confident young man Rachel had met with Cooper the previous day. His eyes flickered around the room and he fidgeted nervously and became very defensive.

'Why do you need to know?' he replied curtly, his Scottish accent seeming more pronounced than it had been the day before.

'We are simply trying to eliminate from our investigations anybody who knew the murdered people,' replied Rachel with firm composure. 'You knew Vicky Page and Joan Henderson and I understand you also found the body of a person killed in June, who we believe may be connected to their deaths.'

'But I thought Joan and Vicky were killed yesterday, why ask me about my movements on Tuesday?' Charles responded, his brow furrowed to emphasise his confusion. 'I told you yesterday I didn't know the man killed in Hasslebury and surely you can't believe the death of that poor old soul who was hit by the car is connected to Joan's or Vicky's deaths?'

'If you could just answer my questions, Mr Charles, I would be most appreciative,' Rachel replied firmly.

He took a deep breath. 'It's Adam,' he replied calmly. He was clearly trying hard to compose himself. 'Nobody calls me Mr Charles.'

Rachel was also keen for Charles to gain some composure. She smiled reassuringly but said nothing.

'Well, on Tuesday I was in here quite early,' he continued. 'It's Joan's day off on Tuesday so I tend to get here at about seven thirty. I think I was here at about that time this week, too.'

'Can anybody corroborate this?'

'I was here on my own until about eight fifteen,' replied the vet. 'Then I think the staff all started to arrive.'

'But until eight fifteen you saw nobody else?

'Actually I tell a lie,' said the vet excitedly, 'the first person I saw on Tuesday was Dennis Preston. He's the local RSPCA man. He arrived at ten past eight. I remember, as he asked me the time.'

'What was he doing here?'

'He was collecting a dog we'd been treating. He was taking it back to the compound, I think.'

'What about yesterday? What time did you get into work?'

'About eightish,' replied Charles a little vaguely.

Rachel scribbled down his answer, as she had with all his previous comments.

'Do you live far from the practice?'

Adam Charles shook his head. 'No, I live about twenty minutes' drive away, in Ruffwood.'

'That's the tiny hamlet the other side of Hasslebury, isn't it?'

'That's right. I rent a small cottage there. I've lived there for about four years.'

'Do you live alone Mr … sorry, Adam?'

Adam Charles grinned; he was now more relaxed than earlier. 'Yes, it's just me and the cat,' he quipped

* * * *

Carmichael arrived at Trinity Veterinary Practice at 9:15 a.m. He strode confidently up to the reception desk, introduced himself and asked the young woman behind the desk if he could speak with the proprietor, Harvey Romney.

'Please take a seat and I'll see if he's free,' replied the receptionist who, judging by the way she behaved, was clearly a temp drafted in to cover for Vicky Page.

'Mr Romney, a gentleman from the police is in reception to see you,' Carmichael heard her say over the phone, before she paused to take in his reply.

Looking a little sheepish, the receptionist placed her hands over the mouthpiece. 'Is it possible for you to come back later?' she enquired with some trepidation.

Carmichael stood up and walked the three or four paces to where the receptionist was standing. Taking the phone from her hand, Carmichael put the receiver to his ear.

'Mr Romney,' he announced in a clear but positive voice. 'I am Inspector Carmichael. I'm leading a murder investigation and if you are not out here in five minutes I'll press charges against you for obstructing the police in their investigations. Do I make myself crystal clear?'

Chapter 25

Carmichael barely had time to make himself comfortable on the waiting-room sofa before the door burst open and the diminutive figure of Harvey Romney marched towards him.

'I run a busy practice here, Inspector,' he remarked angrily. 'I fully understand the importance of your investigation, but I take great exception to the way you just spoke to me.'

Carmichael rose out of his chair and glared at Romney.

'Your receptionist has just been murdered,' he snapped. 'I would have thought that would take priority over anything else you have to do today. Be assured, I'll not take up any more of your precious time than is necessary, but I insist that you answer any questions I may have for you.'

It was apparent to Carmichael that Harvey Romney was not used to people telling him what to do, but it was also clear that the pompous little vet was not about to push his luck any further with Carmichael.

'This way,' Romney said brusquely as he pointed towards the double doors. 'We can use my office.'

Carmichael could see that Romney's lip had been cut and his right eye was showing signs of bruising.

'Have you been in a fight, Mr Romney?' he asked as he started to walk towards the doors.

'It's nothing serious,' replied Romney dismissively. 'I had an unfortunate altercation with a door frame earlier today. There's no lasting damage.'

'Really?' replied Carmichael, who gave Romney a look which told him in no uncertain terms that he didn't believe a word of it.

'It looks for the world like someone's clouted you.'

Romney visibly bristled. He was clearly agitated by Carmichael but chose to ignore the inspector's comment, electing to merely gesture with his right arm once more towards the door.

* * * *

At 9:25 a.m, and for the second time in two days, Lou Henderson entered the viewing room at the mortuary to formally identify a body the police thought to be his wife. However, unlike on the previous occasion, this time there was no mistake. The pale but pretty face revealed when the attendant had lowered the white shroud belonged without question to Joan. Henderson's desolate, aching, aimless stare confirmed this fact long before he muttered:

'Yes, that's my Joan.'

With a show of uncharacteristic empathy, Watson allowed the distraught Henderson a few moments before gently taking hold of his arm and guiding him away.

'Let's get a cup of coffee,' he said sympathetically as the two men departed the room.

* * * *

Rachel Dalton's interview with Adam Charles concluded at about the same time Carmichael started to question Harvey Romney. Unable to get through to her boss on his mobile, Rachel decided to send him a text message and then called Cooper.

'Hi,' she announced when her call was taken. 'It's Rachel. How are you getting along at Davidson's?'

Cooper sighed down the phone. 'We've not found anything of significance yet, but we've still lots of the house and his studio to check over. How did you get on with Adam Charles?'

'He was a lot more nervous today,' replied Rachel. 'I'm not sure he's our killer, but his alibis for Tuesday morning and for yesterday morning are not strong enough to rule him out. He's adamant he didn't know Davidson, but he could be lying.'

'Really? Did he tell you anything else?'

'Yes, he did,' replied Rachel enthusiastically. 'He told me he lives a few miles from Hasslebury, so in theory he could have easily carried out Davidson's murder and got to work before anyone else turned in.'

'Right, so what are you planning to do now?'

'I'm not sure. I tried to call Carmichael but he's not picking up.'

'Well, if you're at a loose end I could do with another pair of hands here.'

Rachel smiled. 'OK,' she replied cheerily, 'I'll be with you in about thirty minutes.'

*   *   *   *

Given his disrespectful behaviour, Carmichael had predictably taken an instant dislike to Harvey Romney. He did not appreciate being made to wait at the best of times, but given the circumstances he was furious at Romney's conduct and made no attempt to hide his feelings during the interview.

'So, when did you last see Vicky Page?' he asked pointedly.

'It would have been at about six on Wednesday evening, just before she went home.'

'Did she drive home?' Carmichael asked, his eyes fixed on the vet's.

'Normally she does, but on Wednesday her father picked her up. Her car was in the garage, so he took her home.'

'And did she tell you what the police wanted to talk to you about?'

Romney shook his head. 'No. However, I suspect it was about Etorphine and our procedures regarding drugs.'

'Why do you say that?' enquired Carmichael, who was surprised Romney was aware of their interest in identifying the source of the Etorphine.

Harvey Romney maintained a smug look on his face. 'Well, on Wednesday evening Joan Henderson called me to tell me about the visit she'd had and she also confided in me that they could not account for a bottle.'

'Did you and Joan talk often?' probed Carmichael.

'We're competitors,' admitted Romney, 'but we are, or should I say were, on very friendly terms. I respected Joan as a vet and as a person. It's really terribly distressing to hear that she's been murdered.'

'So who informed you that Joan was dead?'

Romney frowned quizzically. 'I was told yesterday. I got a call from Adam Charles after your officers had paid a visit to the Park Road Practice.'

'I see,' replied Carmichael pensively. 'So when did Joan call you?'

'It was on Wednesday evening,' he replied. 'She was very concerned about the missing bottle and called on the off chance that we had borrowed it but it hadn't been recorded properly at their end.'

'And had you?'

Romney shook his head. 'No, we do sometimes help each other out when we are running short of certain drugs and also occasionally with other equipment, but we've never borrowed any Etorphine from Park Road.'

Carmichael paused for a few seconds while he considered his next question.

'Tell me about Vicky Page.'

'What would you like to know?' replied Romney with another puzzled frown.

'As a start, maybe you can tell me how long has she worked here, what enticed her here from Park Road, where I understand she had been working previously, and what sort of person was she?'

Romney started fiddling with his pen. 'She had been here about a year and she joined us because we poached her from Park Road,' replied Romney with a self-satisfied grin. 'I offered her twenty per cent more than she was getting at Park Road. It was a bargain, as she was a really good receptionist.'

'And a good-looking girl, too!'

'I'm not sure I like what you are insinuating, Inspector. Our relationship was purely businesslike.'

'I'm sure it was,' replied Carmichael with a forced smile.

Romney rubbed his cut lip, which instantly suggested to Carmichael that his injury may well have been a result of an altercation with someone close to Vicky.

'Are you sure your injuries were caused by a door?'

Romney immediately gazed away, which suggested to Carmichael that the vet was feeling uncomfortable.

'Absolutely. It was just a silly accident.'

'So what sort of person was Vicky?'

'She was organised, she was personable, and in short, bloody good at her job.'

'And was she in a relationship with anyone?'

'Not that I knew of,' Romney replied dismissively.

Carmichael nodded then slowly rose to his feet. 'OK, thank you, Mr Romney. That will be all. I'll let you get back to your busy practice.'

Relieved that the interview had lasted for only a few minutes and keen to prevent the conversation being extended any further, Romney walked rapidly towards the door and opened it wide to allow Carmichael to leave.

'If I can be of any further help,' he remarked cockily, 'please do let me know.'

Carmichael glared at the smug vet and started to leave. As he reached the door he turned around.

'There is one thing you can do for me. I'd like you to come into Kirkwood Police Station at some stage today and give one of my officers a statement about your movements on Tuesday morning, Wednesday evening and Thursday morning of this week. I'd also like you to confirm what you were doing on the morning of 4th June.'

Romney's smug expression evaporated into one of frustration and anger.

'Today!' he exclaimed. 'I've a full schedule today and, to be honest, I've no idea what I was doing on the fourth of bloody June. I don't even know what day that was.'

It was Carmichael's turn to look smug. 'It was a Wednesday,' he replied coolly. 'And one of my colleagues will be available to take your statement until eight or nine this evening, so you can come after work if that suits you better.'

Carmichael didn't hang around to allow the vet to reply; he turned on his heels and, feeling satisfied at having ruined Romney's day, made a swift exit.

Chapter 26

Watson had given Henderson thirty minutes to compose himself before he felt comfortable enough to broach the subject of his movements when the four deaths had occurred.

He'd only known the American for a few days but he'd already formed a strong impression about his character, which he knew could be volatile and aggressive. Watson did not relish the thought of a confrontation with Henderson, but knew he needed to establish his whereabouts, if only to eliminate him from suspicion.

'If you feel ready I'd now like to ask you about your movements on Tuesday morning when Aiden Davidson was killed,' he said in as friendly a manner as he could muster.

Henderson turned his eyes on the sergeant and, for a brief moment, Watson thought he was about to get a broadside from the grief-stricken widower.

He need not have been concerned as Henderson was in no mood to argue. 'I was at home with Joan,' he replied meekly. 'She has Tuesdays off and I try to work from home on that day, if I can. Particularly when I know I'm going away later in the week. As I was due to go to York the next day for the sales meeting, I was at home with her.'

'Can anybody else corroborate this?'

'Only Joan could have. Nobody else.'

'And what time did you leave for York on Wednesday?'

Henderson stared aimlessly at the coffee cup in his hand. 'It must have been about four in the afternoon. I had arranged to meet a few colleagues at six thirty and, as it takes a good couple of hours to get to York, I left around four.'

'Did you drive there alone?'

Henderson just nodded.

'So, what did you do on the Wednesday evening when you got to York?'

'I checked into the hotel and then met my two colleagues,' replied Henderson. 'We had our meeting. Then the others all arrived, we had dinner, a few drinks in the bar and then we went to bed.'

'What time did you turn in on Wednesday?'

Henderson shrugged his shoulders. 'I've no idea. I'd say about eleven, maybe a bit later.'

'And on the Thursday morning you had breakfast at what time?'

'It would have been about seven thirty when I got down there.'

'That's when you got the text from Joan's mobile?'

'That's correct.'

'When was the last time you spoke to your wife?'

'It was at about eight or nine on Wednesday evening,' replied Henderson. 'She called to tell me that you guys had paid her a visit about some missing drugs. She was quite upset as she'd discovered that some had gone missing from the practice.'

'What did you advise her to do?'

'Oh nothing. She'd already phoned the officer that had visited her to tell them by the time she called me. I just told her not to worry and that it would be all right.'

'Did Joan mention anything about Vicky Page coming over to stay with her?'

Henderson shook his head. 'No,' he replied firmly. 'And, as I've said before, I did not even know that young lady.'

'That's fine,' Watson said. 'We will of course need you to provide us with the names of the people you met at the hotel in York, but everything you have told me seems reasonable and will help us to eliminate you from any suspicion. But you do understand we need to ask you these questions. As Inspector Carmichael said earlier, it's just the standard procedure we have to follow.'

Henderson nodded. 'I understand. If it helps you get the guy who killed Joan, I'll help you all I can.'

'There's just the other date I need to check out with you,' said Watson. 'Wednesday the fourth of June. Can you tell me where you were on that day?'

Henderson frowned. 'I'll need to check my calendar,' he replied with irritation 'But I'm fairly certain I was in Denver, Colorado on business all that week. As I recall, I flew out on Sunday the first, flew back on Friday the sixth, getting back to Manchester airport on the seventh.'

'That's great, thanks. I'll need that trip corroborated, too, but that's going to be helpful to us.'

Henderson nodded. 'Was someone else killed that day?'

'I really can't say,' replied Watson uncomfortably. 'All I would say is once we've established you were out of the country that week it will help us with our enquiries.'

*   *   *   *

Carmichael noticed he had a text as soon as he got back into his shiny black BMW. Before starting his engine he read Rachel's message, then called her mobile.

'It's Carmichael,' he announced abruptly as soon as she had answered. 'I got your text. So do you think Adam Charles is a possible suspect?'

Rachel was halfway to Davidson's house when she took the call. 'Yes, he might be,' she replied. 'He's not got much of an alibi for any of the murders. Although, if he is the killer, I'm not sure what his motive would be.'

'Well, I have a new suspect.'

'Who's that?' enquired Rachel eagerly.

'Harvey Romney, the senior practitioner at Trinity. Did he have your business card?'

'I've never met him. I went there the other day, but he was busy so I just left a card with the …' Rachel paused, 'with Vicky Page.'

'It seems that he's always too busy,' remarked Carmichael caustically. 'But is it possible that Vicky could have given him your card?'

'I suppose so. I certainly asked her to.'

'I would expect, in that case, she did. According to Romney, she was very efficient at her job.'

'So what makes you think Romney is a suspect?'

'Because I don't like him. He's a cocky little runt. That may not be very professional, I know, but he's staying on the list until he can give us a plausible alibi for the dates in question.'

'Right,' replied Rachel, who was not sure what to say.

'Anyway have you any news on the trace on that mobile that sent you the text earlier?'

'Er no, not yet. I've not had a chance to chase it up. I'll call them right away.'

'Make sure they know how important it is, Rachel. I suspect we'll find it's Vicky Page's mobile, but if there's even the slightest chance the killer's slipped up and used his own phone, we need to be on to it.'

'OK. I'll make sure they know how critical this is.'

'So where are you going now?'

'I said I'd give Cooper a hand at Davidson's. Is that OK?'

'Fine. When you see Cooper tell him to call Malcolm Page. I want to know how Vicky got over to Joan Henderson's. According to Harvey Romney, her car was at the garage. My guess is that her dad must have dropped her off. If that's the case, find out what time she got there.'

'OK.'

'Actually, I might join you at Davidson's later,' continued

Carmichael. 'I'm heading back to the station first. I want to do some digging on the identity of the first victim since neither you nor Marc seem to be able to identify him.'

'I'll see you later then, sir,' replied Rachel, who was more than a little miffed at the implication of Carmichael's words, but bit her lip. She didn't see anything to be gained by arguing the point with the boss.

'Let's wait to see how successful you are, Mr Hercule Poirot!' she said through gritted teeth once the call had ended.

Chapter 27

Watson shook Lou Henderson's hand firmly at the doorway of the mortuary.

'What are your plans now?' he enquired, with a wealth of genuine sympathy in his voice.

Henderson shrugged his shoulders. 'I'm not sure. I'll probably head back to the hotel and wait there until you guys tell me it's OK to go home.'

'Hopefully that won't be too much longer. I'll let you know as soon as the scene-of-crime officers are through.'

'Thanks, I'd appreciate that,' said Henderson as he started to amble away towards his car.

The burly American had only ventured five or six strides before he turned back to face the sergeant. 'I hope for his sake you find Joan's killer before I do,' he announced, his eyes fixed on Watson as he spoke. 'If not, then I pity him when I'm through with him.'

Watson stood in silence as Lou Henderson continued to walk slowly to his car. He had no doubts about the credibility of Henderson's warning and was certain the grieving widower would have the capacity to carry out his threat should the opportunity present itself.

*   *   *   *

Two police cars sped through Moulton Bank, lights flashing and sirens wailing. They had been summoned by Siobhan

Ballentyne, fearful of the ageing bearded gentleman who had been hammering on her front door for the past ten minutes.

'Open the door, you bloody witch,' he shouted as he kicked and thumped on the psychic's large oak door. 'You have questions to answer – let me in.'

The two police cars pulled up outside Siobhan Ballentyne's house and four uniformed PCs swiftly made their way up the drive to confront the irate vet.

'It's not me you should be manhandling,' Page shouted as he was dragged down the path and bundled into one of the police cars. 'It's that bloody witch. She knows who killed my Vicky. It's her you should be arresting.'

From inside the house, Siobhan watched the proceedings through her spyhole. Once the police car containing her aggressive unwanted visitor had disappeared from sight, she gingerly opened the front door where two of the police officers were waiting to talk to her.

'May we come in?' enquired PC Wainwright with a reassuring smile.

Siobhan ushered the two policemen into her hallway and, once inside, closed the door behind them.

* * * *

The time on Carmichael's digital clock flashed at 11:44 when he arrived at his desk at Kirkwood Police Station.

With his office door closed and a hot mug of coffee at the ready, Carmichael opened up the file on his desk and started to read the case notes relating to the hit-and-run on 4th June.

Twenty minutes and half a mug of coffee later, the silence was broken when Watson rapped loudly on the door and entered the room.

'Sorry to disturb you,' he remarked. 'I just wanted to let you know that Henderson gave a positive ID on Joan's body

159

and the SOCOs have sent through the report on Joan's mobile.'

Carmichael finished the sentence he was reading then looked up from the file. 'What did the report say?'

'Unfortunately there were no prints on the mobile. However, we do know that on Wednesday evening Joan made four calls all in a very short space of time.'

'Go on,' encouraged Carmichael, who was interested to learn who the murdered vet had been talking to.

'The first was at eight fourteen,' continued Watson. 'That was to Harvey Romney. It lasted about eight minutes.'

Carmichael nodded. 'That ties in with what he told me this morning.'

'She then called Rachel's mobile, and then, almost immediately that call was over, she called her husband. That call lasted twenty minutes. Finally at eight fifty-five, she called Vicky Page's mobile number.'

Carmichael pondered for a few seconds. 'That just about ties in with what we knew already,' he concluded. 'So were there any texts other than the one sent to Lou on Thursday morning?'

Watson shook his head. 'That was the only text message on her mobile. So either she never texted or she deleted all her text messages.'

Once again Carmichael took a few seconds to consider what he'd heard. 'What about Lou Henderson. Did you discover anything more from him?'

'Yes,' replied Watson, who by this time was sitting on the chair opposite his boss. 'He's a cast-iron alibi for the first death,' he remarked, pointing at the open file on Carmichael's desk. 'He was in the US on business that week. I've just spoken to his work and they have verified that he was three thousand miles away ... so he's certainly not a suspect.'

'Good work! At least we can now cross him off our list, not that he was ever a very strong contender.'

'But as you've said many times, we should focus on relatives first before we widen the net.'

Carmichael gave a wry smile. He was impressed that Watson had bought into one of his favourite rules. 'What are you going to focus on now?' he enquired, putting emphasis on the word *focus*.

'Well, as it happens, the uniformed lads have just told me that they have detained Vicky Page's father,' Watson replied with enthusiasm in his voice. 'Apparently, he was causing a real nuisance of himself hammering on Siobhan Ballentyne's front door earlier this morning.'

'Really?' Carmichael said with surprise. 'Why was he doing that?'

'We're not sure,' replied Watson. 'But I plan to interview him once we've finished, to find out.'

Carmichael nodded sagely. 'Let me know how you get on. It must be related to Vicky's death.'

Watson quickly stood up. 'That's exactly what I think.' His excitement was clear.

Watson was almost at the office door when Carmichael caused him to turn around.

'I've been looking through the case notes on the hit-and-run in June that you attended and there's one other thing I wanted to ask you, Marc,' he said.

'What's that?' Watson enquired.

'Well, it was just seven thirty-seven in the morning and you mentioned that he was dressed shabbily but that he was clean and looked like he'd recently had a shower.'

'Yes, that's correct,' replied Watson, with a confused expression on his face. 'What's concerning you?'

'Well,' continued Carmichael, who stood up and sauntered over to the ordinance survey map of that part of Lancashire. 'If he was walking in this direction at such an early time, I think it's safe to assume that he must have come from one of only twenty or thirty houses.' As he spoke, Carmichael moved his hand slowly around the isolated houses in the Hasslebury area. 'Those houses include the row of cottages where Aiden Davidson lived.'

Watson nodded. 'Yes, that makes sense,' he confirmed. 'But we interviewed all the people in those houses and we drew a blank.'

'I'm sure you did,' added Carmichael. 'But the coincidence is just too great to believe that he didn't come from one of those houses. And my guess is that a certain nosey old dear who lives in one of those cottages will know more than she's maybe cracked on about before.'

'Betty Wilbraham?' remarked Watson.

'Exactly,' replied Carmichael. 'Rachel and Cooper are already at Davidson's house, so I may just go and join them and, while I'm there, have a chat with Aiden's peculiar next-door neighbour.'

Chapter 28

Cooper and the uniformed officers had spent all morning in Aiden Davidson's house looking for any scrap of evidence to help them discover who he was working for, but after three hours' searching they'd found nothing.

So when Rachel Dalton cheerily breezed into the house her welcome was understandably muted.

'There's not a shred of evidence to link Davidson to the forgeries let alone identify who his associates were,' remarked Cooper gloomily.

'What about the studio?' asked Rachel.

'We've not touched that yet. That's this afternoon's job.'

'Do you want me to make a start in there now?'

Cooper thought for a moment. 'Why don't we both do that. We can leave the uniformed guys to finish off in here.'

'That could have been Marc talking there,' quipped Rachel with a smile intended to lighten Cooper's gloom.

'Good God!' exclaimed Cooper. 'If I'm now starting to sound like Marc Watson, that's a really bad state of affairs. Maybe I should ask for a transfer.'

Rachel laughed. 'It's not that bad, I promise you!' she said reassuringly.

* * * *

Having been informed by PC Wainwright that Siobhan Ballentyne did not want to bring a formal complaint against

Malcolm Page, Watson decided to try to take a sympathetic approach to his questioning.

'You're not under arrest and we do not intend to press charges,' Watson began. 'However, we would like to understand what you were doing at Siobhan Ballentyne's house earlier today and why you were so angry.'

An hour in the custody suite had allowed Malcolm Page to calm down significantly, but he remained unrepentant.

'That witch was playing with her head. She went to her for help, but all she did was mix her up.'

Watson's screwed up face demonstrated the level of his confusion. 'What do you mean?' he gently probed.

Malcolm Page took a deep breath, which suggested to Watson that the old vet was about to unburden himself of an important piece of information.

'Vicky suffered from anxiety and this problem was having a devastating effect on her life,' announced Page, who was clearly choosing his words carefully. 'Siobhan Ballentyne was recommended to her as someone who could help her. And she seemed to do the trick, but ever since she went to see that witch she changed.'

'In what way?'

Page stared at the desk top. 'She became more self-assured, but she also became more distant. She'd always been a shy but honest and open girl. However, after she started seeing the Ballentyne woman, she became secretive and a far less agreeable individual.'

'So what did Siobhan Ballentyne do to change her personality so much?'

'Hypnosis,' replied Page irately. 'She brainwashed her and completely changed her personality.'

It was clear from the expression on his face that Watson wasn't totally convinced about the story he was hearing, but it was undoubtedly something Malcolm Page believed.

'What sort of things did she start doing?'

'She became deceitful. She'd tell me she was doing one thing, but then later I'd find out she wasn't.'

'Like what?'

'Her relationship with Harvey Romney for one,' exclaimed Page. 'I confronted her about it on more than one occasion and she denied anything was going on, but I'm sure they were in some sort of relationship. Why else would she have left the Park Road Practice to work for him?'

'Have you spoken to Mr Romney about this?'

Page's eyes narrowed and he gave out a faint smile. 'As it happens we had words this morning. But he's denying everything, the slimy little wart!'

'I'm sorry to appear a little dim. But your daughter was in her late twenties and unmarried. Surely she could choose who she dated.'

Page looked deep into Watson's eyes. 'Yes, but not Romney. He's married and renowned for his philandering ways. I'm not having another of my girls messed about by him.'

'*Another!*' exclaimed Watson. 'So has he had a relationship with your other daughter?'

'Oh yes! Sarah and he were at veterinary college together. They were an item for three or four years and were engaged to be married.'

'What happened?'

'Sarah found out he'd been seeing someone else and called it off three days before the wedding,' replied Page. 'That's the sort of man he is.'

* * * *

Cooper and Dalton looked into the painter's studio from the open doorway.

'Where shall we start first?' Rachel asked.

Cooper gazed thoughtfully around the cluttered room. 'Well, if I were planning to conceal something in here, I'd probably have a secret compartment somewhere that would be hard to find.'

The two officers scanned the room to locate a suitable hiding place.

'What about that stage at the back of the studio?' Rachel suggested. 'Maybe there's a loose floorboard on there somewhere.'

'Sounds a reasonable bet to me,' replied Cooper. 'Let's start there.'

Chapter 29

Carmichael was halfway to Davidson's house when Watson called. He listened intently while Watson briefed him on his interview with Malcolm Page.

'So Romney was after both sisters,' remarked Carmichael. 'Why doesn't that surprise me?'

'If the father is to be believed, yes,' replied Watson. 'But of course at different times.'

'I'm not sure his relationship with the elder sister is particularly relevant,' Carmichael observed. 'But I'm sure Romney is involved somehow.'

'You may be right, I'm more interested in the link between Vicky and Siobhan Ballentyne.'

'You're right,' Carmichael agreed. 'That bloody woman's name keeps coming up.'

'What do you want me to do now?'

'Is Page still with you?'

'Yes, he's in the custody suite.'

'Well, get a full statement from him. Include his movements on the 4th June and this week,' said Carmichael. 'Also find out if he did drive Vicky to Joan Henderson's house on Wednesday. I know Cooper had that task, but I suspect he's not got around to it; especially with Page being out and about terrorising Harvey Romney and Siobhan Ballentyne all morning.'

Watson laughed. 'OK, I'll get on to it straight away.'

'Thanks, Marc. We'll have our end of day debriefing at five o'clock this afternoon. I'll see you then.'

'Right you are, sir,' Watson responded respectfully.

* * * *

It took Cooper less than five minutes to locate the loose floorboard on the small raised area in Davidson's studio.

'Rachel,' he shouted enthusiastically. 'I've found it!'

Rachel hurried across to where her colleague was kneeling and watched as he extracted a small metal box from within the cavity under the loose plank of wood.

'Is it locked?' Rachel asked.

Cooper tried the metal latch. 'Bingo!' he exclaimed as, to his astonishment, it opened immediately.

'Wow!' said Rachel as Cooper pulled out several thick wads of twenty-euro banknotes and, from underneath the banknotes, a memory stick. 'There must be thousands of euros in there.'

'Yes, but it's what's on the memory stick that I'm interested in.'

To Cooper's surprise, Rachel took out her laptop from her bag. 'Let's check it out,' she said eagerly.

'Do you always carry a laptop with you?' enquired Cooper in amazement.

Rachel smiled. 'Yes, how else can I keep up to speed with my Facebook page!'

Having never had children, Facebook hadn't yet reached the Cooper household, which was apparent by the look of confusion on his face.

Rachel switched on her laptop and inserted the memory stick. Within a few seconds details of all Aiden Davidson's clients and, more significantly, the name of his partner in crime appeared on Rachel's tiny computer screen.

*   *   *   *

Carmichael had intended to find Cooper and Rachel as soon as he arrived at Ivy Cottages, but when his car pulled up and the first thing he saw was Betty Wilbraham's curtains twitching, he decided to pay the nosey neighbour a visit first.

Chapter 30

Carmichael leaned forward on the worn-out settee in Betty Wilbraham's dishevelled living room and took a small sip of coffee from the grubby mug he'd been given a few seconds earlier.

'I've been looking back at the case notes from the hit-and-run that happened back in June a few miles down the road,' he said calmly. 'And I'm puzzled.'

'Really?' replied Betty, whose body language without any question told Carmichael she was feeling awkward and very nervous. 'As I've said before, I didn't know anything about it.'

Carmichael took another sip of coffee, but this time more substantial. 'To be honest,' he announced, his gaze never wavering from his agitated hostess, 'that doesn't stack up. Shall I tell you why?'

Betty was becoming more uneasy. She said nothing, but her expression was pained and her guilt was clear to see by the way she couldn't stop wringing the palms of her hands together as if she was trying to crush the life out of something in her grasp.

'Our poor victim was dressed shabbily but he was clean,' continued Carmichael. 'He certainly had not slept rough; in fact, we believe that he'd showered that morning. He was killed at seven thirty-seven in the morning while walking away from Ivy Cottages. Our guess is that he either left one of these cottages or walked past them at around seven in the morning. Are you following me so far?'

Betty's eye-line dropped downwards and fixed on Carmichael's shoes.

'My guess is that our man spent the night at one of these cottages,' Carmichael added, his tone clear and calm. 'And having got to know you fairly well over the last few days, I believe that it's almost inconceivable that you know nothing about this man.'

Betty's nostrils took a deep intake of air, then she raised herself up from her threadbare armchair and ambled over to the Welsh dresser. Slowly and carefully she slid open one of the drawers, took out a faded photograph and passed it over to Carmichael. Having given him the picture, she then returned to her armchair without saying a word.

Carmichael looked at the photograph, which, although in colour, was clearly at least thirty or forty years old.

'Who are these people?' he enquired as he looked at the picture of a young girl aged about ten and an older boy who looked about fifteen or sixteen.

'It's my brother, Damien,' she replied. 'It was taken when we were children back in Ireland. It was Damien who was killed that morning and you're correct: he did stay here the night before he died.'

*　*　*　*

Rachel was buzzing with excitement as she dialled Carmichael's mobile to share their discovery. 'You do realise that he'll be insufferable when he finds out who was behind the identity frauds,' she quipped to Cooper as Carmichael's mobile started to ring.

Cooper smiled. 'As long as he's happy, then I'm happy,' he replied philosophically.

*　*　*　*

'Can you excuse me?' Carmichael said as he saw it was Rachel calling. 'Do you mind if I take this call somewhere private?'

Betty Wilbraham, who still looked decidedly edgy, pointed in the direction of the kitchen. 'You can go in there.'

'Hi, Rachel,' Carmichael said, 'just bear with me a second while I go somewhere private.'

Once inside Betty's kitchen, Carmichael pushed the door shut. 'I'm free to talk now,' he informed his excited DC.

Carmichael listened intently as Rachel updated him on the contents of Aiden Davidson's memory stick.

'I knew it,' remarked Carmichael. 'My gut told me that Romney was up to his neck in all this.'

As he spoke, Carmichael could not help observe a familiar leaflet pinned to Betty Wilbraham's cluttered notice board. It was a copy of the flier that Penny had shown him the day before promoting Siobhan Ballentyne's White Vixens meetings.

'I'm actually just next door with Betty Wilbraham. Tell Cooper to bring Harvey Romney into the station.'

'Will do,' said Rachel. 'Do you want me to join him?'

'No. He can take one of the uniformed officers with him. I need you to join me. I've found out from her the name of our hit-and-run victim and I've just seen something else that we need to follow up with our friend Betty.'

* * * *

Carmichael decided to call Watson and bring him up to speed while he waited for Rachel to arrive.

'Marc, it's me,' he whispered. 'There have been a few developments here that I need to tell you about.'

Watson listened carefully as his boss outlined the details of his conversation so far with Betty Wilbraham and the news Rachel had just given him.

172

'I've finished with Malcolm Page,' remarked Watson. 'So what do you want me to do from now until our debrief?'

'You can help Cooper interview Romney. But until he arrives try and see if you can find out anything about Damien Wilbraham. All I know so far is that he would have been in his late fifties or early sixties. Betty told me they were born in Ireland, so you may have to do some digging there, too. I doubt you'll be able to get that much in the next two or three hours, but start the ball rolling.'

'Will do,' replied Watson. 'See you at five.'

Chapter 31

Penny Carmichael had spent the morning at home pottering around. She had lots of things she wanted to do, but she was feeling a little delicate after all the wine she'd consumed the evening before and had wisely decided to take things easy.

She was having her third or maybe fourth coffee break and listening to some opinionated oaf spouting forth on the *Jeremy Vine Show*, when the door bell rang.

Penny put down her coffee mug, walked slowly down the hallway and just as the bell rang for the second time, she gently opened the front door.

'I'm sorry to bother you,' said the plump young woman, whose face Penny recognised but could not quite place. 'Is this where Inspector Carmichael lives?'

Penny could see the visitor was apprehensive, which made her also feel a little uncomfortable. 'Yes,' she replied cautiously. 'But he's at work at the moment.'

'I need to speak to him,' replied the young woman. 'It's quite urgent.'

Penny suddenly remembered where she'd seen the woman before. 'If you leave me your name and contact number, I'll ask him to call you,' she replied, while at the same time pulling the door towards her to leave no space between her, the door and door frame.

The flustered woman lifted up her handbag and started to rummage inside. After a few seconds she extracted an eyeliner pencil and proceeded to scribble her details on the back of a scrap of paper.

'Sorry to bother you,' she said as she handed over the crumpled paper and scurried away down the path.

* * * *

Rachel Dalton was only a matter of a few feet from Betty Wilbraham's front door when she felt the gentle throb of her mobile in her trouser pocket, indicating that a text message had just arrived.

Hi Rachel
Have you thought about that drink? Let me know when you're free. I'm available tonight or tomorrow.
Dennis

Rachel had no desire to start any sort of relationship with Dennis Preston. It wasn't that she found him physically unattractive, quite the opposite. It was simply that she didn't fancy him and it was just too soon after Gregor. There was absolutely no way she wanted to jump into another relationship, not until she was sure her head was clear from the last one.

Rachel placed her mobile back in her pocket and knocked loudly on Betty Wilbraham's front door.

'I think that will be DC Dalton,' remarked Carmichael, who returned from the kitchen clutching the leaflet he'd seen on Betty's notice board.

Betty Wilbraham opened the door and ushered Rachel Dalton into the house.

'Before we talk a little more about your brother Damien,' said Carmichael once all three of them had been seated, 'can you please tell me a little about this leaflet?'

Betty Wilbraham looked perplexed. 'It's a session that

Siobhan Ballentyne hosts every Friday evening,' replied Betty. 'I occasionally go if I feel I need some support.'

'So what sort of support are you given?' Carmichael asked.

By the look on her face Betty was clearly mystified as to the basis of Carmichael's interest, but saw no reason to avoid answering his question. 'It's just an opportunity to discuss issues that may be concerning you with a small group and on some occasions get some one-to-one support from Siobhan.'

'So you know Siobhan Ballentyne well?' Carmichael enquired.

Betty shrugged her shoulders. 'I know her fairly well. I certainly don't go every week, but I'd say once a month.'

'And are you planning to go tonight?'

'I wasn't,' replied Betty curtly. 'But I may well do now. I'm feeling pretty stressed to be honest.'

'Did you talk with Siobhan and her group about your brother?'

'Not the group, but I did tell Siobhan that he'd visited me.'

'Does she know he'd been killed by a hit-and-run driver?' Rachel asked.

Betty shook her head. 'No, I never told her that.'

'Are you certain?' Carmichael asked.

Carmichael looked across at Rachel, raised his eyes skyward then turned back to face Betty Wilbraham. 'I'm going to leave you to give Rachel a full statement about your brother, his visit here in June and the morning he left. I need you to tell her everything, Ms Wilbraham, do you understand?'

Betty nodded. 'I understand.'

'I also want you to tell Rachel, in detail, everything you can remember telling Siobhan Ballentyne about your brother's visit and also about the female visitors Aiden Davidson had.'

'I never spoke to Siobhan about Aiden,' replied Betty resolutely. 'I'm sure about that.'

Carmichael nodded. 'OK,' he replied firmly but reassuringly. 'But I need you to tell DC Dalton everything this time.'

Betty nodded. 'Am I in trouble?'

Rachel smiled. 'You should have told us the whole truth earlier, but I'm sure it won't be so serious if you're totally candid with us now.'

Carmichael stood up and walked over to the front door. As he did so, he beckoned Rachel to join him.

'I'm going to talk to Siobhan Ballentyne again,' he said in a whisper. 'Get as much as you can from Betty and we'll pick this up at the debrief later.'

'Right you are, sir.'

'Show her the photographs of Joan Henderson and Vicky Page,' Carmichael added. 'I'd be interested if either were regular visitors to Aiden Davidson's house.'

Rachel nodded. 'OK, I'll see you later. Enjoy your meeting with Psychic Siobhan.'

Carmichael puffed out his cheeks. 'To be honest, she gives me the creeps,' he replied. 'But she's got quite a few questions to answer, that's for sure.'

* * * *

Carmichael was just about to start his engine when his mobile rang and Penny's number came up on the screen.

'Hi, darling,' he said. 'How are you?'

'I'm fine,' replied Penny. 'I just wanted to let you know that you had a visitor earlier.'

'Who was that?'

'Do you remember me telling you about the woman who ran out of Siobhan Ballentyne's session?'

In truth, Carmichael had no idea what his wife was talking about, but didn't want her to think that he hadn't been listening. 'Yes,' he lied.

177

'Well, it was her, she came here. She left her telephone number and asked whether you could call her urgently.'

'Did she say what it was about?'

'No, but she looked really anxious. I got the impression it was serious.'

'Why didn't she just call the station?' Carmichael asked, in a tone of voice normally reserved for his team.

'Steve, I don't know,' Penny remarked crustily. 'I'm just passing on the message.'

'OK,' replied Carmichael. 'Give me the number and I'll call her now.'

'Her name's Pauline Squires and her number's 07784 178178.'

Carmichael wrote down the number on one of the pages of a crumpled-up road map that had lain in his door pocket. 'Remind me,' he said as tactfully as he could, 'why did she storm out of Siobhan's gathering?'

Penny knew at once that her husband had clearly not been listening properly when she'd told him about the meeting she and Susan Watson had attended on Tuesday.

'Siobhan maintained that she had Pauline's mother in the room and that her mother was telling her to do the right thing about something,' said Penny in a slow and deliberate manner. 'This completely freaked Pauline out and she got up and rushed out.'

'So do you think that's got anything to do with what she wants to talk to me about?'

'I've absolutely no idea, but it might do.'

'OK,' replied Carmichael. 'As it happens, I was just on my way to see Mystic Meg, her name is coming up far more than is healthy for my liking, but I'll call Pauline Squires first. She may have something more that I need to add to my list of discussion points.'

'Good luck! I can't wait to find out what's going on.'

Carmichael smiled. 'It might be another late one tonight.

We're making some progress with the murders, so I suspect our debrief will last quite a while.'

'Well, I suppose that's good news,' replied Penny. 'I'll see you when I see you.'

Chapter 32

From his stationary car, Carmichael dialled the number Penny had given him. It rang for about fifteen seconds before clicking into the answering service:

This is Pauline Squires. I can't take your call at the moment but please leave a message and I'll get back to you as soon as I can.

Carmichael hated the impersonal nature of voice messages and often refused to leave them, but on this occasion he knew it was necessary.

'Good afternoon,' he said slowly. 'This is Inspector Carmichael. I understand that you need to talk to me urgently. Please either call me back on this number or contact one of my colleagues at Kirkwood Police Station.'

He ended the call, put his mobile down on the passenger seat and started the car's engine.

* * * *

'I'm really upset with you,' Rachel told Betty as soon as she heard Carmichael's car disappear down the lane. 'You had several opportunities to tell us it was your brother who'd been killed, but you chose not to. Why on earth did you keep this from us?'

Betty was clearly feeling guilty about her behaviour, an emotion that she communicated vividly by her inability to maintain eye contact with the young DC.

'I'm sorry,' she replied quietly. 'I just didn't want to be involved.'

Rachel stared angrily at the dishevelled and decidedly pathetic-looking woman. 'Not involved!' she exclaimed. 'He was your brother.'

'Well, I didn't ask him to visit me,' replied Betty offhandedly. 'I hadn't seen him for well over twenty years. We were never close and he was always bad news. I decided years ago that I didn't want him to have any part in my life and him dying didn't change that one iota.'

Rachel couldn't believe what she was hearing, but was smart enough to understand that her best chance of getting Betty to tell her everything was to adopt a more conciliatory approach. She took a deep breath and put on her best reassuring smile. 'OK,' she said calmly. 'What's done is done, but you do understand that we need to know everything, don't you, Betty?'

Betty Wilbraham slowly raised her eyes so that her gaze met with Rachel's. 'I understand, What do you want to know?'

*   *   *   *

Harvey Romney was incandescent with rage when Cooper informed him that he was required to accompany him and PC Dyer to Kirkwood Police Station.

'Am I under arrest?' he snapped back at Cooper.

'No,' replied Cooper calmly. 'However, should you refuse we'll arrest you on suspicion of being involved in fraud.'

'Fraud! What a load of rubbish. This is police harassment!'

'We can discuss all this at the station,' continued Cooper with the distinct air of someone who was not about to be intimidated in any shape or form.

'I'm calling my lawyer,' shouted Romney as he grabbed his mobile and marched towards the open door. 'I'll be making a formal complaint about this. It's bloody ridiculous and a complete waste of my time.'

Cooper remained composed, allowing Romney to storm out of the practice and into the car park.

'I assume, as I'm not under arrest, I can drive my own car to the police station?' Romney enquired.

'I'd prefer you to ride with me and PC Dyer,' remarked Cooper, who was two paces behind him. 'If necessary, we'll arrange transport for you to get home once we've finished talking to you.'

Cooper's wording made it quite clear to Romney that he might not be coming back in the immediate future, which unnerved the previously aggressive individual.

'I'm saying nothing more until my lawyer's present,' Romney announced as he clambered into the back of Cooper's car.

'That's perfectly fine,' replied Cooper, who was pleased at the prospect of a reasonably quiet car journey to Kirkwood Police Station.

* * * *

During his twenty-minute drive to Siobhan Ballentyne's house, Carmichael pondered long and hard how he should approach the interview. He was certain that the psychic was a clever con artist, but equally he remained unconvinced that she was a significant player in the various deaths under investigation. He was, however, sure that she knew more than she was telling him. It would have been inconceivable for someone whose name was cropping up as frequently as Siobhan's not to know much more than she was making out. Carmichael's big problem, though, was how to get her to release that information. Based upon his previous meeting, he knew that normal questioning would be unlikely to get her to divulge much.

With a little reluctance, Carmichael decided to try a

different strategy, one that would play more on Siobhan's mammoth ego. Although he was not the most gifted flatterer, he knew that this was almost certainly going to be his best approach on this occasion.

* * * *

Having realised she had to come clean, Betty Wilbraham sat back in the armchair and, with her gaze fixed firmly on a point a few inches above her faded lounge curtains, got herself ready to talk freely about her past, something she had not done willingly for over twenty years.

'I was born in a small village in county Cork,' Betty began. 'Damien was my only sibling. He was seven years older than me. Our mother did have another child between us, but that baby died at birth.'

Rachel remained quiet and still as she listened intently.

'Damien was forever in trouble,' continued Betty. 'He was always in scrapes and getting told off by my father, but when he was young it was just devilment really. Stealing apples from the orchards of Mr Finnerty's farm or pinching the milk bottles from the doorsteps … that sort of thing.' As she spoke Betty smiled gently. 'But when he got into his late teens he became worse. He would get drunk with his mates, and he then started stealing money from my parents and he also got into drugs. I'm not sure what the final straw was but one day my father and he had an almighty row. There was shouting and screaming by both of them. I was upstairs but I could hear their shouting quite clearly.'

Betty stopped for a few seconds as if it was painful to relive those memories.

'So what happened then?' coaxed Rachel gently.

For the first time in minutes, Betty looked directly at Rachel. 'Damien punched my father. He broke my father's nose and walked out.'

183

'Did you see him again?'

'Only once. It was after my parents had both died. He came to see me to claim his inheritance. But he had been left nothing. My father's will was very specific, everything went to me.'

'So what happened?'

'I gave him a thousand pound to get shot of him. That was over twenty years ago and until June that was the last time I saw him.'

'I see. So did he ask for money when he came in June?'

'Of course. I was so shocked when I opened the door that day. After the last time, I sold the house in Ireland as soon as I could and moved here. I never thought he'd find me.'

'So what happened when he came?'

'He wanted money of course,' Betty replied with an air of inevitability. 'I told him I had none to give him, which is true. I begrudgingly allowed him to stay a night, then at seven the following morning he left.'

'So why did you not come forward when we were trying to identify him?'

Betty stared back into Rachel's eyes. 'Because I was pleased to at last be rid of him,' she replied, with an eerie honesty in her voice. 'I was free at last.'

'Other than Siobhan Ballentyne, who else knew about Damien?'

Betty shook her head. 'Nobody. And Siobhan didn't know that much.'

'What about Aiden Davidson?'

Again Betty shook her head. 'I suppose it's possible that Aiden might have seen him when he came calling that day. But he never mentioned him to me and I certainly didn't mention Damien to him.'

As Betty was talking, another text message popped through on Rachel's mobile. It was Dennis Preston again.

'Excuse me,' Rachel said as she opened up the latest text.

Hi Rachel
Have you thought about that drink?
Dennis

Rachel's irritation was etched on her face.

'Is there anything wrong?' enquired Betty with genuine concern.

Rachel switched off her mobile and thrust it into her trouser pocket. 'No it's nothing of any great importance … What about the RSPCA man, Dennis Preston?' Rachel asked.

Betty thought for a moment. 'No, Dennis is a good friend but I didn't mention Damien to him either.'

'OK. As Inspector Carmichael said earlier, you will need to make a formal, full and honest statement, Betty. Do you understand?'

Betty nodded. 'Yes, I understand. Will I be in trouble for not being more open before about Damien?'

'I'm not sure,' replied Rachel truthfully. 'It won't be up to me, but there may be some consequences.'

By the expression on her face, Rachel could see that Betty was worried. 'My best advice to you, Betty, is to be completely transparent with us from now on. If you cooperate completely, I'm certain that will have a major bearing on what happens to you.'

Betty nodded. 'I'll certainly help all I can.'

Rachel gave her a reassuring smile. 'Before I take your statement, I'd like to show you a couple of photographs. I want you to look at them very carefully and tell me if you recognise either of the two women.'

Rachel took out the photographs of Joan Henderson and Vicky Page and laid them on the arm of Betty's easy chair.

Betty studied the photographs carefully.

'I've never seen that one before, but the other one was a frequent visitor to Aiden's house.

'Are you sure?'

'Absolutely,' replied Betty unequivocally. 'She was the one I was talking about yesterday. For the last six months she'd visited him at least once a week.'

Chapter 33

When she opened her front door Siobhan Ballentyne was shocked to see Carmichael standing in front of her.

'What a pleasant surprise,' she remarked with her customary smile. 'I certainly wasn't expecting it to be you, Inspector.'

Carmichael could feel his shoulders tensing and under normal circumstances would probably have made a disparaging comment regarding the irony of her statement, given that she was a celebrated clairvoyant, but, in keeping with his game plan, resisted such a temptation.

'I'm so sorry to intrude unannounced,' he remarked with his best manufactured smile on show. 'I would really like your help if it's a convenient time for you?'

'Of course,' responded Siobhan, who was clearly flattered at being asked by the police for help. 'As I said to both you and your lovely wife, I'd be more than happy to help you, Inspector. Do come in.'

* * * *

The strength of Harvey Romney's relationship with his legal advisor was evident by the speed at which his brief arrived at Kirkwood Police Station. Within thirty minutes of Cooper's battered Volvo pulling to a halt in the car park, he and Watson were able to start their interview – such as it was.

'First of all,' announced Cooper. 'I want to confirm that as yet no charges have been made against you, Mr Romney. However, following information we've received earlier today, we want you to answer some questions.'

'What information would that be?' enquired Romney's brief.

Cooper gazed sideways at Watson before answering. 'As your client is aware, we are investigating several suspicious deaths in the area and, as a result of those investigations, we have also discovered that one of the victims was engaged in fraudulent practices. At this stage we are not able to say whether the fraud is linked to his death, but we are keeping an open mind and we are keen to understand more about the fraud.'

Romney sat, arms folded, with his eyes raised to the ceiling. 'I have absolutely no idea what you are talking about,' he announced firmly. 'What fraud and why are you questioning me?'

'Does the name Aiden Davidson mean anything to you, Mr Romney?' Watson enquired.

'Davidson, Davidson,' said Romney, his eyes still looking upwards, but this time in a theatrical gesture as if he was looking for some divine intervention. 'I don't think so. Who was Aiden Davidson?'

'Well,' replied Cooper with a smirk of satisfaction. 'You are correct to say *was*. Mr Davidson is one of the people whose deaths we are treating as suspicious. It's interesting you chose the past tense given that you maintain you didn't know him.'

Romney angrily fixed his stare at Cooper. 'I've said all I'm prepared to say. Either charge me or let me go.'

Cooper smiled. 'OK,' he said calmly. 'Let me tell you and your legal advisor what we have found. I then suggest we leave you two gentlemen to have a private discussion for twenty minutes, then maybe we can resume our discussions. How does that sound?'

Romney and his lawyer looked at each other for few seconds.

'I think that would be agreeable to us,' replied the brief. 'So, what is it you claim to have found?'

* * * *

Carmichael sat down on one of Siobhan's luxuriant sofas and took a sip of coffee from the china cup that had been handed to him by his host. To his surprise and irritation, Mr Swaffie appeared from nowhere and, without warning, jumped up on to Carmichael's sofa and rested his emaciated hairy head on Carmichael's thigh.

'He's clearly very comfortable with you, Inspector,' remarked Siobhan with obvious delight. 'He's normally very agitated around men, but he likes you.'

Although Carmichael's overriding desire was to turf the dog back on to the floor, that course of action was at odds with his strategy so, with a forced smile, he reluctantly stroked the dog's bony head with his free hand.

'There are a few things you could help me with,' he said as he continued to pet the canine.

'Enquire away, Inspector,' replied Siobhan excitedly.

'I'd like to understand how your powers work,' he remarked, carefully placing the china cup on to the small wooden table at the side of his sofa. 'For example, when you spoke with my wife earlier in the week, how did you come to tell her that I needed to follow my instincts regardless of what others may say and that the message was no hoax.'

Siobhan smiled self-righteously. 'I gather information from many sources,' she explained, 'through relatives and friends who have passed over to the other side, but also from Guthrie.'

'Your guardian angel?'

'Yes, that's correct.'

'And it was Guthrie who gave you that particular message?' asked Carmichael, who, as he spoke, heard a long-drawn-out noise emitting from the rear end of the dog, as it continued to stare longingly up at him.

'Yes,' Siobhan replied, apparently oblivious to the sound of the gas emanating from her beloved dog. 'It was true, wasn't it?'

'It was,' confirmed Carmichael, swallowing hard and trying valiantly to ignore the foul smell starting to enter his nostrils. 'It was very accurate, too, given you had never met me or my wife before.'

Siobhan was beside herself with joy at hearing the inspector confirm the strength of her powers. 'I'm so pleased you're now taking a much more open-minded view of my psychic gift,' she proclaimed with glee.

Carmichael was also feeling extremely pleased. Despite having to endure the flatulent dog, which appeared to have taken a shine to him, it seemed as though his conciliatory approach was working perfectly. 'I wouldn't go so far as to say I'm a complete convert,' he fibbed. 'However, as I learn more about your world I'm certainly becoming more willing to accept that your powers may be a help to us.'

'That's wonderful,' exclaimed Siobhan, as she leaned forward and picked up Mr Swaffie.

She proceeded to walk over to the door, dog in hand. 'I'm afraid you'll have to go outside,' she remarked to her hairy friend. 'I'm sure Inspector Carmichael would be happier if you left us.'

Carmichael put on a forced smile but was secretly delighted to be seeing the back of the scrawny, flatulent mutt.

'How else can I help you?' Siobhan asked, once she'd successfully ejected Mr Swaffie into the hallway.

'What about the other comment you made to me when we met? You mentioned that a woman who cared more about animals than people knew more than she was saying.'

'Yes, I remember.'

'Would that woman have been Betty Wilbraham?'

'That's the thing,' replied Siobhan with a look of sorrow on her face. 'It's impossible for me to be more accurate. Remember, I'm only passing on what Guthrie tells me.'

'But it could have been. And, of course, you know Betty Wilbraham, don't you?'

Siobhan, for the first time, looked a little wary. 'I do know Betty,' she replied carefully. 'But Guthrie didn't give me a name.'

Carmichael nodded. 'We're sure it was Betty,' he replied 'and she's giving us a fully detailed statement as we speak.' Carmichael took another sip of coffee, but never once took his eyes off Siobhan.

'Well, I'm glad Guthrie and I helped,' added Siobhan, who appeared to have regained her poise once more. 'What else can I help you with?'

'Actually, I'd really like to know more about the White Vixens,' Carmichael added. 'My wife's very interested in coming to one of your sessions, actually maybe the one tonight.'

'Really?' replied Siobhan, who was now becoming sceptical about Carmichael's apparent road to Damascus conversion. 'I got the distinct impression when I mentioned it to her that she was less than keen.'

'No, I'm sure she's planning to come,' added Carmichael who retained a straight face but inside was loving winding up the psychic. 'Especially if there's a possibility of being hypnotised. She's always wanted to be put under.'

Siobhan's smile briefly deserted her. 'Well, she's more than welcome of course, but if she wants to have a one-to-one session under hypnosis she may want to arrange a separate appointment.'

Carmichael smiled and took a large gulp of coffee. 'Does the name Vicky Page mean anything to you?'

'Yes,' replied Siobhan. 'She was one of my clients.'

'As you may know, she was found murdered yesterday,'

continued Carmichael. 'I'd really like to know why she came to you and how you helped her.'

Siobhan shuffled uncomfortably in her chair. 'Under normal circumstances the sessions I hold with my clients are totally confidential,' she said with what Carmichael took to be her serious face. 'However, in the circumstances, I think I can share with you the underlying cause of her visit.'

'Which was?'

'An inferiority complex in relation to her sister,' replied Siobhan. 'She had been made to feel totally inadequate when compared to Sarah, I think mainly by her father.'

'I see. And were you able to help her?'

Siobhan grimaced. 'We were making progress but it was a deep, deep-seated problem and it was always going to take time for her to completely overcome her issues.'

'And what remedy had you recommended?' Carmichael enquired.

'We were fighting on various fronts. Through positive thinking, through techniques to enhance esteem and through encouraging her to confront her fears.'

'I see,' said Carmichael. 'And when did you last see her?'

'It would have been last Friday at the Vixens meeting.'

'And how did she seem last Friday?' Carmichael asked.

'She was in fine form. To be honest she was as happy as I've ever seen her.'

'So, why was Malcolm Page so angry this morning?' continued Carmichael.

'You'd need to ask him that. However, I'm sure his emotions are very raw given that Vicky has been murdered.'

Carmichael nodded. 'I suppose that's true.'

'Is there anything else I can do to help you?'

'There's just one more question,' he said as he stood up from his chair. 'What is the ethical position in your profession regarding the use of information gleaned from somebody under hypnosis for other purposes?'

'That would be absolutely immoral.' replied Siobhan robustly.

Carmichael smiled. 'Just as I thought.'

*   *   *   *

As soon as twenty minutes had elapsed, Cooper and Watson returned to the interview room to talk once more with Harvey Romney.

'Have you had enough time?' Cooper enquired.

Romney was looking far less brash than earlier and his arms folded position had been replaced by a less aggressive chin-in-hand demeanour.

'My client', began the brief, 'is prepared to make a full and detailed statement in writing, which we will prepare and give to you in the morning.'

'That's appreciated,' replied Cooper. 'However we'd really like some answers today; otherwise we may have to arrest your client and keep him in custody over night.'

'On what charge?' snapped Romney, who was unable to stick to the game plan he'd agreed with his solicitor.

'Fraud and perverting the course of justice are the two obvious ones that spring to mind,' interjected Watson. 'Although murder or an accessory to murder are also charges that we can't rule out at some stage.'

'Certainly the fact that we are primarily investigating four suspicious deaths will be a big factor against us releasing you until we are confident your involvement is minimal,' added Cooper.

Romney gestured to his brief to start being more forthcoming.

'My client denies any wrongdoing,' announced the brief. 'He was an associate of Aiden Davidson but denies any involvement in any form of fraud and is certainly totally innocent of murder. His statement will support that.'

193

'So what about the printouts we found in Mr Davidson's house that show he was being paid significant sums of cash on numerous occasions by your client?' Cooper asked.

'And what about the numerous calls that were made between your client and Aiden, evidence of which we found when we checked his mobile phone statement?' added Watson

'We admit that calls were made between my client and Mr Davidson,' replied the brief, 'but there is no crime in that. And in the absence of any evidence about any payments other than these printouts, we respectfully feel that you have no case against my client and request that he's released immediately.'

Cooper shook his head. 'I'm sorry, but I must insist on Mr Romney providing us with a full written statement about his movements when the four deaths occurred and his involvement with Aiden Davidson, *before* he leaves the station. Otherwise we will detain him and charge him on the basis of his involvement in fraudulently providing documents to illegal immigrants.'

Romney looked ready to explode. He slammed his fist on the table in front of him and looked towards his brief. 'Let's get this sorted and get out of this damn place,' he shouted. 'We can produce a statement here as well as we can at home. If that's what they want, let's do it!'

Pleased to be getting their way, Cooper and Watson stood up.

'We'll leave you to it,' remarked Watson as the two officers exited the interview room.

Chapter 34

'Steve, you must be joking!' exclaimed Penny down the phone line. 'You seriously want me to go to Siobhan's White Vixens meeting?'

'Yes,' insisted Carmichael. 'I don't need you to bare your soul or anything like that, just observe what's going on. Just see how she operates.'

'You must be insane! She'll spot I'm not for real straight away. If I go, I've got to have a genuine issue. And one I am happy to share with all her Vixens!'

'Good point,' replied Carmichael, who hadn't really considered what sort of problem Penny could discuss. 'I know,' he said excitedly, 'tell her you're concerned about one of the children.'

'No way. I'm not involving them, even if I do make something up.'

'Then what?' enquired Carmichael.

Penny remained flabbergasted by her husband's request. 'Leave it with me, I'll think of something. But this will cost you, Steve, and I don't mean just a refund of Siobhan's fee. And I'm not expecting that to be that cheap either.'

'Fantastic! I'll see you later and you can tell me all about it!'

Penny, still reeling at her husband's bizarre request, hung up the phone and wandered off down the hallway in a daze.

'Maybe this is the time to approach him about a dog for Natalie,' she muttered to herself.

*　*　*　*

It was just five minutes before the evening debrief when Rachel finally sent her text reply to Dennis Preston. She didn't want her reply to be ambiguous in any way so made it short and precise.

Thanks for the offer, but the answer's no!
DC Rachel Dalton

As was the norm, the debriefing scheduled for five o'clock started dead on time.

'Well, I think we're making some progress,' Carmichael announced. 'At long last we've established the identities of all four victims and we've also identified Harvey Romney as Aiden Davidson's accomplice in the identity frauds. So, as I said, good progress.'

'We are still waiting to see Romney's statement,' added Cooper. 'But I think we have enough to charge him.'

'Good,' replied Carmichael. 'We need to find some of their customers. In my experience, when these illegals are caught, they have no qualms about spilling the beans, especially if they've been charged a packet for their documents, which I'd fully expect from Romney.'

Cooper nodded. 'I'll pick up on that one,' he volunteered.

'But unfortunately,' continued Carmichael, 'we've no obvious candidate for our killer.'

'Well, if we are working on the assumption that it was someone who had access to the Etorphine missing from the Park Road Veterinary Practice, and also someone whom I gave my mobile number to,' observed Rachel, 'that narrows it down to just the Park Road employees and, if that's the case, then my money's on Adam Charles. He ticks all the boxes.'

'What do you mean?' asked Carmichael.

'Well, he hasn't a strong alibi for any of the murders this

196

week and he was the person who reported finding Damien Wilbraham.'

'What about a motive?' asked Carmichael.

Rachel shrugged her shoulders. 'I can't think of one, but to be honest I can't think of a strong motive for anybody to have killed all four people.'

'I agree,' remarked Cooper. 'Adam Charles has to be on our list.'

'OK,' agreed Carmichael. 'Who else do we have as suspects?'

'Romney has to be a candidate for Davidson's murder,' suggested Watson. 'Although he hasn't admitted anything, it was he who Betty overheard arguing with Aiden on Monday. They were involved together in the fraud. Maybe they fell out and Romney killed him.'

'I have to admit I'm not one of Romney's greatest fans,' Carmichael remarked. 'But why would he kill Vicky Page and Joan Henderson? And we've absolutely no link established between Romney and Damien Wilbraham.'

'I may have some information that could change that,' interrupted Rachel, with smug enthusiasm. 'When I showed Betty Wilbraham the photos of Vicky and Joan earlier this afternoon she said that Joan was a frequent visitor to Aiden's house. What if she was also involved in the fraud?'

Carmichael was considering what Rachel had just disclosed when Cooper chipped in. 'Well, I still think we may be looking for *two* people,' he pronounced. 'Maybe it was Joan who helped Romney kill Aiden Davidson, then Romney killed her and Vicky, too.'

'It's possible, I suppose,' replied Carmichael.

Watson shook his head. 'I don't think so,' he remarked. 'Lou Henderson told me he was with his wife on Tuesday morning so, assuming he's telling the truth, she couldn't have been Davidson's killer.'

Carmichael thought for a few moments. 'Let's take this step

by step,' he said calmly. 'Let's just start with the premise of Romney acting in isolation. Let's see what sort of alibis Romney supplies us with for the four murders. If they're shaky, we will have to delve a little deeper. In the interim we need to consider whether we have any other strong candidates.'

'Well, based upon the fact that many murders are carried out by their spouses, the obvious candidate for Joan's death should be her husband Lou Henderson,' suggested Cooper.

'No, it's not Lou,' replied Watson with confidence. 'He's a cast-iron alibi for Damien Wilbraham's death – he was in Colorado – and it would have been a really busy night for him to get to his house from his hotel in York, commit the murders, then get himself back to the hotel in York in time for breakfast. He didn't even know Vicky or Damien Wilbraham either, so I'm certain we can rule him out.'

'Also, I've never given him my mobile number, so I agree it can't be him,' added Rachel.

'But he knew Davidson, and we've just found out his wife was visiting Davidson,' Carmichael remarked, 'so I think we should still keep him on our list, albeit I agree that he's not as strong a suspect as Adam Charles or even Harvey Romney.'

Watson looked dumbfounded. 'If you say so,' he replied. 'But I'm certain he's not involved in any of the deaths.'

For once Carmichael found himself secretly agreeing with Rachel and Watson, but Watson was right when he'd said spouses were frequently the killers, and until he was one-hundred-per-cent certain that Lou Henderson was not the killer, he wasn't going to cross his name out completely.

'Anyone else?' Carmichael asked.

The three officers returned blank looks that suggested they had no other strong contenders.

'What about Malcolm Page or even Betty Wilbraham?' Carmichael asked, more in hope than anything.

'Betty can't drive,' replied Rachel. 'So she couldn't have killed her brother.'

'And I don't see her having the strength to haul Davidson's body to the railway bridge and drop it over either,' added Cooper.

Carmichael shrugged his shoulders as if to demonstrate he concurred with their observations. 'Maybe so,' he admitted.

'But, in theory, Page could be our man,' remarked Watson. 'I'm not sure what his motive would be for the murders, but we've not checked his movements and he would have access to Etorphine.'

'I can't see him killing his own daughter,' chipped in Rachel with a look of resistance on her face.

'I agree with Rachel,' added Cooper. 'But we should check him out, too.'

Carmichael wrote the names of Adam Charles, Harvey Romney, Lou Henderson and Malcolm Page on the whiteboard in bold red letters.

'Is that it then?' he asked.

For a split second Rachel considered suggesting Dennis Preston. However, she resisted the urge. He may have become a pest as far as she was concerned, but that wasn't a strong enough reason to put his name forward.

'OK,' continued Carmichael. 'In that case, I suggest we break for a few minutes to get a coffee and to allow Marc to see if Harvey Romney has finally completed his statement.'

Watson got up and rushed out of the interview room.

'I haven't seen him move that fast in ages,' Rachel muttered in Cooper's general direction.

Cooper grinned. 'No, the last time I saw him shift that quickly', he quipped, 'was when I told him that the canteen was selling off their meat pies at half-price!'

*　*　*　*

Even as she rang Siobhan Ballentyne's doorbell, Penny could not believe she had allowed herself to be hoodwinked into attending a White Vixens meeting. Neither could Siobhan Ballentyne by the look on her face as she opened the door.

'Do come in, Mrs Carmichael,' she said gushingly as she ushered her into the house. 'Your husband told me that you might be joining us this evening. It's so wonderful to see you.'

* * * *

Back at Kirkwood Police Station, the four officers had reconvened and Carmichael was quickly scanning over Harvey Romney's statement, which Watson had just handed to him.

When he'd finished, Carmichael looked up at his colleagues with an exasperated expression. 'Looks like Romney's toughing it out,' he remarked. 'He is willing to admit that he knew Aiden Davidson, but is denying any involvement in the forgeries.'

'What about his alibis for the times of the four deaths?' Cooper enquired.

'He's claiming he was on a course in Harrogate when Damien Wilbraham was killed,' replied Carmichael. 'He says he would have been travelling to the practice at seven thirty-seven on Tuesday, when Davidson was killed, and he maintains that on Wednesday evening, he was at home with his wife.'

'So, he's not our man then!' remarked Rachel.

'Well, he's maintaining he knows nothing about the forgeries either,' Watson pointed out.

'We need to check his story. Can you take care of that, Marc?' Carmichael asked.

Watson nodded. 'Will do, sir,'

Carmichael sighed. 'So we've four suspects, but only Adam Charles who seems to have a weak alibi for each of the murders. Furthermore, he had Rachel's mobile number and he had the opportunity to take the Etorphine from the practice. Is that correct?'

Although Rachel and Cooper both nodded their agreement Cooper still appeared unconvinced. 'I think there were two people involved in these killings,' he remarked.

'You could be right,' agreed Carmichael. 'But for now let's focus our efforts on the four suspects we've identified and, in particular, Adam Charles.'

Cooper shrugged his shoulders. 'You're right, I've no firm evidence to support it being two people; it's just a feeling I have in my gut.'

'I'm the last person to argue against gut feelings,' said Carmichael with a smile, 'I follow them all the time. But let's just stick with the four suspects as if they have been working alone for now.'

'What I can't work out', said Rachel, 'is what the relevance of seven thirty-seven is and why, in each of the text messages, the killer keeps taunting us about it?'

'Yes, I agree,' Cooper added. 'And why did we not get a text for the first death?'

'I'd have thought that was an easy one,' said Watson. 'For the messages we've had so far the killer has used the mobiles of the people he killed.'

'So?' enquired Rachel.

'Well,' said Watson firmly, 'I suspect Damien Wilbraham, being a scruffy old sod, probably didn't own one. Our killer couldn't taunt us. Not unless he was stupid enough to use his own mobile.'

His three colleagues sat in silence for a few seconds agog at Watson's hypothesis.

'Actually, that makes perfect sense,' replied Carmichael. 'And bloody obvious now you've mentioned it. Good thinking, Marc.'

Watson looked particularly smug. He wasn't used to being praised by the boss and was only too happy to let both

Rachel and Cooper see the full majesty of his self-righteous grin.

'That reminds me, Paul,' continued Carmichael. 'Did SOCO get back to you regarding any fingerprints on Joan's phone and did they manage to find out where Vicky had been sleeping on the night she and Joan were killed?'

Cooper nodded. 'There were no prints found on Joan's phone. They maintain that Vicky had been sleeping in the spare bedroom, but there's no sign of any of her possessions and even more bizarrely her bed had been tidied up to make it look like it hadn't been slept in.'

'Why on earth would someone do that?' Carmichael enquired.

'I've no idea,' replied Cooper, with a faint shake of his head. 'But SOCO are certain Vicky had been in the spare room.'

Carmichael thought for a few moments. 'We need to find Vicky's things, particularly her mobile,' continued Carmichael. 'That's something I'd like you to follow up on, Rachel.'

'OK,' replied Rachel, although she had no idea how she was going to set about that assignment, given that she was sure the phone and the rest of Vicky's possessions would have been dumped by now.

'And I'd also like you to check out which of our suspects either owns, or has access to, a white car,' Carmichael added. 'Damien Wilbraham was hit by a white car, so let's find it.'

Rachel nodded again. 'Will do.'

Carmichael looked at his watch: it was 5:55 p.m. 'Which of you are on duty this weekend?'

'I'm on tomorrow,' replied Cooper.

'Me too!' added Watson.

'OK, in that case why don't you two get yourselves home?' remarked Carmichael with uncharacteristic charity. 'Rachel and I can tidy things up this evening, given that we're the lucky ones who have the weekend off.'

Never one to look a gift horse in the mouth, Watson grinned, grabbed his jacket and made a dash for the door. 'That suits me. Have a great weekend, everyone, and I'll see you tomorrow, Paul.'

'I think he was even quicker this time,' Rachel muttered in Cooper's ear.

'What do we do with Romney?' Cooper asked.

'Oh yes, I forgot about him,' replied Carmichael. 'We may have enough to charge him as it is, but let's hold fire until Marc has checked out his alibi, and you've spoken to some of Davidson's customers. Let him go for now, but call me tomorrow and let me know what you discover and we'll review the situation then.'

Cooper nodded and headed off to give Romney and his brief the good news.

'So, what loose ends do you want us to tidy up this evening?' Rachel enquired as soon as they were alone.

'I'd like you to make contact with a woman called Pauline Squires,' Carmichael said. 'Penny said she came to my house earlier today looking worried about something. I've tried to call her but got no answer. Can you try her and find out what's worrying her? It may have nothing to do with this case, but I'd like to find out what's perturbing her before we break for the weekend.'

Carmichael handed Rachel the torn-out page from his road atlas where he'd scribbled down her number.

'I'll call her now,' Rachel dutifully replied.

'And while you're doing that I'll go and update Chief Inspector Hewitt,' said Carmichael, with a look of despondency on his face.

Chapter 35

Hewitt leaned back in his hefty leather chair, his spider-like hands clasped firmly behind his scrawny neck. 'So, there's some progress,' he concluded with a pompous air of astuteness. 'You've at least an identity for all four bodies, but you're still a fair way from apprehending our murderer.'

'I don't agree,' argued Carmichael calmly. 'We've got a number of suspects and I'm convinced that the murderer or murderers, as there may be two people involved here, are within days of being identified and I'm confident we'll have this case wrapped up within days.'

Hewitt remained in the same superior pose. 'I hope you're right, Steve,' he said in a way that Carmichael took to mean '…I think you've no chance.'

'Anyway,' said Carmichael, who was still composed and outwardly unruffled, 'I just thought I'd give you an update before the weekend.'

Hewitt removed his hands from behind his neck and sat forward. 'Well, thanks for doing that, Steve,' he muttered. 'I've every confidence in you, but please get this person before there are any more deaths. The last thing I want is the top brass asking awkward questions. You need to get this one closed out PDQ.'

Carmichael stood up, smiled back at his boss and left the office. Once outside he raised his eyes to the heavens and shook his head. 'I despair sometimes with that man,' he whispered to Angela, Hewitt's charming PA. 'How on earth do you remain so … so sane?'

'It's easy,' replied Angela with a warm smile. 'You do get used to him after a while. He's not so bad.'

Carmichael's face clearly showed that he begged to differ. 'Anyway, when he gets very difficult,' continued Angela, 'I just imagine I have a lever next to the desk that opens a trap door beneath him. There's many a time the tigers below have had a hearty meal thanks to me.'

Carmichael's eyes opened widely. 'Angela!' he said with astonishment. 'I've never seen this side of you.'

Angela winked back at Carmichael. 'Oh there's a great deal you don't know about me,' she replied with a mischievous grin.

*   *   *   *

Rachel's attempt to call Pauline Squires had exactly the same result as Carmichael's call earlier. She also left a voicemail and with her jacket on and ready to go home, she was just scribbling a note to her boss to advise him of her failure when her mobile indicated that another text message had been received.

Rachel finished the note before looking down at the text message.

'Bloody man,' she said out loud, just as Carmichael appeared at the door.

'I hope you're not talking about me,' he remarked jovially.

'Oh no,' replied Rachel. 'It's some bloke who's starting to become a real pain.'

'Anyone I know?' enquired Carmichael.

Rachel considered whether she should tell her boss about Dennis Preston's incessant texting, but thought better of it.

'No,' she replied with a forced smile on her face. 'It's just one of those things us single girls have to cope with.'

Carmichael accepted her answer without question. 'OK then,' he remarked. 'Have a nice weekend and I'll see you on Monday.'

Rachel smiled again and walked towards the door.

'Oh, I nearly forgot,' she said, turning half around to face the boss. 'I couldn't raise Pauline Squires either. I left you a note. Do you want me to call her over the weekend?'

Carmichael thought for a few seconds. 'No,' he concluded with a shake of his head. 'If she doesn't return our calls or come into the station, it can't be that important. It can wait till Monday. You get yourself home and enjoy your weekend.'

'Thanks, sir,' replied Rachel as she disappeared out into the corridor. 'You, too!'

* * * *

Penny could not wait to get out of the White Vixens meeting at Siobhan Ballentyne's house.

'That deserves a bloody expensive meal, Inspector Steve Carmichael,' she muttered to herself as she started the car engine and headed back home.

* * * *

Carmichael's drive home was peaceful and uneventful. To his delight the roads were quiet and he completed the 23.2-mile journey in a little over thirty-two minutes. With a self-righteous smile he pressed the small button on his car fob to lock the doors on his black BMW and strolled purposefully up the slender path to his front door.

In the distance he could hear the faint sound of a siren, but had no inkling whatsoever of the frantic attempts of the paramedics as they struggled desperately to revive Pauline Squires, who lay lifelessly in the back of the speeding ambulance.

Chapter 36

As soon as Rachel arrived home, she flung her jacket on the armchair, put the kettle on and, as she waited for it to boil, started to compose a text message to send back to Dennis Preston. She was almost halfway through when she had a change of mind.

'I'll call the fool,' she muttered under her breath as she pressed the call button.

His mobile rang just once before he picked it up. 'RSPCA, Dennis Preston speaking,' he said in a confident clear voice.

'It's DC Dalton,' announced Rachel as calmly as she could. 'Don't you understand the word *no*?'

*   *   *   *

'So how did it go?' enquired Carmichael as he placed his arms on his wife's shoulders and looked down into her angry eyes.

'It was bloody awful, if you really want to know,' replied Penny, who was determined not to allow her husband to make light of her ordeal at Siobhan Ballentyne's White Vixens evening.

'Really?' replied Carmichael, who was genuinely surprised at Penny's irate demeanour. 'What on earth went on?'

'It was like being at a convention for anxious housewives,' replied Penny. 'And, as a result of the hour and a half I spent with Siobhan's ladies, I know all about Mrs Mason's insecurities following her father's suicide twenty years ago, the fact that some old dear called Annie can't accept the death of her husband in the 1970s and that another poor young woman called Stella can't cope with relationships ever since some boyfriend put his hand up her skirt when she was fourteen.'

'So, a bit of an ordeal,' remarked Carmichael.

'Ordeal!' shrieked Penny. 'It was painful and I felt so awkward. I must have been out of my mind to agree to go.'

'So, other than these poor ladies' worries and hang-ups, did you glean anything from Siobhan that might help the case?'

Penny rolled her eyes and shook her head. 'Nothing. All we did was sit in a circle, share our problems and offer advice to each other.'

Despondently, Carmichael wandered over to the fridge and removed a bottle of wine. 'Care for a drink?' he asked as he lifted the bottle so Penny could see it.

Penny smiled back in his direction. 'A large one, please. But don't think you can fob me off with a couple of glasses of wine to try and make it up to me. As an absolute minimum I want a meal at The Fisheries tomorrow evening, I want you to seriously consider buying Natalie that dog she keeps harping on about and …' As she paused Penny held out her hand. 'I also want the forty-five pounds this evening's embarrassing fiasco cost me.'

Carmichael raised his hands up in mock surrender. 'Of course, a meal at The Fisheries and a full refund is the least I can do.' he remarked, trying hard to hide any smile that might appear. 'It's a deal.'

'And what about Natalie's dog?' Penny asked sternly.

'I'll have to think about that,' he replied. 'A dog is a massive commitment.'

'Well, don't take too long thinking it over, because I'd like one, too!'

Carmichael didn't feel it was the right time to argue his case against getting a dog, so chose to cut short the conversation and pour his wife a large glass of wine. As he did, a thought suddenly entered his head.

'What issue did you make up to share with the Vixens?'

Penny picked up her glass, took a large swig and gave her husband a smug self-satisfying smile. 'I'm afraid that's between me and the rest of the Vixens,' she remarked, her eyes expressing her unabashed delight. 'But let's just say you'd have been proud of my inventiveness.'

Chapter 37

Rachel had just clambered into her hot bath when her mobile started to ring.

'Please God, tell me it's not him,' she said through gritted teeth as she leaned across and picked it up off the wicker chair where she'd dumped it seconds earlier.

'DC Dalton?' enquired the male voice at the end of the phone.

'Yes,' replied Rachel, who was both surprised and relieved that it wasn't Dennis Preston's voice she was hearing.

'It's PC Dyer here,' continued the caller. 'I've just picked up the voice message you left earlier today on Pauline Squire's phone. I thought you should know that she's been rushed into Kirkwood Hospital.'

Rachel sat bolt upright so suddenly that the foamy water formed a tidal wave that travelled the length of the bath before cascading over the end and on to the floor.

'What happened?'

'It's a suspected overdose, they're pumping her stomach as we speak.'

'Thanks for letting me know,. I'll get over as soon as I can.'

She flung the mobile back on to the wicker chair and sank slowly back into the bubbly water.

* * * *

It took just two large glasses of wine and a number of heartfelt apologies from her husband before Penny started to see the funny side of the day's events.

'Who do you think is behind the murders?' Penny asked as she cuddled up to Carmichael on the sofa.

Carmichael sighed. 'We're not sure,' he admitted awkwardly. 'Our strongest candidates are either Harvey Romney, who is the owner of Trinity Veterinary Practice or, more likely, a man called Adam Charles, who's one of the vets at Joan's practice.'

'So, why do you think they may be your killer?'

'Neither have strong alibis for the times of the murders. In fact, Charles was the person who reported the first death back in June. Both had access to Etorphine, and we're certain Romney was involved in a fairly major identity fraud scam with Aiden Davidson.'

Penny took a sip of her wine. 'What about a motive?'

'Our theory with Romney is that he fell out with Davidson over the fraud and possibly, with Joan Henderson's help, killed Davidson. Then he killed Joan, maybe to keep her quiet.'

Penny hesitated a moment as she absorbed all that her husband had just told her. 'You think Joan was involved in the fraud, too?' she asked, the pitch in her voice slightly raised to indicate her surprise.

In truth, Carmichael was not totally convinced with this particular theory, but he nodded to indicate that Penny's sceptical summation was correct.

'And Vicky Page was just in the wrong place at the wrong time?'

'Correct,' replied Carmichael, who was impressed at how quickly his wife was picking up the gist of this particular hypothesis.

'What about this guy, Adam Charles? What motive did he have?'

Carmichael shifted uneasily on the sofa. 'That's not quite so obvious,' he replied with a slight tinge of irritation in his voice. 'He's certainly got the most obvious means, but we don't yet have a plausible motive for him. However, it's one of our priorities.'

Penny took another sip of wine. 'What I don't understand is what the hit-and-run has in common with the other deaths and why the time of seven thirty-seven in the morning is such an important time?'

Carmichael shrugged his shoulders. 'Join the club,' he remarked sombrely.

* * * *

It was almost 9:50 p.m. when DC Rachel Dalton arrived at Kirkwood Hospital and, within ten minutes, she had located PC Dyer, who was in Mountbatten Ward where Pauline Squires had been admitted.

'She's stable but still unconscious,' PC Dyer told Rachel in a whispered voice. 'The ward sister told me that her condition is still serious but no longer critical.'

Rachel decided to wait at Pauline's bedside. She had no idea why Pauline Squires would want to speak with her boss, but she wanted to be at her bedside to talk with her as soon as she woke up from her drug-induced stupor.

Rachel gazed at her watch and, for a split second, considered calling Carmichael to let him know what had happened. But it was almost 10 p.m., so decided that, until Pauline came round, her boss couldn't do anything, so thoughtfully elected to leave him to enjoy what was left of his evening at home.

'Do you want a cup of tea?' asked the nurse who had been instructed to check on Pauline every fifteen minutes. 'You may be in for a long wait.'

Rachel returned a forced smile of resignation. 'I've

nothing better to do this evening,' she replied wryly. 'And a cup of tea would be great, thank you.'

*   *   *   *

'Do you fancy watching *Catch Me If You Can?*' Carmichael asked, as he sat with his wife on the small sofa in their front room.

'Now!' replied Penny. 'It's already ten-thirty. It will be well after midnight when it finishes.'

Carmichael shrugged his shoulders. 'It's probably a long shot,' he confessed. 'But given the link with the text messages we've been receiving, I think I should watch it. You never know, it might even be entertaining.'

Penny shook her head as if to emphasise her bewilderment at Steve's suggestion. 'OK,' she replied with a smile. 'But if we're having an evening at the cinema I'm getting something to munch. You set up the film and pour me another glass of wine, while I get the popcorn.'

Ten minutes later Steve and Penny, like two love-struck teenagers, were sitting quietly together in the half-gloom engrossed in the film, each with a glass of wine by their side and a large bowl of popcorn wedged between them.

213

Chapter 38

Saturday 19th July

The smell of bacon being cooked filled Rachel's nostrils as soon as Carmichael's front door opened.

'Oh hi,' remarked Penny, who was shocked to see DC Dalton on her doorstep.

'Is Inspector Carmichael in?' Rachel asked somewhat timidly.

'Yes, come in,' replied Penny while at the same time drawing the door wide to let their visitor enter.

'Thanks,' said Rachel. 'I'm sorry to bother you so early on Saturday but it's quite important.

Carmichael didn't notice Rachel as she entered the kitchen. His back was to the door as he merrily turned the contents of the frying pan, dressed in shorts, T-shirt and an apron with a cartoon of Winnie the Pooh on the front; a present Jemma had bought him for Christmas.

'You've a visitor,' announced Penny, who was a few feet behind Rachel.

Carmichael looked back over his shoulder and was clearly surprised to see Rachel standing by the kitchen table.

'What's happened?' he asked, knowing there was no way Rachel would pay him a house call on Saturday morning unless it was something serious.

'It's Pauline Squires,' replied Rachel. 'She was rushed to hospital last night.'

'What?' exclaimed Carmichael, who jettisoned the spatula into the frying pan and turned round to face Rachel. 'Don't tell me our killer has targeted another victim.'

The sight of Winnie the Pooh emblazoned on Carmichael's apron caught Rachel a little off guard. She was tired, having only slept for a few short spells the night before in the less-than-comfortable hospital chair and was keen to update her boss, then get home and get some decent kip. 'It's an attempted suicide,' replied Rachel. 'An overdose. There's no suspicion of any foul play.'

'Is she all right?' Carmichael enquired.

'She keeps coming in and out of consciousness. The doctors don't feel she's likely to have suffered any permanent damage, but she's still not capable of telling us why she tried to kill herself.'

'Have you been with her all night?' Penny asked.

Rachel stifled a yawn. 'Yes, since about ten o'clock.'

Carmichael didn't see his DC losing a night's sleep as being any cause for undue concern. 'And has she said anything in that time?' he asked.

'Not too much. She hasn't come round properly all night, but she kept mumbling that she was a murderer.'

Carmichael frowned. 'But who has she murdered?'

Rachel shrugged her shoulders. 'I've no idea. I just thought you needed to know, given that she was so keen to speak to you.'

'She was also really disturbed last Tuesday at the psychic meeting when Siobhan Ballentyne told her she needed to do the right thing,' added Penny, who at the same time gestured to Rachel to sit down.

'That bloody witch,' announced Carmichael angrily. 'Her name keeps coming up!'

Penny took the pause in the conversation as her cue to offer Rachel some sympathy for having had such a long night.

'Would you like a cup of tea, my dear?'

215

'Oh, yes please,' Rachel replied.

'Actually, I bet you haven't eaten yet either,' Penny added. 'Do you want a sausage and bacon sandwich?'

Carmichael's expression was a clear sign that he wasn't keen to share his breakfast. However, when the young DC accepted his wife's generous offer, he sensibly didn't argue his point.

'Who is with Pauline now?' he asked as he joined Rachel at the kitchen table, allowing Penny to take over the cooking duties.

Rachel smiled. 'I spoke with Cooper earlier and he arranged for a WPC to sit at Pauline's bedside.'

'Good,' replied Carmichael. 'I'll call him later and make sure he tells me as soon as Pauline comes around.'

As Penny finished cooking the contents of the frying pan and started to stuff the bacon and sausage between slices of thick white bread, Carmichael poured out three mugs of tea.

'Do you think Pauline Squires is connected to the other murders?' Rachel enquired as she lifted the mug to take a sip.

'I've absolutely no idea,' replied Carmichael, who was truly perplexed by this unexpected development. 'But, after breakfast, I'm going to see that meddling psychic again, and this time she either tells me the truth or I'll charge her with withholding evidence and wasting police time.'

Penny placed the plate of sandwiches on the table between her husband and Rachel.

'If you're about to take on forces from the other side, you'd better make sure you do it on a full stomach,' she teased, with a wry smile and a sly wink in Rachel's direction.

'And maybe it will have more impact without the Winnie the Pooh apron!' added Rachel before biting deep into a hot sandwich.

* * * *

216

Cooper had arrived at Kirkwood Police Station at 8:15 a.m. and, by the time Marc Watson slowly ambled into the office, he had already arranged for a WPC to sit vigil at Pauline Squires' bedside and had located two of Aiden Davidson's customers.

'Nice of you to make an appearance!' Cooper announced sarcastically as his colleague finally plonked himself at his desk.

Watson showed no obvious signs of guilt at arriving over an hour after his fellow sergeant.

'I doubt I've missed much,' Watson replied, his indifference conspicuous in his delivery. 'Checking out Romney's alibi is not going to be that easy on a Saturday. If he was at a convention in Harrogate when the tramp was mown down, it's unlikely that anyone will be around today to talk to. Those sort of places don't tend to work on Saturdays. Not like mugs like us.'

'You won't know unless you try,' replied Cooper, who, as he spoke, sprang out of his chair. 'Anyway, I won't be here to find out. I'm going over to Newbridge. I'm going to talk to the proud owner of one of Aiden's forged passports. A lady who now calls herself Alma Stone, but who, thanks to Aiden's meticulous records, I think is really an Iranian Kurd called Alimah.'

With a purposeful air Cooper strode towards the door.

'Oh, if WPC Berry calls from the hospital, can you get her to call me on my mobile?' said Cooper as he made his exit.

'Berry!' remarked Watson. 'Isn't she the one with the pert–?'

Cooper missed the end of his colleague's sentence. The office door had already slammed shut behind him and he was five or six yards down the corridor before Watson could finish.

'I wonder what Berry is doing at the hospital?' Watson mumbled to himself, before picking up the phone and dialling 118 118. 'Can you put me through to the Harrogate Convention Centre?' he asked the operator.

* * * *

When Carmichael spotted Siobhan Ballentyne's shocked face as she opened the door, he just couldn't help himself. 'You look surprised to see me,' he announced irreverently. 'I'd have thought someone with your powers would have foretold my arrival, or is Guthrie still asleep?'

Siobhan quickly gathered her poise. 'Do come through, Inspector,' she said, completely ignoring his opening comments. 'It's so good to see you again.'

Carmichael strode confidently into the hallway and through into the sitting room.

'May I offer you some refreshment?'

'No, thank you,' replied Carmichael, who sat down on the sofa. 'I just want you to sit down and start telling me the truth. I've no time for any of your usual claptrap. My patience is at an end with you and, without any of your normal flannel, I want to know what you know and how you came by the information.'

Siobhan sat down opposite Carmichael.

'I can assure you, Inspector, I've shared all ...' Siobhan started to say before she was abruptly interrupted.

'Let me make myself crystal clear. I don't care whether you have psychic powers. I don't believe you do, but my opinion is irrelevant. I'm not here to challenge your spiritual abilities; I'm here to find out what you know that's relevant to the murder investigations I'm conducting. Do you understand?'

For a split second Siobhan thought about arguing her case, but the stern look on Carmichael's face quickly made her change her mind. 'What specifically do you want me to tell you?' she replied somewhat sheepishly.

'Well, let's start with Pauline Squires and the message you

218

gave her at the meeting on Tuesday,' suggested Carmichael. 'What was it that you were asking her to come clean about? I can guess how you got the information, but I want to know what it was you were referring to?'

Siobhan Ballentyne looked nervous. No matter how hard she tried, she couldn't maintain the fixed eye contact which was normally one of her trademarks. Edgily she fiddled with her rings and Carmichael could see that she was feeling uneasy, something he found perversely enjoyable.

'Before I tell you anything,' she said, her voice wavering slightly as she spoke. 'I am not a fraud. I am a third-generation psychic and I do hear voices from those who have passed over. But OK, I admit that occasionally I do use other sources of information to help my clients.'

Carmichael's initial instinct was to interrupt and challenge this watered-down confession, but he elected to stay silent and allow Siobhan to continue to unburden herself.

'With Pauline Squires I discovered, from a confidential session I'd had with another client, that she was responsible for the death of a man by careless driving. In the meeting I was just trying to get her to do the right thing.'

Inside, Carmichael felt elated that at long last he'd managed to get Siobhan Ballentyne to discard her usual cool and collected stance.

'So, who told you about the hit-and-run?'

Siobhan's torso recoiled back into the comfy armchair. 'I can't tell you that, I'm afraid,' she remarked indignantly. 'That would be breaching client confidentiality.'

Impassively Carmichael stared back at the ruffled psychic. 'This is a murder enquiry,' he replied firmly. 'And, unless you are totally candid with me, I will charge you with obstructing the police in their enquiries and withholding evidence.'

Siobhan Ballentyne stared back at Carmichael, her irritation and resentment etched across her face.

'I'm deadly serious,' Carmichael added.

* * * *

Cooper leaned against the bonnet of his clapped-out Volvo to take the incoming call. As he put his mobile to his ear, he watched with a degree of empathy as two uniformed officers escorted Alimah (aka Alma Stone) from the squalid-looking corner shop where she had been working since arriving illegally six months earlier.

'Cooper,' he said.

'It's WPC Berry here,' remarked the person at the end of the line. 'I thought I'd let you know Pauline Squires has regained consciousness. The doctors are saying it's OK to talk with her.'

'That's great news,' replied Cooper, who was having a productive morning. 'I'll come straight over.'

Chapter 39

His interview with the crestfallen psychic now over, Carmichael walked briskly towards his car. He had not heard the door close and could feel Siobhan's eyes burning into his shoulder blades.

'I may use other sources of information to supplement my client's experience,' she shouted at him as he reached the gate, 'but I do have psychic powers.'

Carmichael stopped and half turned to catch her eye. 'Remember what we agreed,' he shouted back at her. 'I want a full statement from you today, Ms Ballentyne.'

Siobhan's anger was patently evident in her face.

'I'm no fraud,' she shouted, her anger palpable in her voice.

Carmichael chose not to respond. Slowly he turned his back on the charlatan clairvoyant and strode over to his car.

He felt no guilt from the distress he'd caused the psychic, and was more than happy to leave her to fume on her doorstep with her pathetic excuse of a dog at her heels.

As his BMW pulled away from Siobhan's house, Carmichael switched on the radio and he settled back in his seat, pleased with his performance and looking forward to a quiet drive to the hamlet of Hasslebury. However, his peaceful journey was short-lived. Having travelled no more than half a mile, his mobile rang.

'Hi, sir,' came the familiar voice of Cooper. 'Are you OK to talk?'

'Yes,' replied Carmichael. 'I'm on my way to see Betty Wilbraham again. I've just had a very frank and illuminating discussion with Siobhan Ballentyne. And from what she told me, we need to think about this case from a completely different angle.'

'Really? ' Cooper remarked with excitement. 'Well, I've had a good morning, too. I've been talking to one of Davidson's customers and she's confirmed that she was put on to Davidson by your friend Harvey Romney. It was him she paid and she's willing to testify to that.'

'I bloody knew he was involved,' said Carmichael with unabashed euphoria. 'And he may also prove to be our killer, too.'

'Why's that?'

'Because Siobhan Ballentyne has just told me that Pauline Squires is our hit-and-run driver,' replied Carmichael. 'It was she who killed Damien Wilbraham. That phoney psychic found that out from Betty Wilbraham when she hypnotised her.'

'What?' exclaimed Cooper. 'But how does that make Romney the killer?'

'Because it means that our murderer didn't kill Damien Wilbraham, so anyone with an alibi for the first death is back on our list of suspects. And that leaves Harvey Romney and Adam Charles as our prime suspects.'

'I see,' replied Cooper. 'But what about all the texts we received about seven thirty-seven?'

'Red herrings,' replied Carmichael bluntly. 'Whoever killed Davidson, Joan Henderson and Vicky Page wanted to hide their murders by trying to associate them with the hit-and-run. And as that happened at seven thirty-seven, the killer just tried to link all the other deaths in some way to that time.'

'And that would explain why there wasn't any text message after Wilbraham's death,' added Cooper.

'Precisely,' replied Carmichael. 'And what's more I spent a

couple of hours watching that film *Catch Me If You Can* last night and, having seen it, I'm equally convinced that the reference he made to it in his texts is just another ploy by the murderer to wrong-foot us.'

'So, why are you going to see Betty Wilbraham?'

'I need to know what she knew about her brother's death. She certainly told Siobhan Ballentyne more than she has told us, so I need to make sure she's not withholding anything else. Anyway, what are you doing?

'Oh, I'm on my way to the hospital. WPC Berry has just informed me that Pauline Squires is now conscious.'

'Good. Hopefully she'll confirm what Siobhan Ballentyne told me earlier, namely that she is the hit-and-run driver.'

'What about Romney and Charles?' enquired Cooper. 'Do we arrest them?'

Carmichael considered the question for a few seconds. 'I think so. I'll call Marc and get him to organise bringing them both in. I want to charge Romney with the fraud, and both men need to answer questions about the three unsolved murders.'

'OK,' replied Cooper. 'Do you want me to do anything else after I've met with Pauline Squires?'

'I'd like to get the full team together at the station this afternoon before we start any formal interviews,' said Carmichael. 'So, once you've spoken with Pauline Squires, get yourself back to Kirkwood.'

'What about Rachel?' Cooper asked. 'She's supposed to be off today. Do you want me to ask her to come in, too?'

'Yes. Tell her we'll be starting the debrief at three o'clock. I know it's her day off but she needs to be there, too.'

* * * *

Marc Watson's morning had been as far from awe-inspiring as it could get. To his surprise, he'd managed to speak with someone at the Harrogate Convention Centre who was able to verify Harvey Romney's attendance on the day Damien Wilbraham had been killed, but outside of that he'd achieved precious little. So when Carmichael called him to bring him up to speed and then instruct him to organise for Adam Charles and Harvey Romney to be brought in for questioning, he leapt at the opportunity. Thirty minutes later, having briefed the uniformed officers who were to arrest Adam Charles, as well as those he'd selected to accompany him in apprehending Harvey Romney, he rushed into the car park.

As Watson scurried towards the awaiting patrol car, he almost didn't spot the forlorn figure of Lou Henderson.

'Mr Henderson, what are you doing here?'

'I've come to talk to you about Joan,' he replied in his distinctive American drawl. 'I want to start arranging her funeral and I would like to know when her body will be released.'

On hearing these words and seeing how distraught Henderson looked, Watson felt his adrenaline levels subsiding.

'I'm not sure,' he said with genuine sensitivity. 'I'm just on my way out. Can I maybe call you later?'

'Forget it!' snapped Henderson angrily. 'I've had it with you guys. You show me the wrong body, you don't tell me anything about how you're doing finding her killer, and now you can't even spend a few moments with me trying to sort out her funeral. This wouldn't happen in the States.'

'I'm sorry,' replied Watson sympathetically. 'I can't tell you more about our progress, but I will tell you that we made a big breakthrough earlier today and we're getting close to making an arrest.'

'Oh really?' responded Henderson with a look of disbelief on his face. 'So what's this big breakthrough?'

'I can't tell you that,' Watson replied. 'But all I will say is

224

that we've established he's been trying to fool us. He's used the text messages to try and get us to link the murders of Joan, Vicky and Aiden Davidson with another death last month. We're now pretty sure that that death isn't linked with your wife's murder and, as a result, the nets now closing in on him.'

Lou Henderson didn't look convinced, but said nothing.

'I'm sorry,' Watson continued. 'I will have to go, I'm afraid. I'll check the situation with Joan's body when I return and I'll call you.'

Although he felt uneasy leaving Henderson standing alone in the police station car park, Watson made his way hastily to the awaiting car, which, within seconds, sped off as its occupants hurried away to apprehend Harvey Romney.

Chapter 40

As his black BMW glided serenely along the winding country roads leading to Betty Wilbraham's house, Carmichael calmly and methodically considered which of the men Watson was bringing in for questioning was the most likely killer.

Having not yet met Adam Charles, it was hard to make a judgement on him, but he was certainly a strong candidate. He worked with Joan, knew Vicky and would have had access to the Etorphine. Furthermore his alibis were weak and, having been the person that found Damien Wilbraham, Charles would have known the time of his death, so he was certainly in possession of enough knowledge to have instigated the seven thirty-seven deception. But, as yet, there appeared to be no obvious motive for Adam Charles to murder either victim.

With Harvey Romney he also had a suspect that now had poor alibis. He knew all three victims, he had access to Etorphine and, now that they appeared to have established that Romney was involved in the fraud with Aiden Davidson, he certainly had a motive for his death.

As he weighed up the evidence for and against the two suspects, his thoughts were abruptly interrupted by the sight of Dennis Preston's RSPCA van careering towards him in the centre of the road. Carmichael slammed on his brakes, spun the steering wheel towards the high grassy bank to his left, and waited for the impact.

It seemed to take forever for his BMW to come to a halt,

by which time Dennis Preston had disappeared around the bend and out of sight.

'That's it!' exclaimed Carmichael out loud. 'As soon as I've finished with Betty Wilbraham, you're nicked.'

* * * *

When Cooper arrived outside Pauline Squires' small private ward, WPC Berry was already waiting for him.

'The doctors say you can only have ten minutes with her,' the pretty young constable told him. 'She's still quite groggy.'

Cooper smiled and nodded. 'I doubt we'll need much more than that,' he replied before pushing the door firmly and entering the room.

He found Pauline Squires lying flat on her back staring at the ceiling.

'This is Sergeant Cooper,' announced WPC Berry in a whisper. 'He needs to ask you a few questions.'

Pauline Squires turned her head to face the two officers.

'Will I go to prison?' she asked in a trembling voice.

Cooper chose to ignore her question. 'I just need you to tell me what happened, Pauline,' he said in a firm but kindly voice. 'I just need to know what happened that morning.'

* * * *

Carmichael rapped loudly on Betty Wilbraham's door. To his surprise, it opened almost as soon as his fist had finished its final thud.

'You'd forget your head if it were loose,' remarked Betty, her smiling face indicating that she was expecting her caller to be someone dear to her. 'Oh, it's you,' she continued when she saw Carmichael standing in front of her. 'I thought you were someone else.'

'Sorry to disappoint you, Mrs Wilbraham,' replied

227

Carmichael with a forced smile. 'I need to ask you a few more questions, I'm afraid.'

Betty, whose expression was now far more sedate, opened the door wide, stood back and beckoned her visitor inside with a swift movement of her head.

Carmichael then saw she was carrying an empty plastic cat box.

'I assume you were expecting the RSPCA man,' he remarked as he walked into the house. 'Was it you he was visiting just now?'

'He forgot to take this with him,' replied Betty. 'He brought a hedgehog in it last week. He called in to see how he was doing and was supposed to take it with him.'

'I see,' replied Carmichael, who followed Betty into the front room. 'Forgetful *and* a bad driver,' he mumbled, not expecting Betty to be able to hear.

'I expect his thoughts are elsewhere,' retorted Betty almost angrily. 'He seems preoccupied with your young colleague at the moment.'

'Do you mean DC Dalton?' enquired Carmichael with genuine surprise.

'If she's not told you, then I shan't,' replied Betty curtly. 'It's their business.'

For a split second Carmichael considered pushing Betty to tell him more, but elected to leave it. He hadn't come to talk about Dennis Preston's possible infatuation with one of his officers, but made his mind up to speak to Rachel himself to find out what Betty was talking about.

Carmichael sat down on the threadbare settee and waited for a few seconds while his host also made herself comfortable.

'I'm here to ask you a few more questions about the morning your brother was killed,' he announced in a stern voice. 'I want you to think hard before you answer my questions and I want you to tell me the whole truth.'

228

* * * *

Pauline Squires looked pathetically up in Cooper's direction.

'It was an accident,' she proclaimed in a feeble voice, tears streaming down her cheeks. 'He just shot out from nowhere. I braked hard and tried to swerve, but it all happened so quickly.'

'Why didn't you stop?'

'I did,' replied Pauline more firmly. 'But he was dead. It was obvious. He had blood coming from his ears and nose. It was terrible.'

'But why didn't you report the accident?'

Pauline Squires shook her head and started to cry. 'I just panicked,' she replied, her words punctuated with loud uncontrollable sobs. 'I was frightened.'

At that point a nurse appeared at the doorway and, seeing Pauline in such distress, rushed over to comfort the sorrowful patient.

'You're going to have to leave,' she ordered, her eyes fixed firmly in Cooper's direction. 'She's in no state to answer any more questions today.'

Cooper nodded and with a sudden movement of his head beckoned WPC Berry to join him outside.

'Calm down, my dear,' the nurse said sympathetically to her patient as the two police officers made their exit.

'Can you remain here for now?' said Cooper as soon as they were out or earshot. 'We'll need a statement from her as soon as she's in a less distressed state. Can you sort that out?'

WPC Berry nodded. 'No problem, Sergeant,' she replied obligingly and with a broad smile and a gleam of her bright-white teeth.

* * * *

'Betty,' Carmichael announced, in a manner which gave more than the hint he was about to chastise the dishevelled lady. 'Despite having a number of opportunities, I now know that in your previous statements to my officers and me, you've been extremely economical with the truth. It's high time you started telling us the whole truth, don't you agree?'

Betty Wilbraham leaned back in her armchair and made direct eye contact with Carmichael. 'What do you want to know?' she asked in a way which suggested to Carmichael that not only was he right in thinking she had more to tell him, but that, more encouragingly, at long last she was going to be totally forthcoming.

'Let's start with your brother's visit on Tuesday 3rd June,' said Carmichael calmly. 'Tell me again what happened between him arriving and leaving the following morning?'

Betty exhaled loudly then, as if to further demonstrate her readiness to cooperate, she took a deep breath and started to talk.

'It's pretty much as I told Rachel yesterday,' she said, her voice shaking a little as she spoke. 'I was so shocked when I opened the door that day. I never expected to see Damien again. I never thought he'd find me here.'

'You said in your statement that it had been twenty years since you last saw him,' continued Carmichael. 'How did you know it was him?'

'It was him all right,' replied Betty. 'He was older for sure, but I was in no doubt it was him and when he called me Patsy that confirmed it. My name's Patricia and, apart from our parents, both of whom are now dead, he was the only person who ever called me Patsy.'

Carmichael nodded to demonstrate he believed what he was hearing. 'In your statement you said he asked for money.'

'Yes, but he got none,' responded Betty firmly.

'But you let him stay the night?'

Betty nodded. 'Yes, against my better judgement, I did. But

he was out of here at seven the following morning, I made sure of that.'

Carmichael looked directly at Betty. 'I believe what you're telling me, but there's more, isn't there?'

Betty looked uneasy but remained silent.

'I think you followed your brother that morning, Betty, and I believe you saw the accident. Is that what happened?'

Betty's gaze descended floor-wards. 'Yes, I wanted to make sure he caught the train,' she replied nervously. 'I kept out of sight, but I followed him down the lane.'

'Then what happened?' Carmichael asked pointedly, his laser-like eyes fixed on Betty.

'I was in the bushes at the side of the road,' said Betty. 'I stood on a branch and it snapped. Damien heard the noise and, as he turned, he lost his footing.'

Betty looked in some distress as she recounted the story.

'He stepped out from the pavement into the road just as the white car came around the corner. I could see the woman behind the wheel trying to brake, and as she did, the car swerved a little, but it still hit him and threw him into the air. He hit the ground with an awful thud.'

Betty fiddled nervously with the solitary ring on her left index finger.

'The woman stopped and went to see if he was alive,' continued Betty. 'But it was clear he was dead and after a few seconds she climbed back into the car and sped off.'

'Did you recognise the woman?'

'Yes,' replied Betty meekly. 'It was Pauline Squires. She used to work on the mobile library van until they ran out of funding and it stopped coming.'

'Did she see you?'

Betty shook her head. 'No, she didn't, I stayed out of sight in the bushes.'

Carmichael scratched his chin for a few seconds before continuing his questioning. 'We didn't find anything on

Damien that enabled us to identify him,' he said, his eyes continuing to remain fixed on Betty. 'I think that after Pauline had gone you went over to your brother's body and took from him anything that might help us discover who he was. Is that correct, Betty?'

'Yes,' replied Betty. 'I just didn't want to have anything to do with him. But I realise now that was wrong of me.'

Carmichael shook his head slowly but maintained his gaze at Betty.

'What I don't understand is why you chose to tell Siobhan Ballentyne.'

A puzzled look appeared on Betty's face. 'I told her he was my brother at one of our sessions,' she confessed. 'I was troubled by what had happened and I hoped Siobhan would help me cope with things. But I didn't tell her about Pauline Squires. I kept that part secret.'

Carmichael opened his eyes wide. 'Well, she knows. She's told me so.'

Betty lifted her palms upwards and shrugged her shoulders. 'I don't know how she could have known.'

Carmichael thought for a few moments. 'You told Siobhan Ballentyne under hypnosis.'

'Surely, that's illegal!' remarked Betty, her irritation evident in her voice.

'Unethical and immoral, for sure,' replied Carmichael. 'But she's broken no laws that I can think of.'

'Unlike me!' Betty remarked.

Carmichael paused briefly before answering. 'Yes, I'm afraid your decision to remove all traces of identity from your brother's body is a serious matter. I will have to take you back with me to the station, where you will be charged with perverting the course of justice as a bare minimum.'

'I'll get my coat,' said Betty, who slowly pulled herself up and out of her armchair.

As Betty's pitiable frame ambled over to the array of well-worn coats that hung untidily on the metal hooks in her tiny hallway, Carmichael clambered out of the sofa and waited patiently a few steps behind.

'There's one other question I'd like to ask you,' he said calmly. 'You told DC Dalton that you'd observed Joan Henderson visiting Aiden Davidson's house. Can you tell me how many times you saw her and what sort of time of day she visited?'

Betty half turned as she slowly threaded her left arm into the coat sleeve. 'I didn't know who she was until Rachel told me. She came many times over the last six months. Always during the week and normally she'd arrive mid-morning and leave late afternoon.'

'Do you know if it was always on a specific day?'

Betty pondered upon the question as she put her right arm into the coat sleeve.

'I'm not sure if it was always the same day,' she replied. 'But she had paid him a visit on the day that Damien turned up. That was a Tuesday, as you know.'

Chapter 41

When Carmichael entered the incident room it was dead on three o'clock. Rachel Dalton, Paul Cooper and Marc Watson were all seated as he breezed past them and plonked himself down on the corner of the table nearest the open window.

'Thanks for coming in on your day off,' Carmichael said, his comment directed at Rachel who was still feeling the after-effects of spending most of the previous night at Pauline Squires' bedside.

'No problem, sir,' she replied without hesitation, although the yawn that followed served merely to underline her weariness.

'At last I think we're making some headway,' continued Carmichael, who appeared to be in an untypically cheery mood. 'So, who's going to start?'

'I can if you want,' replied Cooper.

'What have you got for us?' Carmichael asked with a look of keen anticipation.

Cooper, who was still feeling rather pleased with himself, cleared his throat before starting to share his news. 'First of all,' he announced, 'I've managed to trace a couple of women who benefited from Aiden Davidson's little sideline. I've spoken to one of them, a lady from Iran who now calls herself Alma Stone, and she's confirmed that it was Romney who put her on to Davidson and who took payment from her.'

Having been at home tucked up in bed for the last four hours, Rachel looked surprised at Cooper's news. 'So do we think he's the killer, too?' she enquired, her words and gaze directed at Carmichael.

'He's certainly now a strong candidate,' he replied. 'Marc's arrested him and I want you and Cooper to question him again as soon as we've finished the briefing.'

By the look on Rachel's face, it was clear she was excited at that prospect.

'Anyway, Paul, that's not all,' Carmichael added, his eyes now fixed on Cooper. 'Tell us about your conversation with Pauline Squires.'

Cooper paused for a few seconds before continuing. 'I didn't speak to her for too long,' he remarked. 'And I'm waiting for WPC Berry to bring her statement, but what she did tell me was that it was she who accidentally knocked down and killed Damien Wilbraham.'

'That's been confirmed by two other people, too,' added Carmichael. 'Siobhan Ballentyne, who extracted the information from Betty Wilbraham while she had her under hypnosis, and by Betty herself, who informed me earlier that she'd followed her brother that morning and saw the accident.'

'The lying old cow!' announced Rachel indignantly. 'She never mentioned any of that in her statement to me yesterday.'

'I know,' replied Carmichael. 'She's been very economical with the truth so far. But she's downstairs as we speak giving a full and complete statement, which will include her admission of taking from her dead brother's body anything that would have helped us identify him.'

'Why on earth did she do that?' Rachel enquired with a perplexed expression etched across her face.

'So he couldn't be traced back to her, I suspect,' interjected Watson.

'Precisely,' confirmed Carmichael. 'She didn't want him spoiling the cosy life she'd established here.'

'Just her and her hedgehogs,' mumbled Rachel.

'Well, Dennis Preston, too,' added Carmichael deliberately to see how the young DC would react. 'I think our Betty has a crush on the young RSPCA man.'

'Oh really!' replied Rachel with surprise.

'So I suspect,' replied Carmichael with an air of mischievousness in his voice. 'But I'm also led to believe our Mr Preston has his sights set elsewhere.'

Rachel's embarrassed look confirmed to Carmichael, as clearly as anything, that Betty's flippant comment from earlier that day had been right on the button.

'You have an admirer,' remarked Watson, who saw this as being great ammunition to make fun of the poor WDC.

'Don't sound so surprised,' remarked Rachel pointedly. 'But, for your information, it's all one-way I can assure you of that.'

'And it has to be,' stressed Carmichael sternly. 'He may not be a strong suspect, but Preston's linked to the case and while the investigation is ongoing there's to be no personal involvements with anyone connected to the case, by any of us.'

Rachel understood clearly what her boss was saying and nodded her head to signify her acquiescence.

'And in any case,' continued Carmichael, 'I'm planning to charge him with dangerous driving. He's an absolute bloody menace when he's behind a wheel. He's nearly killed me twice in the last week.'

'Dennis the menace,' remarked Watson childishly, much to Cooper's obvious amusement.

Carmichael ignored the comment, electing to keep his attention on Rachel for a few more seconds before turning to Watson. 'So what do you have for us, smart arse?' he asked.

Watson shrugged his shoulders. 'Nothing as grand as Cooper,' he confessed. 'I did establish that Romney had been in Harrogate at the time of Damien Wilbraham's death but, as we now know it was Pauline Squires who mowed him down,

236

I guess that's now irrelevant. Other than that, I can confirm we've brought in Romney and Charles, neither of whom is very happy.'

'Anything else?' Carmichael asked.

'Only that I bumped into Lou Henderson in the car park earlier,' continued Watson. 'He's pretty hacked off, too. Understandably he wants to know when we will be releasing Joan's body.'

Carmichael shook his head. 'I can't see that happening for a good few days at least,' he replied thoughtfully. 'I'll go over to see him tomorrow and talk it all through with him. Actually, I should also speak to Vicky Page's father. I suspect he's going to want to know about his daughter, too.'

'Do you want me to join you?' enquired Rachel.

'Yes, thank you, Rachel,' replied Carmichael. 'I'll do the talking but, as a feminine touch may prove helpful, I'd welcome you being with me.'

'Are we now sure that there's no seven thirty-seven connection with our murders?' Cooper enquired.

Carmichael considered his question for a split second. 'Well, if Pauline did kill Damien, as appears to be the case, then it does suggest that whoever killed Aiden Davidson, Joan Henderson and Vicky Page was trying to throw us off the scent by giving the impression that Damien Wilbraham's death was linked to theirs. I'm afraid the mention of seven thirty-seven and *Catch Me If You Can* appear to have both been a deliberate attempt to mislead us.'

'So why mention them in the texts?' enquired Watson.

'I'm not sure about *Catch Me If You Can*, but I can only think of one reason why he'd mention seven thirty-seven,' Rachel announced, 'That's because whoever the killer is had a cast-iron alibi that placed him well away from the murder scene when Damien Wilbraham was killed.'

'That's precisely what I'm thinking, too,' replied Carmichael.

'Well, although your alibi theory certainly applies to Harvey Romney,' remarked Watson, 'it doesn't hold water for Adam Charles. He found Damien Wilbraham, so he'd have nothing to gain from making the association. In fact, surely it would have been in his interest to play down such an association if he's the killer.'

'You make a valid point, Marc,' replied Carmichael, with a gentle nod of his head. 'I think Romney is much more likely to be our man. However, Charles hasn't a good alibi for any of the deaths. Charles knew that Damien Wilbraham was killed at seven thirty-seven, he worked with Joan Henderson, he knew Vicky Page, he had access to the Etorphine and he also had Rachel's mobile number. With all that stacked against him, we can't discount him yet.'

'But now we believe the death of Damien Wilbraham isn't linked to the other deaths, there must be others who we should now be adding to our list,' Rachel suggested.

'I agree,' interjected Cooper. 'We should not discount other people from either the Park Road or Trinity practices.'

'There's also Lou Henderson and Malcolm Page,' continued Rachel. 'What about them?'

'Henderson's a possibility,' conceded Carmichael. 'I'm not sure what his motive would have been and getting hold of the Etorphine wouldn't have been that easy for him, but he's got to be on our list, I agree. I'm not sure about Malcolm Page, though.'

'I disagree,' remarked Watson. 'I think Malcolm Page is actually a more likely candidate. He had easy access to the drug, he knew all three of our murder victims and he's not got an alibi for any of the three murders either.'

'But did either Henderson or Page know Rachel's mobile number?' Cooper asked. 'Whoever sent the text to Rachel on Vicky's mobile must have been one of the people who Rachel interviewed and who had her card.'

'If so, that would certainly rule both Henderson and Page

out,' Rachel conceded. 'I've never given either of them my mobile number.'

'Let's stick with Romney and Charles for now,' announced Carmichael, who could not see any value in continuing this line of conversation. 'Both Lou Henderson and Malcolm Page need to be considered, too, but let's focus on the two gentlemen we have downstairs for the moment. Do we all agree?'

'Agreed,' replied Cooper without hesitation, his assent being acknowledged positively by his two colleagues who, like a pair of toy dogs on the back seat of a car, jointly nodded their compliance.

'OK,' continued Carmichael, checking the time on his wrist watch. 'Let's leave it there, get downstairs and have a few strong words with our two detainee vets and reconvene back here at five fifteen. Hopefully we'll know more by then.'

Chapter 42

'So, can I have a dog?' Natalie asked Penny, for what seemed like the thousandth time in the last few months.

'I don't know,' replied Penny exhaustedly.

'Do you think there's a chance?' exclaimed Natalie, seeing the change from a straight 'no' – the answer she'd received consistently in the past – to 'I don't know' as being a significant shift in her mother's standpoint on this most important issue.

'Your dad's not keen on us having a dog,' Penny expanded. 'You know that.'

'But if it was up to you, would you let me have one?'

Penny could see where this was all leading: she'd been there countless times over the years with her three offspring and she was too smart to allow her youngest to trap her so easily.

'I'll talk to your father again,' she said in a tone that shouted out loud and clear that she was about to cut short the debate. 'But don't build your hopes up, Natalie, I'm sure he'll say no.'

* * * *

Carmichael was looking forward to meeting Adam Charles and, although his instinct was telling him the vet being interviewed by Rachel Dalton and Cooper in the small room a few doors down the corridor was the most likely candidate as their killer, he decided to adopt an aggressive style from the outset.

'Good afternoon, Mr Charles,' he said as soon as Watson had completed the necessary introductions for the purpose of the recording. 'You are here because we have already established that you have links with three people who have been murdered; namely, Aiden Davidson, Joan Henderson and Vicky Page.' As he spoke, Carmichael fixed his stare straight at the uncomfortable-looking young man. He didn't want to miss any slight movement or gesture that might give away his guilt or suggest he was being anything less than truthful. 'Do you understand?'

Adam Charles sat forward in his chair, his arms resting on the table in front of him. 'I understand completely,' he replied, his voice trembling a little as he spoke. 'But I'm not your killer, Mr Carmichael.'

'I'm told that you've said in previous interviews you didn't know Aiden Davidson,' continued Carmichael, his eyes never flinching from scrutinising Charles's every movement. 'Would you like to reconsider that statement? And while you do, please also consider that to mislead us in our investigations is a serious offence.'

Adam Charles edged back a little in his chair. 'I don't need to reconsider,' he replied forthrightly. 'I have never met Aiden Davidson. I'm certain.'

'OK,' remarked Carmichael. 'Tell me about your relationship with Vicky Page?'

'I knew her from when she worked at Park Road, we were colleagues and good friends,' replied Charles without any hesitation.

'Were you having, or did you ever have, a romantic relationship with Vicky?' enquired Carmichael, his question delivered within a second of Charles having answered his last.

'No,' replied Charles who, as he spoke, moved his body

241

even further away from Carmichael. 'We were just work colleagues.'

'But you fancied her though, didn't you?' continued Carmichael, who was keen to keep the questions coming thick and fast.

Adam Charles shuffled uneasily in his chair and dragged his fingers nervously through his hair. 'When she worked at Park Road I did invite her out on a date a couple of times,' he admitted, his cheeks reddening slightly as he spoke. 'But she made it clear she wasn't interested and that was that.'

Carmichael turned his head to face Watson. 'Unrequited love, Sergeant,' he remarked with a hint of sarcasm in his voice. 'How many cases have you investigated where unrequited love was the motive?'

Watson shook his head gently from side to side before he answered. 'Dozens,' he replied.

'No way,' shouted Charles. 'I asked her out twice, she said no and that was that. Don't start making out there's anything more in it than that.'

'Do you have a partner at the moment?' continued Carmichael.

'What's that got to do with anything?'

'Please answer the question,' Carmichael insisted.

'No, I don't,' snapped Charles. 'What does that prove?'

'So, when you were trying to get Vicky to go out with you,' continued Carmichael, 'was Vicky dating anyone else, to your knowledge?'

Adam Charles took this as a good opportunity to pause and catch his breath. 'Not that I was aware of when we were working together, but I know Dennis kept asking her out, too.'

'Dennis!' repeated Carmichael. 'Who's Dennis?'

'Dennis Preston,' replied Charles. 'He works for the RSPCA.'

* * * *

Rachel and Cooper waited silently as Harvey Romney and his solicitor whispered to each other at the back of the room. Having shared with Romney the salient points of his meeting with Alma Stone, Cooper had advised Romney of his rights and placed him under arrest. The two officers had then put it to Romney that Aiden Davidson and possibly Joan Henderson were also involved in the fraud and that he had killed both of them. And that he had murdered Vicky Page who, unfortunately for her, had been at Joan's house when he killed Joan.

After almost fifteen minutes, an ashen-faced Romney and his solicitor resumed their places behind the desk opposite Cooper and Dalton.

'My client is willing to amend his previous statement,' announced Romney's solicitor in a tone that suggested he was doing the police officers a huge favour. 'He is prepared to admit some involvement in Aiden Davidson's business activities. However, his involvement was minimal and, as such, we require some assurances from you regarding the extent of the charges you intend to pursue. Furthermore, my client requires you to drop all these ridiculous allegations regarding his involvement in the three murders and for you to assure him that he will no longer be harassed by the police.'

The two officers exchanged a long silent look before Cooper responded.

'I think we should be very clear here,' he remarked calmly. 'We have evidence that identifies your client as much more than a bit player in the fraud. He has already made false statements to us and, in so doing, could face additional serious charges. My suggestion is that you encourage your client to start telling us the truth. As soon as he has, we'll decide what charges he needs to answer, but there will be no deals.'

243

'In that case, I'd like to request some time alone with my client,' replied the solicitor.

Cooper nodded, switched off the recording device and rose slowly up from the table. 'I'll give you an hour,' he remarked before signalling to Rachel to follow him out of the interview room.

'I think he's rattled,' remarked Rachel as soon as they were alone in the corridor. 'He's never going to admit to the murders, but I reckon he'll at last come clean on the fraud.'

Cooper smiled. 'I think you may be right.'

Then, pointing down the corridor, Cooper suggested they spend the next sixty minutes listening to Carmichael's interview with Adam Charles while they waited for Romney and his brief to decide how they would proceed.

* * * *

Carmichael had continued to fire question after question at Adam Charles at a relentless pace. As Rachel Dalton and Cooper took up their seats behind the two-way mirror, they were just in time to hear him précis, to the now very agitated vet, the main points that had come out of their discussions so far.

'To summarise what we've established so far,' Carmichael said in a calm and precise tone, 'you have no corroborated alibi for the time of the murder of Aiden Davidson or for the murders of Joan Henderson and Vicky Page. You knew both Joan and Vicky very well, you admit to having had a desire to become romantically involved with Vicky, but she turned you down, and you had easy access to Etorphine, the drug that was used in all three killings. Is there anything so far that I've said that's incorrect?'

Adam Charles shook his head. 'All of what you say is true,' he confirmed, 'but that does not make me a murderer.'

Carmichael maintained his steely stare, but nodded slightly as if to concede his point.

'Tell me about Joan Henderson,' Carmichael said. 'What sort of woman was she?'

Charles considered the question for a few seconds before responding.

'She was a first-class vet,' replied Charles. 'I learned a great deal from her. She was committed to her work and the practice was her life.'

Carmichael frowned as if he was surprised by the answer. 'What about outside work?' he asked. 'Her marriage, was that a solid one in your view?'

It was now Adam Charles's turn to show signs of astonishment. 'I've no idea,' he replied abruptly. 'I think I only met her husband on one or two occasions and she never really spoke about her life outside the practice.'

'Really?' interrupted Watson. 'Are you saying that in the whole time you worked with her she never talked about anything other than work?'

Adam Charles nodded. 'It does seem weird, I suppose,' he admitted, 'and up until now I hadn't really thought about it but, actually, I've no idea what she got up to outside of work.'

As Carmichael and Watson exchanged a less than convinced look, there was a knock on the door and WPC Berry entered the room.

'Sorry to disturb you, sir,' WPC Berry said quietly as she approached Carmichael's chair. 'I've those statements you asked for.'

'Thank you, Constable,' replied Carmichael, who took the three documents and placed them face down on the table in front of him. 'So what about Vicky Page?'

'Other than you fancied her,' added Watson.

'She was a laugh,' replied Charles. 'I make no secret about the fact I really liked her, but I wasn't the only one.'

'Yes, tell me more about her and Dennis Preston,' Carmichael asked.

From behind the two-way mirror Rachel Dalton's attention

became all the more acute. Despite having absolutely no intention of acquiescing to Dennis Preston's continual advances, she did find him attractive and had found his persistence annoying but, at the same time, flattering. So, although the news that he'd also had eyes for Vicky came as no great shock, Rachel could not help feel a little irked to discover that she was not the only object of his affections.

Adam Charles shrugged his shoulders. 'All I know is that Dennis was really keen on her,' he replied dismissively. 'He bombarded her with text messages and sent her flowers, but she wasn't in the slightest bit interested. I'm not sure if he continued to keep asking her out once she'd left to work at Trinity, but knowing Dennis I expect he did. He's not one for being put off that easily.'

For the first time since the interview had started, Carmichael averted his gaze from Adam Charles as he considered his next move. Then, to the surprise of both Adam Charles and Watson, Carmichael stood up and grabbed hold of the three statements WPC Berry had brought in a few minutes earlier. 'That will be all,' he said, his persona now much more relaxed. 'Thank you for your time, Mr Charles. You're free to go.'

Without waiting for Adam Charles to reply, Carmichael headed out of the interview room and down the corridor, closely followed by Sergeant Watson.

'Why are you releasing him?' Watson asked in amazement as they marched quickly down the passageway.

'He's not our man, Marc,' replied Carmichael decisively. 'I'm certain. He's just someone who knew two of the victims, with uncorroborated alibis and access to Etorphine. He's no guiltier than you or I.'

'Do you think it's Romney?'

'I'm not sure. But we need to consider Dennis Preston now, too. He's popping up too frequently for my liking.'

As soon as he spotted the rest of his team walking swiftly

behind them, Carmichael slowed down to allow them to catch up.

'What's Romney saying?'

'We've given him an hour to talk some more to his solicitor,' replied Cooper. 'So for the last ten minutes we've been listening to your interview with Adam Charles.'

'He's not involved. However, the interview was really useful.'

'Why do you say that?' Rachel asked.

'It highlighted firstly that we know absolutely nothing about the private lives of Joan Henderson and Vicky Page,' Carmichael remarked, 'which we need to address as a matter of priority.'

'And secondly?' enquired Cooper.

'Secondly, we need to find out more about this RSPCA man,' added Carmichael. 'His appearance all over the place is too much of a coincidence for my liking.'

'So what's the plan?' Cooper asked.

Carmichael looked at his watch and thought for a moment. 'How much have Romney and his brief still got left out of their hour?'.

'About forty minutes,' replied Cooper.

'OK, this is what we do ...'

Chapter 43

Carmichael sat alone behind the glass of the two-way mirror as Cooper and Watson entered Interview Room 1 to finish the interrogation of Harvey Romney.

Given that it was her day off, that she had got precious little sleep the night before, and that she had an important assignment later that evening, Carmichael had told Rachel to get herself home, and had asked Watson to accompany Cooper for the completion of the interview.

As the two officers settled themselves down and ensured the recording equipment was functioning correctly, Carmichael quickly texted Penny:

Hi have booked a table at The Fisheries for 8:30 tonight. See you later XXX

Having sent the message, Carmichael started to scan through Siobhan Ballentyne's latest statement, one of the three documents WPC Berry had handed him previously.

'So, Mr Romney,' began Cooper. 'Have you finally decided to tell us the truth?'

Romney's brief nodded gently to his client as a signal for him to reply.

Harvey Romney, who looked decidedly nervous, cleared his throat. 'I'm willing to admit my involvement in Aiden's forged passport scam,' he said. 'However, I refute completely any involvement in any of the murders. I will cooperate fully with you with regards to the forgeries, but I have absolutely nothing to tell you about the three murders you're investigating.'

'OK,' replied Cooper. 'Tell me about the forgery scam with Davidson.'

Romney glanced over towards his solicitor who, for a second time in a matter of minutes, nodded knowingly in his client's direction.

On the opposite side of the two-way mirror Carmichael looked at his watch. He decided that he would wait a further thirty minutes to hear what information Cooper and Watson could glean out of Romney and, while he was doing that, he'd continue to read Siobhan Ballentyne, Betty Wilbraham and Pauline Squires statements in a little more detail.

Harvey Romney spent the next twenty minutes meticulously outlining his part in the forgery racket. Although he maintained stoutly that his own role was minor, he was not afraid to implicate others who had been involved, including, to Carmichael's amazement, his ex-fiancée Sarah Page.

'Vicky's sister was the contact on the Continent?!' Cooper queried.

'Yes,' replied Romney. 'She's the person who was really driving this.'

'But I thought she'd broken off your engagement to her just days before your wedding,' added Cooper, with a degree of confusion in his voice. 'How come you're still business partners?'

'I called off the wedding because she was so controlling,' replied Romney. 'But when she contacted me about this little scam with Aiden, it seemed just too good an opportunity to turn down. Anyway we didn't have to meet: she was in Holland and I was here. We didn't even need to hand over any cash to each other as she took her cut in Amsterdam, direct from the client, and I took the second payment here, which included Aiden's cut.'

'What about Vicky Page?' enquired Cooper. 'Was she involved?'

'Not directly. To my knowledge she wasn't aware of what was going on, but when this all started I promised Sarah that I'd find Vicky a job at my practice on a ridiculously high salary. Sarah called it my payment to her for being included in the scam.'

'And I bet having a pretty girl on the payroll wasn't going to be too much of a hardship for you either,' remarked Watson sarcastically.

'She wasn't interested in me,' replied Harvey, rather ruefully. 'I admit I did try, but she wasn't in the slightest bit interested.'

'She clearly had good taste,' Carmichael muttered to himself as he continued to listen to the interview in the room next door while also reading the other statements.

'You argued with Aiden on the day before he was killed,' continued Cooper. 'What was that all about?'

Romney's initial instinct was to deny having an argument, but another pointed look from his solicitor changed his mind.

'He wanted a bigger share of the money. He was already getting sixty per cent of the UK payment, so I wasn't having any of that.'

'But, according to you, Mr Romney, you didn't do anything,' said Watson. 'So I'm not sure what you did to deserve forty percent.'

The interview room fell quiet for about ten seconds while Cooper and Watson decided what to ask next.

'Tell me about Joan Henderson,' Cooper remarked. 'What sort of person was she?'

'Good question,' Carmichael mumbled to himself from behind the glass.

'She was an extremely good veterinary,' replied Romney. 'Exceptionally committed to her job and well respected within the region.'

Cooper nodded. 'What about outside of work? What sort of life did she lead?'

'I didn't know her that well. Our paths only really crossed at work. Outside of her being married to Lou, I don't know much more.'

'And was that a happy marriage?' enquired Watson.

'I'd say so. They were very different people: she was quite a reserved, private person and, if you've met Lou you'll know he's the gregarious type, always the centre of attention, always has something to say.'

'You almost sound as though you don't care for him much,' said Cooper.

'He's OK,' replied Romney offhandedly. 'I'm not a big fan of Yanks. They talk a good talk, but in my experience they're usually full of hot air.'

'Really? You've met quite a few then, have you?'

'Enough,' retorted Romney. 'Anyway, as I said, I don't dislike him; he's just not my cup of tea.'

'But what about Joan?' added Watson. 'Was *she* your cup of tea?'

'Actually, she was. I liked her a lot.'

'Tell me about that call you received from her on Wednesday evening,' Cooper asked. 'How did that go?'

'As I told Inspector Carmichael,' continued Romney, 'she sounded very concerned about the police calling on her that day and was very worried that she couldn't account for the missing Etorphine.'

'Did she mention anything about Davidson in that call?' Cooper enquired.

'No,' replied Romney without any hesitation. 'I'd have remembered if she had.'

'With him being your meal ticket, I guess you would,' remarked Watson caustically.

As he finished his sentence, Carmichael entered the room.

'For the purpose of the recording,' remarked Cooper in a

251

slow audible voice, 'Inspector Carmichael has just entered the interview room.'

Carmichael positioned himself behind Cooper and Watson but remained standing. 'I've got two questions. Firstly, to your knowledge, was there any relationship between Joan and Aiden Davidson?'

Romney screwed up his brow. 'Not that I was aware of,' he replied. 'I don't even know if they knew each other. I know Lou and Aiden drank together at The Drunken Duck, but I wasn't aware of Aiden and Joan having met. Why, do you think they were at it?'

'We don't know,' replied Carmichael. 'I just thought you might.'

'Well, I don't,' responded Romney abruptly. 'So what's the other question?'

Carmichael paused for a second before he continued.

'Tell me about the friendship between Vicky and Joan?' he asked.

'Vicky idolised her,' replied Romney. 'Joan was her role model. If I'm honest, I'm not sure what Joan got out of the relationship, given that Vicky could be a bit of a bubblehead at times, but they did seem to get on really well.'

Carmichael nodded slowly as he considered Romney's responses. 'I'll leave you to finish off here,' he remarked to his two officers, before heading off towards the exit.

'One last question,' he said as he reached the door. 'Why did Malcolm Page thump you the other day?'

Romney gave out a faint smile. 'Because the old fool thought that I'd killed her,' he replied with a frankness that surprised Carmichael. 'He was wrong, of course, but I guess in the circumstances we need to make some allowances for him. As I've already told your foot soldiers here, I may be guilty of making some cash from Aiden's forgery racket, but I'm no killer.'

Chapter 44

In spite of it being over fifteen miles from the sea and over forty miles away from a fishing port of any significance, The Fisheries in Newbridge was renowned as being one of the top-ten fish restaurants in the country. It was also Penny's favourite place to eat, so whenever Carmichael felt it necessary to get on the right side of his wife, he'd invariably book a table.

'I think I'll start with tiger prawn, fennel and olive salad,' Penny announced from behind the large menu. 'Then I'll have pan-fried steak of Loch Duart salmon, minted Jersey royals and hollandaise sauce.'

The waiter nodded as if to suggest he heartily approved of her selection. 'And for sir?' he enquired, turning his body by forty-five degrees to face his guest.

Carmichael had already closed his menu and placed it on the crisply ironed red-gingham tablecloth. 'I'll have whitebait and then I'll have the crab cakes.'

Penny smiled and tried hard to stifle her need to giggle. In the numerous times they'd eaten at The Fisheries, her husband had always started with whitebait and, on the odd occasion he hadn't chosen crab cakes, he'd only ever had haddock and chips.

'Would you care to see the wine list, sir?' the attentive waiter asked.

'No, that's not necessary,' replied Carmichael, 'we'll have a bottle of –

'How about an Argentine Viognier?' suggested Penny

before her husband had the chance to say Chardonnay.

'An excellent choice,' remarked the waiter, who looked expectantly at Carmichael to receive his blessing on the selection.

After exchanging a quick glance across at his wife, Carmichael looked up at the waiter. 'The Argentine Viognier it is then.'

Having taken their order, the waiter sauntered away, leaving the Carmichaels alone at their cosy corner table.

'So how was your day?' Carmichael enquired.

'Oh, the usual,' replied Penny rather offhandedly. 'It started off as chaotic as normal, what with ferrying Natalie to the stables and trying to galvanise the other two into some form of useful activity, but as usual, once I admitted failure with Jemma and Robbie, and after about three cups of coffee, it improved significantly.'

Carmichael smiled. 'Don't worry: they'll both be at university in a few weeks' time, then it will be just the three of us.'

'It might be four,' Penny responded just as the waiter reappeared with a bottle of Argentine Viognier in his hand. 'Would you care to taste the wine, sir?' he asked, as if it was obligatory.

'Er, no, just pour,' replied Carmichael, whose bemused expression brought a wry smile to Penny's face.

The waiter slowly poured each of them a large glass of wine, placed the now half-empty bottle into the wine cooler by the table and made a discreet exit.

'Four,' remarked Carmichael in a loud whisper. 'What do you mean?'

Penny didn't reply. Her attention had been diverted away from her husband towards the door of the restaurant, where a young couple had just entered. 'Isn't that Rachel?' she enquired, nodding surreptitiously in the general direction of the duo she had observed.

Carmichael half-turned in his chair to see what his wife was talking about, although in truth he was well aware of Rachel having made a booking for that evening, given that it was his idea.

'Yes, it is,' he replied, turning back to face his wife.

Penny realised immediately that this was no coincidence. 'What are you up to?' she enquired as she picked up her glass. 'Please don't tell me this has something to do with your murder enquiry.'

'I just thought I'd kill two birds with one stone,' replied Carmichael, his tone of voice giving not the slightest hint of any remorse. 'I've instructed the restaurant to place them at the other end of the room, so it won't interfere with our evening.'

'So, I'm a bird you need to kill, am I?' enquired Penny who, despite being slightly miffed, was nevertheless a little amused by the clumsy plot, but more importantly saw it as a possible bargaining opportunity. 'Anyway, who's the handsome young man she's with?'

'That's a man called Dennis Preston,' replied Carmichael. 'He's someone we want to talk to about the murders and it sort of made sense to do it this way.'

Penny shook her head to demonstrate her misgivings about the whole scenario. 'Do you normally get your team to date your suspects?'

'Only Rachel,' replied Carmichael with a large grin. 'You couldn't imagine anyone seriously wanting to have a dinner date with either of the other two, could you?'

'Fair comment,' replied Penny. 'Although I suspect Susan Watson might disagree.'

It was at that point that the waiter returned to the table with two large plates and placed their starters carefully in front of them.

'*Bon appétit,*' he said, before slipping away once again.

* * * *

Although she'd had some reservations about Carmichael's plan, Rachel had agreed almost immediately when he'd asked her to reply to Dennis Preston's next text message with a suggestion that they meet that evening for dinner. His assurances that he'd be on hand in case anything untoward happened were well received by Rachel, but in truth she was not overly concerned about her own safety. She felt totally able to look after herself.

So, when twenty minutes later she received her next text from the RSPCA man, she quickly texted back and suggested they meet outside The Fisheries at 8:45 that evening, knowing full well that Carmichael would already be inside.

As per the plan, Rachel and Dennis Preston were shown to a table at the far end of the restaurant from where Carmichael and Penny were sitting and, as they had agreed, Rachel made sure she was seated facing into the room.

'I've never been here before,' remarked Preston as he took his seat. 'It looks nice.'

'It's my first time here, too,' replied Rachel. 'My boss comes here a lot with his wife and has told me how good it is, so I thought it would be a great place to meet.'

'What made you change your mind?' Preston asked. 'When you called yesterday you sounded pretty adamant that you weren't interested.'

'Don't build your hopes up,' replied Rachel. 'I'm not, but I figured you'd keep texting me, so I thought if we went out once and you got to know me a little better, then maybe you wouldn't be so keen.'

'I see, you're doing this for my benefit,' Preston remarked with a grin.

'Well, yes,' replied Rachel. 'Of course I get a free meal out of it too, but I'm hoping after tonight you'll be less interested in me and will concentrate more on the other ladies in your life.'

Preston laughed. 'What other ladies?'

Rachel smiled. 'I'm a police officer,' she said. 'We know things.'

Preston shook his head as if to suggest she was mad.

'Anyway,' continued Rachel, 'how did you get my mobile number in the first place?'

Preston grinned. 'You dropped a business card in my van the other day when I gave you a lift. At least I think it was dropped, although I wouldn't be surprised if you deliberately left it for me to find.'

'Be assured it was dropped by accident,' replied Rachel curtly.

As she finished her sentence, the waiter arrived and handed them their menus.

'Would you like any drinks?' he enquired.

* * * *

'I can't believe you'd force poor Rachel into having a dinner date with a prime suspect, on her day off, after she's spent the whole of last night at the hospital with hardly any sleep,' remarked Penny as she tucked into her tiger prawns.

For the life of him, Carmichael couldn't see why his wife was making such a fuss. 'She's fine,' he replied, turning around in his chair to try and catch a glimpse of the couple at the other end of the restaurant. 'Besides, he's not really a suspect as such, just someone who keeps popping up in the case all the time.'

Penny shook her head in a disapproving manner.

'Anyway, what did you mean before about there being four of us when the kids go back to uni?' Carmichael added.

'You, me, Natalie,' replied Penny, 'and a dog.'

257

'No way,' replied Carmichael, who almost choked on a piece of whitebait as he spoke. 'Absolutely no way.'

Penny shook her head and nonchalantly passed him his glass of water. 'Natalie's desperate for one,' she remarked. 'And, to be honest, I'd like one, too.'

'What!' exclaimed Carmichael, taking a large swig of water. 'But who'll train it, and feed it, and take it for walks twenty times a day?'

'Well, it certainly won't be you,' replied Penny curtly. 'We all know that. And they get walked about twice a day, that's all.'

Carmichael was staggered by what he was hearing, but felt that with asking Penny to go to Siobhan Ballentyne's Vixens evening and with arranging for Rachel to come to the restaurant with Preston, it probably wouldn't be wise for him to be too forthright in his objection at that particular moment.

'It's been a long day,' he remarked diplomatically. 'Let's discuss it tomorrow, when we're at home.'

'Is that a yes?' Penny retorted with a mischievous smile, remembering how Natalie had made a similar remark to her earlier that day.

'No,' replied Carmichael firmly. 'It's not even a maybe.'

* * * *

'Have you arrested anyone yet for the all these murders?' Preston asked as he took a sip from his glass of Diet Coke.

'I can't talk about the case, I'm afraid,' replied Rachel coolly.

'I understand. I was just curious.'

Rachel took a sip from her glass. 'I guess you knew all three of the victims,' she remarked as calmly as she could.

'I knew Joan Henderson and Vicky Page. I didn't know the

other guy. I'd seen him of course a few times when I'd been round at Betty's, but I'd never spoken to him.'

'I heard you'd …' Rachel paused for a second as she tried to choose the right words. '… been interested in Vicky.'

'Interested?' repeated Preston. 'Who on earth told you that?'

'As I said before, we get to know things. Was it true?'

Preston, for the first time that evening, looked a little ruffled. 'I did ask her out a few times,' he conceded. 'But that was ages ago. She was a nice-looking girl,' he added as if to justify his interest.

'And did she say yes?'

'No,' replied Preston, his tone firm as if to make his reply crystal clear. 'In fact, I don't want to speak ill of the dead, but I don't think she was interested in men, if you get my drift.'

'Are you saying she was a lesbian?'

Preston moved back a little in his chair. 'I'm not certain,' he backtracked. 'But I had my doubts.'

Rachel smiled. 'I get it – any woman who doesn't succumb to your advances is a lesbian.'

'That's not what I said. I just thought she was generally uninterested in men.'

Rachel nodded knowingly. 'What about Joan?'

'Joan was great. She was a fantastic vet and a really nice person, too.'

'How well did you know her?'

'Good God, what is this? Am I being interrogated?'

Rachel took a sip from her glass and smiled. 'That's what it's like when you have dinner with a police officer. We're *always* on duty.'

* * * *

'Rachel and her handsome partner seem to be getting on like a house on fire,' Penny remarked.

'Good,' replied Carmichael. 'Just as long as she's not enjoying herself too much and she remembers to find out what involvement he has with the murders, I don't care.'

'I suspect she's achieving both,' replied Penny with a sardonic grin. 'Anyway, you've not told me how the case is going. Did you make any progress today?'

'Good question. We now know that Aiden Davidson and Harvey Romney were involved in the forgery. And if Romney is to be believed, Malcolm Page's other daughter, Sarah, was also involved.'

'Really!' exclaimed Penny. 'What about Vicky? Was she part of the gang?'

'She may have been. But probably not.'

Penny cut into a new potato with her knife. 'But what about the four murders?'

'We now know that they're not all linked. The first was a hit-and-run accident committed by Pauline Squires. Whoever our killer is deliberately used the time of Damien Wilbraham's death to try and cover his tracks.'

Penny stabbed the half potato with her fork. 'So, who's in the frame?' she asked with a hint of mischievousness in her voice.

Carmichael inhaled heavily through his nostrils. '*I don't know* is the honest answer. However, I suspect it's either Romney, Rachel's young man over there, or it could be someone close to either Vicky or Joan.'

'Like the husband?' suggested Penny.

'Maybe,' replied Carmichael half-heartedly. 'But if it was Lou Henderson, I don't have a motive for him. If he killed his wife and Vicky, he'd have spent the whole night driving from York to his house then back to York. It's possible, I suppose, but unlikely. Then there's the motive. Why would he kill his wife? Also, he says he'd never met Vicky, so why kill her? And why kill Davidson, too?'

Penny had almost finished eating the mouthful of new potato as her husband finished his last sentence. 'He surely could have got the drug. He must have gone to the practice occasionally. Maybe he took it while he was there seeing Joan.'

'But would he have known what drug to take?' asked Carmichael. 'He's not a vet – he sells life insurance.'

Penny shrugged her shoulders. 'Maybe it's your Mr Romney or the handsome RSPCA man,' she remarked. 'At least they'd both know about drugs. That's a certainty.'

*   *   *   *

The waiter deposited the two starters on Rachel and Preston's table.

'Tell me a little about yourself?' Rachel asked. 'I know absolutely nothing about you whatsoever.'

Dennis Preston smiled. 'There's not much to tell,' he replied rather diffidently. 'I'm thirty-two, I was born in Manchester but spent a large part of my childhood in Texas. My dad was in oil with BP and he got posted there. I've always liked animals and initially studied to be a vet but gave it up, travelled the world for a few years, then, about five years ago, came back to the UK became an RSPCA man and … well here I am.'

'Where are your folks now?'

'They split up about ten years ago. Dad's retired and living with a new partner, who's only a few years older than me, in Cheltenham. Mum lives with me on the other side of Kirkwood.'

'You're still living with Mum? Don't you find that weird?'

Preston seemed offended at the question. 'No, I don't,' he snapped angrily. 'My mother's had a hard time; she needs me.'

Rachel could see she'd hit a raw nerve. 'I'm sorry. It's that nosey police thing again. It's in our DNA.'

This seemed to placate Preston, who took a large mouthful of the crab cake he had ordered.

* * * *

It was almost midnight by the time Rachel and Preston finished their meal and the bill had been paid.

'Can I give you a lift home?' Preston enquired.

Rachel shook her head. 'Er, no, it's fine. My car is out the back, so I'm OK thanks.'

'Well, can I walk you to your car?'

'Actually, I need to visit the ladies',' Rachel said. 'Why don't you go? I'll be fine.'

'OK,' replied Preston who looked a little crestfallen by Rachel's apparent rebuff. 'Will I see you again?'

Rachel had been dreading this question. 'We'll see,' she replied vaguely before planting a rather platonic kiss on his cheek. 'I'll call you.'

With that, Rachel headed toward the rear of the restaurant where the toilets were situated.

'Goodnight, Rachel,' Preston said as she was a few steps from the door of the ladies' toilet.

He then turned as if to leave, but suddenly stopped and turned back to face where Carmichael and Penny were still sitting.

'And goodnight to you, too, Inspector Carmichael,' he shouted. 'I hope you had a nice meal. It's wonderful here, isn't it?'

As Carmichael half turned in his seat, he caught sight of the smug grin on Dennis Preston's face, before the RSPCA man turned once more and departed.

'What now, Columbo?' enquired Penny with an expression that said 'I told you so' written across her face.

Chapter 45

Carmichael couldn't sleep. It was one o'clock and in the half-gloom of his attic study, he sat alone in his comfortable armchair. His left hand gently caressed a glass of whisky while he jotted random notes on his desk pad to reflect the haphazard thoughts that were racing around inside his weary head.

After Dennis Preston had departed, Penny and he had spent a further twenty minutes listening to Rachel's detailed account of her conversation with the RSPCA man.

Rachel's conclusion was totally in line with Carmichael's, namely that Preston was an 'odd fish' but unlikely to be a serious suspect for the murders. However, unlike Rachel, Carmichael thought Preston's comments about Vicky's sexuality needed to be taken seriously. After all, she was an attractive woman, seemed not to have a partner, was clearly uninterested in any of the advances made by Adam Charles, Harvey Romney or Dennis Preston, and Carmichael still couldn't work out her relationship with Joan Henderson. Even though SOCO had been sure they had not slept in the same bed the night they were murdered, maybe there was something going on between them, he thought. After considering this theory for a few moments, with no real conclusion, he pushed these thoughts to the pending file at the back of his head.

Carmichael took out a neatly folded A4 sheet of paper from his desk drawer. He opened it up and read the transcripts of the text sent to Norfolk George and those received by Rachel.

He then started to think of the key facts that he and his team had established, which he hoped would focus his attention. To help him, he scribbled them down on the jotter in as organised a list as he could muster. Given his tiredness, and the numbing effect of the wine he'd consumed at the restaurant, combined with the whisky he'd already polished off since arriving home, his list was surprisingly short, just four things:

1 *Killer knew the time of Damien's death was 7:37 a.m.*
2 *He had to have had a cast-iron alibi for the time Damien was killed.*
3 *He had to have access to Etorphine (probably from the Park Road Practice) and know how to use it.*
4 *He had to know Rachel's mobile number.*

Having established these four factors, Carmichael then started to scribble down, this time in a more random fashion, other points that were as yet unanswered but that were significant to the enquiry:

What was the motive?
Why did the killer keep sending texts about his killings and his plans for further murders?
Why did he taunt the police?
What did Aiden, Joan and Vicky have in common?
Where are Vicky's possessions, particularly her mobile?
Were Vicky and Joan lovers?
Is the forgery linked to the deaths?

Carmichael's final list was his five prime suspects, which he listed in order of his gut feeling of their respective probabilities:

1 *Harvey Romney*
2 *Adam Charles*
3 *Dennis Preston*
4 *Lou Henderson*
5 *Malcolm Page*

Carmichael stared at the transcript of the texts and at his three lists for almost thirty minutes. He was sure that within the eleven short sentences and five names he had all the answers, but for the life of him he couldn't work out what it was he was missing. Carmichael drained the contents of his glass in one deep long swallow and, with a sense of frustration and disillusionment, decided to call it a night.

He folded up the jottings he had made, placed them into the desk drawer with the transcripts, and was halfway to the door when it came to him.

'Of course,' he muttered out loud. 'What a fool – it's so bloody obvious.'

Despite it now being very early in the morning, Carmichael didn't hesitate in picking up the phone. During the next thirty minutes he succeeded in waking up four people with four separate, important local calls and, as he was talking, he took out the paper from his desk drawer, carefully unfolded it and boldly underlined one of the five names with two thick lines of black ink.

Chapter 46

Penny was a sound sleeper at the best of times, but that night she was so exhausted that she neither heard her husband getting into bed, nor heard him getting up a little over five hours later. It was only the sound of his car's wheels spinning on their gravel path at 7:00 a.m. that caused Penny to stir. By the time she'd gained full consciousness, her husband, brimming with excitement, was already well on the way to apprehend his assassin.

*　*　*　*

When Watson had received the phone call so early that morning he couldn't believe what he was being asked to do at such an ungodly hour, but he did as he was ordered and, by the time Carmichael arrived, he was already waiting. Little did he realise it was Cooper who had been given the most arduous assignment and one that had taken him almost five hours to complete. It was only when Cooper told him about it, some five minutes before Carmichael's car came swiftly down the long gravel drive of the Lindley Hotel, that Watson appreciated that, in the scheme of things, organising a team of police frogmen at short notice was by no means the short straw.

'I hope his flash of inspiration is right,' remarked Watson before Carmichael got within earshot. 'Otherwise Henderson will make his life absolute hell.'

Having had no more than three hours' sleep and having already driven almost 250 miles that morning, Cooper, for once, shared his cynical colleague's scorn.

'Don't even go there, Marc,' he muttered out of the side of his mouth as the jubilant Carmichael bounded excitedly towards them. 'If he's wrong, given the way I'm feeling right now, I might beat Henderson to it.'

* * * *

Rachel Dalton and the two uniformed officers assigned to her by Carmichael let themselves into Lou Henderson's house through the front door.

'OK,' she said in an authoritative voice. 'Let's go through every cupboard and every drawer. Carmichael specifically told me we have to find anything that will help us pinpoint the motive for these killings. You two look down here. I'll look upstairs.'

Rachel left the two officers and headed up the staircase to search for evidence.

She had only just reached the first-floor landing when she was called by one of the PCs.

'Is this the sort of thing we're looking for?' he shouted up to her, waving a large sealed envelope with the words 'FOR THE ATTENTION OF INSPECTOR CARMICHAEL' marked across the front in bold black ink.

Rachel walked slowly down the stairs and took hold of the envelope. 'I'm not sure,' she replied. 'But I'm certain it's not a love letter.'

* * * *

'It says here that he checked out last night at about seven thirty,' the male receptionist at the Lindley Hotel confirmed, after scrutinising the information on his screen.

Carmichael rolled his eyes skyward and puffed out his cheeks. 'Has his room been cleaned yet?'

The receptionist shook his head. 'I doubt it. The maids don't start their duties until eight, so it should be as he left it.'

'Can we have a key, please?' Carmichael asked. 'We need to look inside.'

The receptionist took a plastic card from the drawer below the desk, placed it into a small electronic gadget at the side of his station and then handed it over to Carmichael.

'It's room 27,' he said. 'It's on the first floor.'

As he took the key from the receptionist's hand, Carmichael's mobile started to ring.

'It's Rachel,' he remarked as he saw her name appear on the tiny screen on his phone. 'You and Marc go up and have a look,' he instructed as he handed the key card to Cooper. 'I'll be up shortly.'

'What about the frogmen?' Watson enquired.

Carmichael held his hand up to indicate that he wanted Watson to wait while he answered Rachel's call.

'Can you just give me a minute,' he said down the phone to Rachel.

He then looked up at the receptionist. 'Have you been on reception every morning this week?'

The confused receptionist nodded. 'Yes, I've been on mornings since Monday.'

'When we came here the other day, Mr Henderson was out on his morning run,' added Carmichael. 'Do you remember?'

The receptionist nodded. 'Yes, that was Friday morning.'

'As I recall,' said Watson with a smirk on his face, 'I didn't get the impression Lou was much of a runner either. He looked completely out of condition.'

Carmichael smiled. 'Then the question is why on earth did he go out running that morning? I'm not a jogger, but if my wife was missing I can't see me going for an early-morning run.'

Cooper and Watson remained silent and the look on their faces indicated that they were still perplexed.

Carmichael felt a warm smug feeling. 'It was when he was out running that Rachel received the last text from our killer sent on Vicky Page's mobile,' he announced in a slow deliberate manner. 'My guess is it was Lou Henderson who sent that text and I'll also wager that he dumped Vicky's phone somewhere out there.'

'You think it will be in the lake behind the hotel,' Watson remarked, having at last twigged why his boss had called him so ridiculously early that morning to draft in the police divers.

'I'm sure of it, Marc.'

Carmichael prolonged the conversation no further. He waved them off in the direction of room 27 and placed the mobile phone back to his ear.

'Sorry, Rachel,' he said. 'What have you found?'

* * * *

Penny had just got out of the shower when the doorbell rang.

'Who the hell can that be so early on a Sunday morning,' she muttered to herself.

She quickly threw on a pair of jogging bottoms and one of her husband's worn old sweatshirts and headed downstairs.

'Oh, it's you,' she remarked, her shock evident in her words and surprised expression. 'What do you want?'

Dennis Preston, dressed in his smart blue uniform, smiled down at her. 'Good morning, Mrs Carmichael,' he replied confidently. 'Did you enjoy your meal last night?'

Chapter 47

'Do you want me to open it?' Rachel asked.

'Yes,' replied Carmichael who sounded as if he'd just been asked the most ridiculous question in the world.

He walked down the corridor to make sure he was well out of hearing and, when he was confident that he was suitably alone, leaned against a cold marble pillar as the young DC opened up the envelope.

Rachel pulled out several items from inside the envelope. The first item Rachel glanced at was a handwritten note addressed to Inspector Carmichael. By the scrawled signature at the foot of the note, Rachel judged this to have been written by Lou Henderson. Her fingers then gently extracted two one-way aeroplane tickets dated Friday 18th July for a flight from Manchester Airport to Cape Town in South Africa. The tickets were made out to Mr Aiden Blandford and Mrs Joan Blandford and were accompanied by a British passport in the name of Joan Blandford. Instinctively, Rachel opened up the passport to look at the photograph, which was of Joan Henderson. Rachel peered into the envelope and saw one item still left inside. It was a photograph which had become lodged in the corner. With her right hand, Rachel tipped the envelope upside down and caught the photograph face down in her left hand. On the back of it someone had written 'my beautiful Joan'.

Rachel turned the photograph over to reveal a black-and-white photograph of a naked woman sat provocatively on a large armchair. Rachel immediately recognised the chair as being the one that they'd found on the raised platform in Davidson's studio and the naked woman was Joan Henderson.

'So,' remarked Carmichael expectantly from the other end of the line. 'What's in the envelope, Rachel?'

Rachel carefully, and in great detail, described every item she'd extracted from the envelope.

'Read out what's in the letter,' he asked.

Rachel held open the handwritten note and started to read it to Carmichael:

Dear Carmichael

I have no idea whether you have already managed to work out why Joan and Davidson had to die; but, in case you have not, the contents of this envelope should answer any questions that you may still have.

I'm not sure if you are married, but I assume you are. If so, can you imagine what it must be like to discover that the woman you love and cherish more than anything else in the world has lied and deceived you? Can you imagine how you would feel if you discover that she has connived to change her identity and plans to fly off halfway around the world with a man you had thought to be your friend? THAT IS WHAT JOAN DID TO ME.

Had I not inadvertently found the airline tickets and fake passports, by now my seemingly upstanding, loyal and trustworthy wife would be in Cape Town with Davidson, leaving me alone, broke and a laughing stock with my friends, colleagues and family. I could not let that happen.

I am sorry to have misled you with the texts, my

reason for including the seven thirty-seven is, I'm sure, clear to you now - it was to buy me some time to successfully end three lives, but also be able to bury my wife before you found out the truth.

The tramp who was killed back in June was nothing to do with me. I just read about it in the local newspaper and, as I was in the US at the time, I knew I would not come under suspicion if I tried to link it to Joan's and Davidson's deaths.

My only regret is that I had to also kill Vicky Page. She was an innocent in all this and I swear I didn't know she was with Joan that night when I came home.

I set out to end three lives, and although I am now already responsible for three deaths, only two are lives that I planned to take. The third will be ended within the next few hours.
Lou Henderson

Carmichael thought for a few seconds.

'Is the letter dated?' he asked.

'No,' replied Rachel.

'My guess is that he wrote it last night,' remarked Carmichael. 'I suspect, after he checked out of here, he must have gone back home and left the package.'

'Where do you think he is now, sir?' enquired Rachel. 'And who is the other person he wants to kill?'

'I can't say for sure,' said Carmichael, 'but my guess is the third life Henderson's talking about is his own.'

'How do you think he'll do it?'

'If he follows the same pattern, it'll probably involve Etorphine.'

'But he used that up on Joan and Vicky,' Rachel reminded him. 'Remember, we found the empty bottle in the boot of the car with Joan's body.'

272

Carmichael thought for a moment. 'Well, if he needs more I can make a good stab at guessing where he'll get it,' he said slowly. 'Get yourself over to the Park Road Veterinary Practice. I'll meet you there in twenty minutes.'

As Carmichael ended the call he was joined by Cooper and Watson.

'There's nothing in his room, sir,' announced Cooper.

'Don't worry,' replied Carmichael. 'He's left a bunch of stuff, including a note confessing everything, at his house. Rachel's just read it out to me.'

'Where's Henderson now?' Watson asked.

'I think he's headed for his wife's practice,' replied Carmichael. 'You stay here, Marc, and supervise the search for Vicky's mobile,' Carmichael added as he started to head for the exit. 'Cooper, you come with me.'

Watson watched his two colleagues disappear before he headed out to join the search party at the lake behind the hotel.

Chapter 48

Rachael arrived at the Park Road Veterinary Practice at 9:50 a.m., just as the Sunday workforce started to arrive and began milling around at the rear of the building. She remained in her car for a few moments until she saw the familiar figure of Adam Charles pull up in his shiny red Mazda sports car. He was clearly the key holder, as once his car came to a standstill, the three nurses who had arrived before Charles picked up their bags and stood by the door.

Rachel would have preferred her boss to be with her before approaching the Park Road staff, but she didn't want to incur Carmichael's wrath by allowing the staff to enter the building and potentially contaminate any evidence.

'Mr Charles,' she shouted as she clambered out of the car. 'Can you just wait there for a moment, please.'

Adam Charles could not believe what he was seeing. 'What the hell do you want now?' he replied, the frustration palpable in his voice. 'Will you lot ever give me a break.'

The three veterinary nurses looked shocked, but said nothing.

'Please don't enter the building,' Rachel shouted as she quickly covered the twenty metres between her car and the back door of the practice. 'Inspector Carmichael will be here shortly,' she continued, her voice a little out of breath. 'You all need to remain outside until he arrives.'

'What's going on?' enquired one of the nurses, suddenly finding her voice.

Rachel put on a forced smile and at the same time shrugged her shoulders. 'I can't tell you any more, I'm afraid,' she continued. 'But you'll all have to wait here until Inspector Carmichael arrives.'

To Rachel's relief, no sooner had she finished her sentence than Carmichael's familiar black BMW made its grand entrance into the car park.

* * * *

Marc Watson sat alone on a small grassy bank and watched the police frogmen as they meticulously searched the lake at the back of the Lindley Hotel. At no stage in the enquiry had he seriously considered Henderson to be the killer. Harvey Romney and Adam Charles had always been far more likely candidates, even after they'd established that the first death wasn't linked.

His thoughts were a million miles away from the job in hand when his attention quickly shifted to the divers in the lake.

'Found it, Sergeant,' shouted one of the divers who had removed his goggles and was standing in the shallows with a small black object in his hand. 'We've got the mobile.'

'Bloody hell, that was quick,' replied Watson, who was swiftly up on his feet and hurried down the hill towards the lake.

* * * *

Cooper had spent the twenty-minute drive updating his boss on his assignment from earlier that morning. When he had taken Carmichael's call, Cooper had been in bed for no more than two hours but, as Carmichael had suspected, he'd not had any alcohol on Saturday evening and was therefore able to make the journey from Lou Henderson's house to the Marriott in York and back again.

As he explained to Carmichael, the traffic at that time of the morning was almost non-existent, so his times were probably quicker than Henderson would have managed. However, even taking that into consideration, it was clear to Cooper that, had he wanted, Henderson could easily have made the return journey well within the timescales between his last sighting at around eleven thirty on Wednesday evening and breakfast at around seven thirty on Thursday morning. He may have even managed a few hours' sleep.

'Unfortunately, they didn't have any security tapes at the hotel, so there's no evidence that he came home that evening,' announced Cooper.

'Thanks, Paul,' Carmichael replied as they came to a halt. 'I appreciate you giving up a full night's sleep. If we can wrap this up quickly, you can get yourself off home. Once we've located Henderson, the rest of us can take over.'

'I have to admit I'm struggling to keep awake at the moment,' admitted Cooper.

Carmichael smiled. 'Well, if I'm correct, I think we may find Lou Henderson in there. I'm not sure he'll be alive, though.'

The two officers clambered out of the car and walked over to where Rachel and the four veterinary workers were waiting.

'Has anyone entered the practice yet this morning?' Carmichael asked.

Rachel shook her head. 'No, I told everyone to wait until you had arrived.'

'Good. Let's take a look.'

He gestured to Adam Charles to open the door.

* * * *

Having successfully completed his assignment, Marc Watson decided to give the boss a call and tell him the good news. As he extracted his mobile from his pocket, a new text message came through. Watson hurriedly opened his inbox and read the text.

'Bugger,' he cursed out loud. 'Carmichael's not going to like this.'

* * * *

It took Carmichael and his team a matter of minutes to find the half-empty bottle of Etorphine. It had been placed on the table in the main operating theatre, on top of a small brown envelope.

Cooper pulled the envelope from under the bottle and, as it was addressed to Carmichael, handed it over to his superior.

Carmichael ripped open the envelope, extracted a folded sheet of notepaper from within and read it out aloud.

By the time you read this it will be over.

Carmichael threw the note down on the table and headed for the exit.

'He's leading us a merry dance again,' he remarked frustratedly as he and his fellow officers were once again outside in the car park. 'That devious bugger is playing games.'

As he tried to gather his thoughts, Carmichael's mobile began to ring.

'Hello,' he bellowed down the line.

'It's me, Marc,' replied a somewhat timid voice from the other end. 'We've located Vicky's phone. It was in the lake where you thought it would be, and I thought you should know I've just received a text from Lou Henderson's mobile.'

'Let me guess,' Carmichael replied. 'It told you he's ending it all.'

'I think that's what he means,' Watson replied. 'All it says is that it's all over now.'

Carmichael glanced down at his watch. It was 10:20 a.m.

'Get yourself back to the station, Marc,' he said, his irritation audible in his voice. 'We'll head back too and meet you there in twenty minutes.'

Chapter 49

The mood inside the incident room at Kirkwood station was one of hushed despondency.

Carmichael, Cooper and Watson sat motionless, each trying to fathom out what their next move should be. Rachel, on the other hand, was absorbed by something on her computer. Her eyes focused on the small screen as she tapped away furiously on the keyboard.

Eventually the silence was broken by Carmichael. 'I was certain we'd find him at the Park Road Practice,' he confessed forlornly. 'Where on earth can he be?'

'Given his track record,' remarked Cooper. 'Can we be sure this latest death he's talking about is his own?'

'I'm not so sure we can,' Carmichael acknowledged.

For a few seconds the room remained silent until Watson suddenly spoke.

'What was it that made you realise it was Lou Henderson who was our killer?'

Carmichael looked up at Watson from his desk. 'It took me a while, but once we knew the first death wasn't connected, Henderson had to be back in the frame,' he said slowly. 'I started to wonder what it was that had prevented us from considering him as a suspect before. After all, as Joan's husband, he had to be one of the first people we should have considered.'

Carmichael then extracted the jottings he'd made the previous evening from his jacket pocket and laid them on the table in front of him. 'It was the text messages that were confusing us,' he continued. 'If you ignore them and just look at the rest of the evidence, Henderson has to be a major suspect.'

Cooper nodded his head. 'You're right, sir. Without the texts, we'd never have been sidetracked by the seven thirty-seven or *Catch Me If You Can* business. It does make sense.'

'It does to a point,' remarked Watson. 'But how did Henderson know about the time of Damien Wilbraham's death being seven thirty-seven? And what about his alibi for the night Joan and Vicky died? He was also in York that evening.'

Carmichael shook his head gently. 'I called Norfolk George last night about the article he'd published regarding Damien Wilbraham's death,' he replied with a wry smile as he remembered how grouchy Norfolk George had been to receive a call in the small hours of that morning. 'He confirmed it had mentioned the time of death quite clearly. Henderson simply read it in the *Observer*. And as for Henderson's alibi on the night Joan and Vicky were killed. He could have easily made the round trip in just over four hours.'

'Two hours five minutes each way,' confirmed Cooper with precision in his voice. 'I should know – I drove it in the early hours this morning.'

'Even if it took him two hours to commit the murders, put Joan's body in the car and drive her car around the corner, he could easily have been back for breakfast at seven thirty-seven,' remarked Carmichael.

'But what I don't understand is why he moved his wife's body from the house and then texted himself saying that it was Joan rather than Vicky in his house?' Rachel enquired from behind her computer screen.

'Glad you're still with us,' remarked Carmichael sarcastically.

280

'I believe that was simply another attempt by Henderson to wrong-foot us. I do genuinely feel that Vicky was unlucky. She was just in the wrong place at the wrong time. But Henderson is a clever sod. All that confusion about the bodies was his doing to deliberately throw us off the scent.'

'Well, it fooled me,' admitted Watson. 'His performance at the morgue when it was Vicky, not Joan, we asked him to identify was very convincing.'

'But, hang on, what about the text message?' Rachel asked. 'How did he text himself from Joan's mobile?'

'That was easy,' replied Carmichael. 'He took it with him back to York. He simply set the message on Joan's phone with himself as the recipient, then, when he had his audience of witnesses, sent it to himself. He probably had a mobile in both of his jacket pockets.'

'But Joan's mobile was found in the house,' Watson added. 'How did he manage that?'

'That's my fault,' Carmichael replied, with a disparaging shake of his head. 'If you recall, I let him go inside the house to collect a few things. He must have planted it when he was in there.'

'The conniving sod!' Watson exclaimed.

The incident room fell deadly silent once more, punctuated only by the clicking noises made by Rachel on the computer keyboard.

'Rachel, I hope what you're doing is connected with the case?' Carmichael remarked caustically.

Rachel looked up from her computer with a broad beaming smile. 'Oh yes, sir,' she replied enthusiastically. 'And what's more, if you can bear with me while I make a couple of calls, I think I may soon be able to tell you where Henderson is. Or, where he may be at some point in the very near future.'

*   *   *   *

Natalie Carmichael's face when she saw the cute small dog sitting neatly in its wicker basket was a picture.

'I don't believe it,' she shrieked. 'Is he really mine?'

Penny smiled back but, fully aware that the outcome was still far from certain, tried to make sure her ecstatic daughter's expectation levels weren't set too high.

'I need to talk to Dad first,' she replied robustly. 'He may say no.'

'Oh how could he?' replied Natalie as she knelt down to fuss the hairy little creature. 'You have to make him let us keep him.'

'I'll try,' replied her mother. 'But it's not going to be easy.'

* * * *

Carmichael, Watson and Cooper eagerly waited for Rachel to end her call.

'Well,' enquired Carmichael. 'What did they say?'

Rachel could hardly contain her euphoria. 'It's confirmed,' she announced, the elation oozing out of her. 'Aiden Blandford, a US citizen, is booked on flight BA1399 from Manchester airport to Heathrow at fifteen thirty this afternoon. He's then booked on flight JJ8089 that leaves Heathrow for Rio at nine fifteen this evening.'

'Aiden Blandford!' exclaimed Carmichael. 'But that was the alias Aiden Davidson was using.'

Rachel shook her head and grinned. 'No that was what Lou wanted us to believe, Aiden Blandford is the alias of Lou Henderson.'

'Brilliant work, Rachel,' Carmichael shouted. 'Making that connection was a stroke of genius. Now, let's make sure he doesn't give us the slip.'

Chapter 50

Lou Henderson waited patiently in the small grey Fiesta he'd hired the day before, at Manchester Airport, in the name of Aiden Blandford.

He had one last act to perform before he was ready to flee the country. With a new identity, all the cash he could gather and all his wife's jewellery, Henderson had parked up out of sight at Thompson Weir. As soon as he was sure the coast was clear, he clambered out of the car and headed for the weir, which was the only fast-flowing body of water in the area.

He carefully placed his small bag down by the side of the rushing water and took out a pair of his shoes, his well-worn Barbour jacket and the note he'd written for Carmichael.

Henderson carefully laid them down by the side of the weir, making sure that the letter was firmly secured under one shoe, so there was no way it could blow away.

Carefully, Henderson removed from the bag the bottle of Etorphine and syringe, both of which he'd taken earlier from the Park Road Practice. He then stabbed the forefinger of his left hand with the needle and, as soon as a small bubble of blood appeared, squeezed hard to force a more plentiful flow. Then, with his right hand, Henderson removed the top off the bottle of Etorphine and, with great care, filled the syringe half full of the immobilising drug, making sure not to get any blood on to the bottle. He then leaned out over the side of the river and with one hard push emptied the liquid into the fast-flowing water. Henderson then replaced the cap to the bottle of Etorphine and, after wiping some of his blood on the end of the needle, placed the bottle and the syringe on to the abandoned Barbour jacket.

His final sham act was to take his mobile from his trouser pocket and send the text message he'd previously written.

Pleased that his deception was now completed, Lou Henderson allowed himself a small smug grin. He then threw his mobile into the rapid current, scampered away to his hired car and drove off in the direction of Manchester.

* * * *

Carmichael's driving was much quicker than normal. Although they'd already contacted the police at the airport, he desperately wanted to be there when Henderson was apprehended.

'So, run it by me again?' Watson asked from the back seat. 'How did we work out that Lou Henderson was Aiden Blandford?'

'You explain it,' Carmichael said to Rachel. 'After all, it was you who twigged it.'

Rachel smiled broadly. 'It was quite easy actually,' she said. 'I just followed the boss's premise that everything Henderson has sent us, the texts and the letter, were aimed to throw us off the scent. Trying to get us to believe the death of Betty's brother was linked to Joan's and Davidson's deaths, the seven thirty-seven nonsense, and the *Catch Me If You Can* references were all red herrings. He even tried to mislead us into believing the body we found at his house was Joan rather than Vicky. In short, pretty much everything he's been doing has been to deliberately get us thinking what he wanted us to think.'

'OK,' replied Watson. 'I get all that, but how did you work out that Henderson was going to use the name Aiden Blandford?'

Rachel's broad grin remained on her face. 'I wondered why only Joan's false passport was in the envelope Lou left at the house. The only conclusion I could come to was that Lou didn't put both in there because he needed to use one.'

'I see,' remarked Watson. 'So am I right in assuming that there were never any plans for Aiden Davidson and Joan to fly to Cape Town?'

'I think he's got it!' exclaimed Cooper.

'That's right,' continued Carmichael. 'In fact, I assume there were never any plans for Lou and Joan to go to Cape Town either. I suspect neither Joan nor Davidson had any idea that Lou had booked any tickets. Why would they, as he was never going to use them? They were booked by Henderson using the false names for one purpose only. To lead us to believe that Joan and Aiden were planning to elope together.'

'And once he'd booked them and got his tickets confirmed,' remarked Rachel, 'it would be easy enough for him to cancel them and booked himself on a different flight as Aiden Blandford, but this time to Rio.'

'But, if they were in a relationship, wouldn't Aiden have told Joan about the fake passports?' Watson asked.

'That depends,' replied Rachel sagely. 'Firstly it may not have been Aiden who forged them but, assuming he did, you have to ask yourself whether Joan knew about his forgery scam. My guess is he probably did forge them for Lou but he didn't tell Joan because she didn't know he was a forger.'

'I agree,' added Carmichael. 'And even if he had, I suspect Lou Henderson knew his wife wouldn't dare mention it to him, as it would have exposed her affair with Davidson.'

'The crafty ...'

As he spoke, Watson saw a new text message coming through on his mobile. 'It's from Henderson,' he remarked.

The car went silent as Watson read the text, first to himself and then out loud:

DEATH NUMBER FOUR IS NOW COMPLETED. IT'S OVER. I'VE ENDED IT ALL – FROM THOMPSONS WEIR.

Carmichael smiled. 'Get some plain-clothed guys down there, Marc,' he instructed. 'But there's no way they'll find Henderson. They'll probably find a suicide note and maybe even his abandoned car, but he's heading to Manchester Airport. And, at long last, we're one step ahead of him.'

Chapter 51

Carmichael's car arrived at Manchester Airport at 12:35 p.m., where they were met by airport security officers and ushered into a small office housing the airport's security screens.

'He's not checked in yet,' announced the senior officer on duty, 'but as the flight doesn't depart until three thirty this afternoon, he's got well over an hour before the official check-in time ends. To be honest, on a Sunday, as long as he's here an hour before takeoff for a local flight, he should make it easily.'

'Will he not have to check his bags in earlier as he's got a connecting flight to Rio?' Carmichael asked.

The security guard shook his head. 'Yes, but an hour should be easily enough time.'

'OK,' replied Carmichael. 'We'll just sit and wait.'

*   *   *   *

Henderson's journey from Thompsons Weir to Manchester Airport was straightforward and uneventful. The traffic was surprisingly light and he arrived at the hire car drop-off point at exactly 1 p.m.

Having handed over the car, with two and a half hours before his flight took off, Henderson carefully placed his two suitcases on to a trolley conveniently abandoned by a previous traveller and calmly sauntered the short walk to the terminal entrance, with the bright sun on his back.

On entering the departures hall, Henderson gazed up at the board to identify the number of the BA check-in desk. Then, having spotted his flight and discovered where he needed to go, he pushed his trolley for a matter of no more than twenty feet and joined the rear of a small queue waiting to check in.

'Spotted him,' shouted Watson, pointing at the rotund, casually dressed man waiting patiently at check-in desk K22.

The head of security looked towards Carmichael to receive his instructions.

'No point in waiting – let's pick him up now,' announced Carmichael enthusiastically. 'All units in the vicinity of check-in desk K22 please detain the chubby, middle-aged, white male wearing light-brown trousers and a green polo shirt.'

With only five other people in the queue, and none of them looking anything like Henderson, it was easy for the four security officers to locate and apprehend their quarry.

Within the space of two minutes, broad smiles appeared on Carmichael and his team's faces as they saw the successful capture of Lou Henderson on the security monitor.

'Got him!' exclaimed Carmichael, who couldn't resist demonstrating his elation at the arrest. 'Now, let's see what he has to say for himself.'

*　　*　　*　　*

Despite being offered the chance of heading home, Paul Cooper and Rachel Dalton wanted to watch Carmichael's questioning of Lou Henderson. So, when at 4:30 p.m. Carmichael and Watson entered the main interview room at Kirkwood Police Station, their two colleagues were already positioned behind the two-way mirror in eager anticipation.

'I understand you've declined to talk with a solicitor,' Carmichael said as he sat down to face the subdued-looking

American. 'I would strongly suggest that you do take some legal advice before we start the interview.

Henderson looked back at Carmichael. 'Thanks, buddy,' he replied blithely, 'but I'm just fine. Let's just get this over with.'

Watson gazed up at the large clock hanging on the wall and switched on the recording device. 'The time is four thirty-two on Sunday 20th July. Interview at Kirkwood Police Station with Lou Henderson. Inspector Carmichael and Sergeant Watson in attendance. We have suggested that Mr Henderson talks with a solicitor, but he has declined that invitation.'

Carmichael looked directly into Lou Henderson's eyes. 'So, Lou,' he said calmly. 'You've been leading us a merry dance these past few days. Can you please tell us, in your own words, what's been happening?'

Henderson considered the question for a few seconds before answering. 'I suppose if I denied everything that's not going to get me far,' he responded with a faint smile of resignation.

Carmichael shook his head. 'Just tell us the truth,' he replied firmly.

Henderson seemed reconciled to his fate, and by his body language he appeared almost relieved it was over.

'Are you guys married?' he asked.

Watson frowned and was about to rebuff the question, when his boss interrupted.

'Yes,' replied Carmichael. 'We're both happily married.'

'I thought I was, too,' remarked Henderson, his eyes staring beyond the two officers in front of him. 'Well, that's until about three months ago.'

'What happened then?' Carmichael enquired.

'I was at Aiden Davidson's house,' he replied. 'We drank together at The Drunken Duck. One evening, after closing time, he asked me back to his for a nightcap. He had some Jack Daniels and I agreed.'

'So, what happened at Davidson's?' asked Watson.

'We were in that outhouse studio of his and he had to go back to the house for something. Some ice, I think it was.'

'And?' continued Watson, who was eager for Henderson to get on with his story.

'Well, when he was out, I opened the desk drawer and there on the top was a picture of Joan,' said Henderson, his face taut with anger and eyes still staring out into the distance.

'The one of your wife that you left in the envelope?' remarked Carmichael.

'Yes, the naked one,' replied Henderson. 'There were some notes, too, from Joan to Davidson. I recognised Joan's handwriting and I can assure you gentlemen that they left no doubt in my mind that the two of them had been having a relationship.'

'Did you confront either of them about it?' Carmichael asked.

'That's not how we do things where I come from, Inspector,' replied Henderson, his deep Southern accent seeming even more evident than usual. 'We address these things in our own way.'

'What did you do?' Carmichael asked.

'I waited my time,' replied Henderson, his gaze now back on the faces of his interrogators. 'I left the photo and notes in the desk and spent the next few weeks deciding how I would get even.'

'And you decided to murder them there and then?' Watson enquired.

'Too damn right I did,' replied Henderson, with no hint of remorse. 'But I wanted to try and give myself a fair chance of getting away with the murders. I also wanted to get away with as much of Joan's money as I could. You see, she was the one with the cash in the relationship.'

Henderson then paused, which led Carmichael to think he may not want to say anything more. He knew any solicitor worth his salt would be trying to shut Henderson up at this stage, so he was pleased Henderson had opted not to have one.

'What did you do, Lou?' he asked, as if he were talking to a friend rather than a murderer.

'I knew Aiden was a forger,' remarked Henderson. 'He was a good one, too. So, one night when we had one too many Jack Daniels, I asked him to make Joan and I some false passports in the names of Aiden and Joan Blandford. I told him I'd pay him £500 for each of them and he agreed.'

'Why did you do that?' Carmichael asked.

'I told him it would be a laugh and that I would surprise Joan with it and suggest we went away under our assumed names for a joke,' replied Henderson. 'But I really wanted mine as a fall-back if I needed to escape after I'd finished what I had to do. If my main plan worked, I'd have no need for either passport. In fact, I was going to ditch it once I'd killed them, but I needed it for my backup plan.'

'What was the main plan?' Carmichael asked.

'To be honest, at first, I wasn't sure how I could do it and get away with it,' continued Henderson with frankness that took Carmichael and Watson by surprise. 'I knew the first person the police would look at would be the husband, so it was a tricky one.'

Watson and Carmichael listened intently. This was not so much an interrogation, rather a full and detailed confession.

'Then I read the article in the local paper. Once I saw that, it came to me right away.'

'That would be about the hit-and-run at seven thirty-seven in the morning,' remarked Carmichael.

'Correct,' replied Henderson. 'And, as I was in US when it happened and there were no arrests, I decided all I needed to do was link my two killings and the only thing I could think of to link them was the time – seven thirty-seven.'

'Your killing time,' observed Carmichael.

Henderson leant back in his chair and smiled. 'You have to admit, guys, it was a smart plan.'

'So let me get this right,' said Watson. 'The plan was for you to kill two people, Aiden and Joan. You sent the texts to the newspaper and to DC Dalton simply to ensure we associated the deaths with the first killing, for which you had an alibi.'

'You listen well, buddy,' replied Henderson. 'You're right on the button.'

'But in your text messages you mentioned four deaths,' Carmichael said. 'So who was the fourth?'

'Nobody,' replied Henderson with a sickly smile of satisfaction. 'That was also a red herring. Had all gone to plan after Joan, that would be it. I'd let you guys think another was going to happen but there was no fourth death. My hope would be that I'd be in the clear. I'd sell everything here, go back to the US and then, in a few months, using the forged passport, disappear for good.'

'You've got to hand it to him,' remarked Cooper from behind the glass. 'It was a bloody good plan.'

Rachel nodded. 'Yes, really cunning.'

'But it started to go wrong, didn't it?' Carmichael said. 'Why was that, Lou?'

'I didn't account for Joan asking her friend over on Wednesday evening,' Henderson replied. 'I'd not planned on having to kill her, too.'

For the first time during the interview, Henderson's face indicated some contrition on his part. 'I truly never knew her and when she came into the kitchen I was as surprised as anyone.'

'But not too contrite to try and confuse us more by switching the bodies around and giving that Oscar-winning performance at the morgue,' remarked Watson.

'I had to think on my feet,' replied Henderson. 'I did a good job too, considering how tired I was.'

Carmichael nodded as if to appear to acknowledge Henderson's skilful deception. 'Why did you tidy up the bed in the spare room, and what did you do with Vicky's things?'

Henderson, clearly flattered by Carmichael's apparent admiration at his resourcefulness, allowed himself a self-satisfied smirk. 'I dumped her stuff in a skip in a lay-by when I was driving back to York. I kept her cell phone – I knew I'd need that later – but her handbag and clothes were of no use to me.'

'And the bed?' enquired Carmichael. 'Why did you try to make out it hadn't been slept in?'

Henderson shrugged his shoulders. 'I figured I'd confuse you a little more,' he replied, his eyes fixed on Carmichael's. 'I bet you wasted some energy on that one, didn't you?'

Carmichael chose to ignore Henderson's question.

'So, why did you change your plan again?' he asked. 'There were now four deaths, which coincidentally fitted your texts. Why then start to make us believe you were the killer but that you planned to kill yourself?'

Henderson smiled. 'That was my backup plan. In my business you always have to have a plan B. I figured my main plan would work, but if not, my fall-back was to try and show that it was Aiden and Joan that were planning to use the false passports, which is why I bought the tickets in their names.'

'Sorry?' interrupted Watson. 'You deliberately booked tickets to South Africa in the names of Aiden and Joan Blandford which you never expected to use.'

Henderson once again smiled at Carmichael. 'Your sidekick's bright, isn't he?'

'Just please answer the question,' replied Carmichael.

'Yes, that's correct,' replied Henderson. 'I bought two flexible one-way tickets to Cape Town a few weeks back, which I needed to convince you guys that Joan and Davidson were planning to use. Of course, once I had received confirmation of the tickets, I didn't need them any more so I exchanged them the other day for a one-way ticket to Rio.'

Carmichael took a deep intake of breath. 'And had it not been for you using the same name to buy your ticket to Rio and the work of a very diligent member of my team, you would have got away with it.'

Henderson sighed. 'I was too smart for my own good,' he conceded. 'I should have gotten Davidson to do me another false passport in a different name. I'd be on my way to Rio right now if I had.'

Carmichael smiled. 'You're probably right, Lou.'

'I've just a few questions,' interrupted Watson. 'Why did you use Etorphine to drug Aiden, Joan and Vicky?'

'I remember Joan mentioning it once,' replied Henderson. 'She said it was what they used on big animals. So I figured it would work on humans, too.'

'How did you manage to get it from the practice?' Carmichael asked.

'I took it last Saturday,' replied Henderson. 'I arranged to pick up Joan from work. I got there early on purpose and, when they were all busy rescuing the life of some poor creature, I just took a bottle. It was easy – the security there is awful – and besides, why would they ever expect the boss's husband to take anything?'

'Tell us about the text messages,' said Carmichael.

'Oh, they were easy,' replied Henderson, who seemed only too happy to share the details of his actions, as if they were something to be proud of. 'I got the telephone number for the reporter from the *Observer* by just contacting the newspaper. It was a breeze to send that from Davidson's phone, which I did just before I left his house. I sent the one from Joan's phone to myself easily enough by having her phone in one pocket, mine in the other.'

'And you dumped that phone at your house when I

allowed you to go inside to collect some clothes,' remarked Carmichael.

'Yeah,' replied Henderson. 'That was really shoddy work, Carmichael. That PC you sent in with me was really lax. You should have a word with him about that.'

Carmichael could feel his blood pressure rising, but tried hard not to show it as he wanted to make sure Henderson told them everything whilst he appeared to be so cooperative.

'One final question,' continued Carmichael. 'How did you get DC Dalton's mobile number to send her the text messages from your wife's mobile and from Vicky's mobile?'

'She gave it to Joan,' Henderson replied. 'It was by the land line when I got home. I was going to text the newspaper again, but when I saw her card I thought I'd contact her. As we'd never met, I figured that might also throw you guys off the scent.'

Carmichael looked at Watson to see if he had anything else to add. When it was clear he hadn't, he looked back at Henderson.

'That will be all for now,' he replied. 'But, once again, I'd urge you to get yourself a solicitor. You certainly need one in my view.'

'Can I ask you a question?' Henderson remarked.

'Of course,' replied Carmichael.

'Which one of your team worked out that I was going to use the Aiden Blandford passport?'

Carmichael turned his head to look at the two-way mirror before returning his stare in Henderson's direction. 'A very tired, but very smart one.'

Chapter 52

After the interview with Henderson, Carmichael gathered his team in the incident room.

'You've done an incredible job,' he said with a mixture of true pride and elation. 'Fantastic teamwork and your commitment's been outstanding.'

Carmichael looked across at Cooper and Rachel, who were clearly exhausted. 'You two get yourselves home. You've both put in a hell of a lot of hours in the last few days, so go home and get some sleep. Marc and I can finish off here.'

Neither Paul Cooper nor Rachel Dalton had any desire to argue the point and, within the space of a few minutes, Carmichael and Watson were alone.

'What a devious mind,' remarked Watson. ' But you've got to hand it to him, having a backup plan, in case we figured out the first death wasn't connected to the murders of Aiden Davidson and Joan, was really astute.'

'There's no doubting that,' replied Carmichael. 'However, what I can't work out is how he knew we'd twigged that little ruse of his.'

'Search me,' replied Watson, who knew full well his conversation with Henderson the day before in the police station car park was the source of that particular nugget of information.

'I could kill a beer,' remarked Carmichael, who didn't notice the embarrassed look on his sergeant's face. 'Let's do a couple of hours here to make a start on the paperwork, then I'll buy you a couple of swift pints. Are you up for it, Marc?'

'Would be rude not to, sir,' replied Watson, relieved that the subject had changed. 'Especially if you're paying.'

*   *   *   *

It was almost 9 p.m. when Carmichael finally arrived home. Although he was shattered, the adrenalin rushing through his veins on closing the case, and the two pints of lager shandy he'd had with Watson in The Railway Arms, meant that he was still upbeat and by no means ready to call it a day.

'Hello,' he shouted down the hallway as he closed the front door.

Natalie came rushing out of the kitchen to meet him. 'Hi, Daddy,' she shrieked as she threw her arms around his neck. 'We can keep him, can't we?'

Carmichael kissed his exuberant daughter's cheek and, after prising himself away from her, shrugged his shoulders. 'What are you talking about?' he enquired. 'What is it you want to keep?'

His question was answered within seconds when the tiny figure of Mr Swaffie came out of the kitchen and bounded towards where they were standing.

'What the hell is he doing here?' Carmichael asked, his voice indicating that he wasn't best pleased.

A nervous-looking Penny emerged from the kitchen. 'We had a visit from the RSPCA man this morning,' she said timidly. 'It would appear Siobhan Ballentyne no longer wants the dog and told Dennis Preston that we would make a good home for him as apparently the dog has really taken to you.'

Carmichael looked down at the fluffy creature resting its head on his shoe.

'Well, I can assure you the feeling is one way,' he remarked dispassionately with a look of revulsion on his face.

'I've been with that dog at Siobhan Ballentyne's house and he smells.'

'He doesn't,' announced Natalie indignantly. 'He's really clean and I'll wash him and groom him.'

'I'm not talking about the outside,' replied Carmichael. 'He's got awful wind. I'm telling you, for a tiny fellow, he can absolutely reek.'

Natalie hastily picked up Mr Swaffie and stormed down the corridor and back into the kitchen, slamming the door behind her, leaving Carmichael and his wife alone in the half-lit hallway.

'Please don't look at me like that,' Carmichael remarked. 'I know you want to keep him too, but he's the most pungent, ugly little animal I've ever seen. If we do get a dog, we need one that's much nicer than that scruffy mutt.'

Penny folded her arms and glared back at him.

'I'm sorry, Pen,' Carmichael continued, 'but I'm taking Mr-whatever-his-bloody-name is back to that crackpot phoney psychic, and he's going back tonight.'

Chapter 53

It was almost 10 o'clock when Carmichael reached Siobhan Ballentyne's house but, despite the late hour, the front door was open and the lights were all on inside.

'Hello,' he shouted through the open door.

After several more 'Hellos', each getting progressively louder, Siobhan Ballentyne appeared at the top of the stairs carrying a packing case.

'Jesus Christ,' she cursed, her voice no longer sounding as refined as normal, this time with a faint but noticeable Midland accent. 'What the hell do you want now?'

Carmichael was certainly shocked by her abruptness, but even more taken aback by the fact that she sounded so different.

'You seem to have picked up an accent,' he remarked.

Siobhan, who by now had descended the staircase and had placed the packing case down on the floor, puffed out her cheeks and shook her head slowly from side to side.

'What is it you want?' she said once again. 'I've written my statement. Can't you leave me alone to finish my packing?'

'Are you planning on leaving us?'

'There's certainly no flies on you, Inspector,' replied Siobhan sarcastically. 'You can spot a clue a mile away.'

'Where are you going?'

'Anywhere but here,' snapped Siobhan.

Carmichael enjoyed a smug smile of satisfaction. 'I guess word of my investigation could well sow some seeds of doubt as to your credibility,' he remarked with unabashed glee.

'Between you and that nutcase Malcolm Page it's certainly going to be challenged,' she replied. 'But, actually, you've both done me a favour. This place is too small for a woman with my talents; it was time I moved on anyway.'

'To peddle your gobbledygook to new unsuspecting victims,' remarked Carmichael caustically.

'Did you get my present?' Siobhan asked, her face beaming with delight. 'I hope you and Mr Swaffie get on together.'

'That's why I'm here,' replied Carmichael. 'I want to know what on earth you are doing dumping that creature on me and my family.'

'After what your wife told me, I thought your family would provide the perfect home for Mr Swaffie. Is it not working out?'

'What did my wife tell you?' Carmichael asked, with some indignation in his voice.

'Hasn't she told you?' replied Siobhan. 'The secrets you have from each other. You'd never know it by just looking at you.'

'The dog's in the car,' remarked Carmichael looking back in the direction of his BMW. 'I've come to give it you back.'

Siobhan screwed up her face. 'No way,' she replied curtly. 'As I told that rather handsome RSPCA man, it's not possible to take him with me. That's why I suggested he took it to Penny. He's yours now.'

Carmichael couldn't believe what he was hearing. His initial thought was to just retrieve the dog from the car and dump it back on the psychic, but he couldn't do it. In spite of his loathing of dogs, he didn't want to put this one at any risk and the Siobhan Ballentyne he was now with was certainly not someone he trusted.

'The sooner you're away from here the better,' he said, his words delivered with a bluntness that left Siobhan Ballentyne in no doubt about his revulsion. 'You are nothing but a fraud. I'll find a decent home for the dog. The poor thing is better off without you.'

Carmichael turned on his heels and marched away in the direction of the car. He had no desire to remain in the psychic's company for a second longer.

'How did I know about Lucy?' Siobhan hollered at him, her voice trembling but overflowing with spite and her Brummie accent even more pronounced. 'If I'm a fraud, how did I know about her?'

Carmichael could feel his body tighten as he heard her words, but he refused to look back.

'She knows, Carmichael,' Siobhan screamed. 'She'll never tell you, but your precious Penny knows. The fool's forgiven you too, but she will never forget. Be assured of that!'

Carmichael clambered back into the car, slammed the door shut behind him and sped off, his heart pounding and his head full of anger.

Chapter 54

Six months later

It was 11 p.m. and Carmichael was sitting on the sofa in his front room, watching TV. As the wind bellowed outside, he felt warm and relaxed with a glass of whisky in his right hand and his wife snuggled up close to him on his left.

'Are you pleased with the outcome?' Penny asked, her eyes remaining fixed on the TV screen.

'Oh yes,' replied Carmichael, who also appeared engrossed in the programme. 'A life sentence would have been better, but twenty-five years for Henderson, in this day and age, is certainly a great result. He could be out in fifteen to twenty, I suppose, but yes, I'm pleased.'

'So, with Harvey Romney and Sarah Page already being convicted of fraud, I guess you've had a result all round,' added Penny, who still kept her gaze on the TV.

Carmichael nodded. 'Yes, they got five years a piece for their little scam, so all in all it was a massive result for the team.'

There was a short pause before Penny spoke again.

'Did Lucy ever see that RSPCA man again?'

The sound of the name Lucy sent a shudder down Carmichael's spine. 'You mean Rachel. Lucy left the team a few years ago.'

'Sorry, you're right; I meant Rachel,' Penny replied without moving her eyes away from the TV.

'No. I suspect, knowing his track record, he would have kept trying his luck, but I don't think Rachel was interested. As far as I know, they never went out after the evening at The Fisheries.'

'Smart girl. I suspect she's waiting for a better catch. A more successful man.'

'Maybe,' remarked Carmichael who continued to watch the TV programme. 'I've no idea; we don't tend to talk about that sort of thing at work.'

Penny nodded. 'So I guess that's all the loose ends tied up in the Henderson case. Just how you like it.'

Carmichael considered his wife's words for a few seconds, then turned to face her.

'Well, almost. There's just one thing outstanding and that's the matter of what you told Siobhan Ballentyne that evening when you went to her Vixens meeting. You never did tell me what it was you said.'

Penny kept her eyes on the TV screen but smiled smugly to herself. 'No, I didn't. That will have to remain a secret between the Vixens, me and, of course, Mr Swaffie.'

As she spoke, she gazed down at the small hairy dog that lay on the floor at their feet.

'Pass me the air freshener,' Carmichael said with desperation in his voice and his fingers clamping his nostrils tight. 'This damn dog's just let loose another one.'